SHADOW
CAMPUS

Kathleen Kelley Reardon

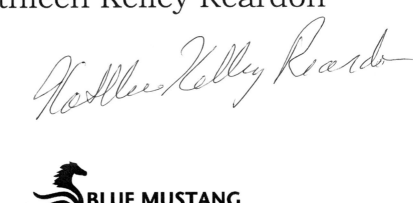

BLUE MUSTANG
P R E S S

Blue Mustang Press
Boston, Massachusetts

Cover painting by Kathleen Kelley Reardon

ISBN: 978-1-935199-17-5
PUBLISHED BY BLUE MUSTANG PRESS
www.bluemustangpress.com
Boston, Massachusetts

Printed in the United States of America

For my mother and father
Elizabeth and John Reardon

Also by Kathleen Kelley Reardon

They Don't Get It, Do They:
Communication in the Workplace –
Closing the Gap Between Women and Men

The Secret Handshake:
Mastering the Politics of the Business Inner Circle

It's All Politics:
Winning in a World Where Talent and Hard Work Aren't Enough

Comebacks at Work:
Using Conversation to Master Confrontation

CHAPTER ONE

The incessant ringing was starting to get to Meg. Every night her architect brother, Shamus, labored over blueprints in his apartment, three thousand miles away on Ridgefield, Connecticut's storybook Main Street. Why, tonight of all nights, was he not there? Finally the machine kicked in:

"Shamus here. Leave a message."

"Shamus, please call right away," she said, trying not to sound desperate. It was too much to ask; she *was* desperate. "It's an emergency, Shamus. *Please* call me."

"Maybe this time he'd check his machine," she thought. He'd walk into his apartment any minute and turn it on. But she knew better. Shamus was the only family she had left in the world but the sibling concern was definitely one-way. She'd have to catch him at home, in the mood to answer. She called again.

"For God's sake, Shamus. Come home." She hung up. *Got to get out of here.* She heard footsteps in the hall. Her heart pounded. "Take it easy," she admonished herself. The university security number was on a faded pink sticker by her phone. She reached for the receiver. The footsteps were getting louder. Her hand began to shake as she punched 2-3-. "Oh God," she gasped. "Oh my God."

There was no easy way out: not even a window in her office. For all the talk at faculty meetings about raising this business school in the U.S. News and World Report's ratings, the building was a dump. Windowed offices were only for associate and full professors. Not that those offices were anything special, but at least there was some way out. Her office was like a closet – an L.A. earthquake death trap.

"*Buenas noches, professor.*" It was Juan, the custodian, speaking to someone in the hallway in a deferential tone. Juan had become like a friend, always stopping by on late nights when she'd be hunched over her computer working on yet another research article for a refereed publication. "Go home," Juan would say. "This is no place for a young woman at night." But tenure was just around the corner, and the whole five years would be for nothing if she couldn't land tenure. So Juan would check on her, often several times a night.

The stairway door creaked and then clacked shut. Muffled voices grew softer. Whoever it was had gone. She put the receiver down, consciously relaxing. Perhaps her imagination had gotten the better of her. This was a university, after all. She gathered her coat and scarf from the hook on the back of her door, put them on, checked to see if she had everything. As she reached for the doorknob, the footsteps came again, this time approaching quickly.

"Juan, is that you?"

"No Meg. It's me." There was no mistaking that voice – deep, soft, charming. He'd once fancied himself a potential radio talk host. "If this gig doesn't pay off," he'd told her one time, "I might still go for it."

"Meg, let's talk. I wasn't thinking. Open the door." An excruciating silence followed. Then he mumbled something. "Come on, Meg." This time his voice was more insistent. It was the same voice he'd used earlier that day.

"Go away. Just go away."

"You know I'm not going to do that, Meg,"

She snatched the receiver from its cradle. She punched in her brother's number.

"Shamus here. Leave a message."

She slammed down the receiver.

The doorknob moved slowly to the left, then right. "It's locked," she shouted. "Get out of here before I call security."

"Let me in. Just open the door and we'll pretend today never happened."

A key slipped into the doorknob. Cradling the receiver against her shoulder, she began punching in the emergency code, 2-3-4-. Her other hand moved in a panic through the staples, paper clips and scotch tape in her top desk drawer.

The door opened. He was smirking, as if taking in the fullness of his victory.

"Get out of here," Meg growled as she raised a long sleek letter opener.

Swinging violently, he knocked it out of her hand, across the room, where it clattered against the door. He lunged at her just as another figure appeared behind him.

"Juan?" she cried.

It was the last sound she made before the room went black.

CHAPTER TWO

Shamus noticed the blinking red light on the decrepit answering machine as he entered his apartment. He rolled his eyes and shook his head as he placed a small bag of groceries on the counter. "Probably Meg," he said to himself. He reached to press the blinking red light and decided it could wait.

His refrigerator door squeaked as he opened it. A few beers, milk, white bread, carrots, some ragged lettuce and the faint odor of pizza were its only inhabitants. He added some soda and a bottle of wine; the rest went into the freezer: frozen peas, burgers and ice cream. His apartment was equally Spartan, a photo here and there, and furniture for use, not for comfort or pretense. This kind of life appealed to him; its simplicity suited his self-image. He'd convinced himself that creative thinking occurs in unadorned surroundings. There was something romantic about this notion. Besides, he didn't have guests, thus no one to impress.

The phone rang. As he walked over to it, he breathed in deeply and again shook his head with annoyance. Once again he'd take on the older brother role – unsuited as he was to it. Both their parents had died in a car accident the year before. Prior to that he'd only spoken with Meg at Christmas or Easter when she'd returned to Connecticut or by phone on the occasional birthday. She'd ventured beyond their roots, living not only in California but Los Angeles, a place Shamus could never bring himself to visit let alone make his home. He'd moved to a small place in Ridgefield from an even smaller one in Danbury. Building houses had made that possible. College wasn't for him. He took a low paying job in construction a year after high school and never looked back. The boss now on most projects, his unglamorous career paid food and rent, provided one or two good friends, and a new challenge with each beginning. It was enough for him.

Lately he and Meg had talked more often. He felt obligated; figured she did too. Despite all those years of their mother saying, "Some day you'll need each other. You're brother and sister. It's a life-long bond," they had little in common and less with the passage of time. He was older by four years, but it wasn't their age difference that kept them at a distance. But they never discussed it. And if he had his way, they never would.

He picked up the phone. "Shamus here," he said indifferently.

"Mr. Doherty? This is Frank Simmons."

"Who?"

The name was vaguely familiar.

"I'm calling about your sister, Meghan."

"Is she okay?" Guilt gripped his stomach for almost not answering. Images of mangled cars and body bags along side a remote road viciously invaded his thoughts. He'd told her to get a large car. Los Angeles was not a place for a subcompact, but she had wanted to save money. She was like their father in that way, favoring frugality over practicality.

"No she's not okay," Simmons said blandly. "You'll need to come out here right away."

"What do you mean?"

"I can only say that you should come. She had an accident – in her office. She is alive. That much I can tell you. It'd be best for you to talk with a doctor."

He remembered Simmons now. The one he and Meg called "Tightass," a man of few words – lecturing in tone, smelling of stale tobacco. The latter, according only to him, his sole vice. He was an associate dean or something.

"What kind of accident?" Shamus demanded. "How is she?"

"That's all I'm at liberty to say," Simmons replied as if he'd practiced before calling.

"She's my sister, God dammit! Is she okay or not?"

"Naturally you're upset, Mr. Doherty," Simmons said distantly – bureaucratically. "I would like to say more, but I've been instructed to ask you to speak directly with the doctor. His name is Michaels. We're all thinking of Meghan at this time of course. You'll want to come soon. She's at Pacific Coast University Hospital. They're expecting you."

"Instructed by whom?" Shamus asked, lowering his voice, trying now to ignore Simmons' tone and focus on information.

"I have the phone number for the hospital."

Shamus scrambled for a pen and sliver of paper. He wrote down the number then absently placed the receiver down. He imagined Meg lying in a hospital. She was probably alone. She had a couple of professor friends. Susan "something" was one, and there was another whose name completely escaped him. Whenever she had described them, he'd always been half listening and half working on blueprints for his next project. Her calls had been an interruption, his interest always forced. Guilt gripped his stomach again and shot to his head. Would he bother if she weren't his only family? If there'd been three of them, perhaps a sister for Meg to bond with, would he have slipped out of their lives to become the firstborn, long lost brother, sorely missed by his sisters for all they fondly imagined him to be rather than anything he ever was? This wasn't the first time he'd asked himself these questions; nor the first time he'd declined to answer them.

* * *

Shamus packed and called the hospital. They provided little additional information. Dr. Michaels was not available.

"I'm sorry, sir," a nurse in intensive care apologized. "In cases like this we're not supposed to give out information over the phone."

"In cases like what?" Shamus persisted.

"I'm sorry," the woman said less apologetically than perfunctorily. You'll have to come to the hospital."

"I'm 3000 miles away."

"I see," she replied. A pause. "As I said, sir, we can't give..."

"I'm her brother, her only family. Please, just tell me – is she conscious?"

There were several seconds of silence at the other end. He reminded himself that the nurse was just doing her job, that anger had rarely gotten him anywhere despite his penchant for its application. He waited.

"She's stable but nonresponsive," the nurse whispered – warmly this time. Shamus pictured her looking about to see if anyone had heard her depart from the script. "That's all I can tell you. I wish I could do more. I truly do."

* * *

As the plane flew over the Grand Canyon the word "stable" replayed in Shamus' mind. His parents had been "stable" after the car crash and neither of them had made it. Their mother had gone first. She'd opened her eyes, smiled in recognition at Meg and Shamus, and then just died. Their father had lived a few more days, but never regained consciousness. They'd been driving cross-country to see Meg. The Grand Canyon was to be their last stop before arriving in Los Angeles. A day later a trucker's brakes gave way. No one was to blame. "Just one of those freak things," the police had told them.

He wondered whether Meg's accident had been "one of those freak things." Or maybe she'd been attacked, God forbid, in one of those dark campus parking structures, had made it to her office and collapsed. He pushed the thought away. Meg was a risk-taker in some ways but she wouldn't be careless. Then again, it was a city. A procession of horrific images pulsated through his mind. He reminded himself that Meg was self-sufficient, capable, the kind you'd want around in an emergency. Only once when they were kids had he felt the need to protect her. She was scrappy. That's the word his friends used to describe her. Some of them actually feared her. Meg's determination was daunting.

Turbulence shook the plane, shifting his attention back to the present. Outside the window were millions of lights from the endless housing tracts of Los Angeles. Hours must have gone by. Shamus had hardly noticed. The same thing had happened when he'd flown to Nevada, where his parents' accident had occurred. Normally he would grip the armrests during turbulence. Only when he'd flown to be with them for the last time, precariously suspended above an abyss of anticipatory grief, had he been indifferent to it. His energy had been focused on getting there – on perhaps undoing some of what had passed between them in the dim hope of reviving what had been lost. But it was not to be. Now Meg was hanging on, perhaps just long enough for him to lose her too. He closed his eyes, envisioned her face and drifted above the ominous darkness of that same abyss.

* * *

Shamus went straight from the airport to the hospital. It was nearly midnight. The new, three-story structure looked more like a regional hospital in some small New England town. A plaque beside the glass doors read 2010. Shamus remembered Meg mentioning a new hospital and medical school being added to Pacific Coast University to supplement two large hospitals in Santa Monica. The spacious lobby was silent. Chairs that had no doubt been teeming with people earlier in the day, platforms for the joy and sadness brought to their inhabitants by the miracles of modern medicine – or the lack thereof – were lined up like a collection of shells.

"I'm sorry, sir, but visiting hours are over," a well-coiffed, silver-haired woman in a pink uniform remonstrated across the lobby from the entrance where Shamus stood.

"I just arrived from Connecticut," he said, approaching her. "My sister, Meg Doherty, is in intensive care." The woman's steel blue eyes softened.

"I'm sure they can make an exception then."

Shamus watched as she donned her colorful glasses, turned to her computer and typed in DOHERTY. Her perfume smelled familiar, elegant rather than sweet. Her hair, nearly all white, was perfectly coiffed. Likely a well-heeled volunteer giving back, Shamus thought. Up popped Meg's name. The woman took a small sheet of paper identical in shade to her uniform and proceeded to write the room number on it. "Go up these elevators to the third floor," she instructed, pointing behind Shamus. "Stop at the reception desk. I'll call ahead to let them know you're coming. If no one is there, go through the door into intensive care and let the head nurse know who you are and the circumstances that brought you here at this hour. Her bark is worse than her bite. Tell her Marianne sent you up." She handed the paper to Shamus, smiled slightly, then pulled her lips tight in sympathy. "My good wishes," she said with a practiced yet sincere tone.

For a moment Shamus wondered if he'd been wrong about people in L.A. He'd always considered them to be vacuously self-absorbed, skating along Venice Beach, evenly and identically bronzed in counterfeit beauty. He pushed the thought aside. The receptionist was, after all, one person. The elevator opened. He rode it to the third floor, turned right, and then right again. The sign at the abandoned reception desk read:

Intensive Care
Family Visitors ONLY
10 A.M. to 8 P.M.
Please Register Here

He passed the desk and pushed open the heavy silver doors. A large woman in her fifties sporting a stethoscope over a blue and white flowered shirt and blue pants – the kind he'd seen in television show operating rooms – approached him with a look of intractable disapproval.

"Yes, may I help you?" she inquired stiffly.

"I'm Shamus Doherty," he said. "I just flew here from Connecticut to see my sister."

Nurse 'Constance,' by her name tag, appeared less than impressed. She was, Shamus thought, solid. Yes, that was the word. Not angry or imposing, but solid like a trained Doberman – restrained yet capable of dreadful ferocity. She smelled of rubbing alcohol and exuded seriousness of purpose. She studied him, apparently not altogether pleased with what she found.

"As you can see on the sign..."

"Marianne sent me up," he interjected with compelling intensity to counter hers. His steely eyes formed an impregnable fortress. "I'm Meg's only family. I've got to see her, even if it's just for a few seconds."

A moment passed. She did not look away. Her body did not move. She studied him. "All right, Mr. Doherty," Nurse Constance said, casting him a 'don't-expect-this-too-often' look. "Follow me. She's in room 312."

Shamus followed dutifully. He was beginning to feel the stress of his flight. The sterile smells and insistent cacophony of pumping respirators took him back to Nevada and his parents' final days. His head ached. As he walked, time seemed to pull backwards as if he'd stepped onto the wrong escalator, looking upward but moving inexorably back. He half expected Meg to come running, breathless, from around the corner: "*Are they all right? Shamus, Are they all right?*"

"Mr. Doherty, are you all right?"

"What?"

"Are you all right?" Nurse Constance repeated, concerned as her job required, more loudly this time.

"Oh, no – I mean yes. I'm just tired."

She nodded, as if reasonably satisfied, then pointed to a room.

"Your sister is in there. Now, don't expect too much. She's on a respirator."

Shamus moved slowly toward the door.

"Should I go in with you?" She waited a moment then took hold of his right elbow like a mother cat nudging a reluctant kitten. They moved as one through the door and to Meg's bedside.

His sister's bed was the only one in the room. Tubes stretched from her arms and nose. An antiseptic odor burned and violated his nostrils, abraded his throat before clenching his stomach. The walls seemed to constrict, the floor to agitate as if to dispel him from the room. He gripped the bar of the bed.

"Her blood pressure is normal," the nurse said, checking the monitors.

"Ah," Shamus replied distractedly. "That's good."

Meg appeared to be contentedly asleep. She'd cut her hair shorter since he'd seen her last; she was blonder too. Shamus reached his hand out to brush a strand away from her eyes, and another from her neck. He jerked back at the sight of a dark bluish-black bruise across her throat.

"What's this?"

Nurse Constance regarded him, puzzled, then looked down at Meg.

"This horrible bruise…" Shamus persisted. He touched Meg's head gently, his pinky finger resting on dried blood in her hair.

"They didn't tell you?" Nurse Constance said, annoyed at someone.

"Tell me *what*?" Shamus shouted.

Nurse Constance frowned. "It's not my place, Mr. Doherty."

"Whose place is it, for God's sake? She's my sister!"

The heretofore unflappable nurse straightened the sheets – buying time. She located the medical chart and looked at it. She peered over her slender reading glasses, examining Shamus – determining, it seemed, if his condition was adequate for the reception of the news she was about to deliver.

"Mr. Doherty, your sister tried to end her life." Her words were simple, emphatic, and intentionally calm – a stark contrast to the intensity of their meaning.

Shamus turned away from her, closed his eyes, and then raised his head to look at the blank ceiling as if doing so might erase what he'd just heard.

"She used a scarf, which is why she is so badly bruised across her neck." The nurse vainly searched Shamus' face for a response, an indication that she should go on.

Shamus simply couldn't fathom what he'd just heard. Meg wasn't a Holy Roller, but compared to him she was devout – maybe compared to most people. For Meg to take her own life was out of the question. The Church no longer held it against you, but there was still God to think about.

Meg would surely have thought of God.

"She's Catholic for God's sake," he muttered.

"I'm sorry, Mr. Doherty." Nurse Constance's words were softer now. She paused, seemed to reflect on what more she might do, briefly touched his right arm, turned and walked from the room. Shamus heard her whispering to someone. He looked up as a silver-haired, gruffly handsome, lab coat-clad man of about fifty-five, chart in hand, strode into the room and over to the foot of Meg's bed.

"How are we tonight, Miss Doherty?" The self-assured stranger did not look up from the chart. "Dr. Michaels here." A few more seconds passed. He looked over at Shamus. "May I speak with you for a moment, Mr. Doherty?"

Shamus dutifully followed him into the corridor.

"Your sister is very ill. Apart from the bruising that you can see, she is in a coma."

"She does have brain activity?" Shamus asked.

The left corner of the doctor's mouth ascended with casual superiority. "Yes. There is brain activity as you call it. But it doesn't mean she'll return to consciousness. Even if she does, she may be unable to communicate."

Perhaps it was the hour, his lack of sleep, the shock of seeing his sister bruised and close to death and for those reasons he restrained the instant dislike for her doctor as best he could. "Is this glum picture based on medical fact?" Shamus asked managing his facial expression, looking directly into the doctor's commanding blue eyes.

The doctor smiled as if being patient with a child. "Medicine is not based entirely on fact, Mr. Doherty. It's based on experience. Experience I have. I suggest we take her off the respirator and see how she does."

Was he hearing correctly? Was he "overreacting to authority" as Meg would say, or was this doctor actually proposing to experiment with his sister's life?

Dr. Michaels studied Shamus' demeanor. Appearing dissatisfied, he looked back at the chart. "At this point the decision is yours, Mr. Doherty," he said flatly.

Shamus leaned over and studied Meg's face as if some solution awaited him there. When he looked up, Dr. Michaels was gone.

Shamus found him down the hall checking another patient's chart. Nurse Constance looked up from her desk at the nursing station. She glanced over at Dr. Michaels and then at Shamus. She placed her finger over her pursed lips warning him to say nothing, before returning to her work.

Shamus took two calming breaths and then returned to Meg's bedside.

"Don't worry about anything, Meg. I've met his type before – imperious, 'all-bow-to-me, I'm a doctor.'"

He looked up to find that they were not alone. An attractive woman of about thirty was standing in the doorway. She was wearing a white lab coat. Her brunette hair was tied back. Errant strands curled along her forehead and lined her face. A stethoscope and her name in royal blue script on her pocket suggested she was likely not as young as Shamus would have guessed. She read Meg's chart for a few moments and then looked up.

"So, I see you met Dr. Michaels," she said. Her expression was sympathetic.

"Yeah. A real prince of a fellow," Shamus quipped.

"He's full of himself, but he knows what he's doing."

"That guy is full of himself and six extra selves."

She smiled broadly; deep dimples punctuated her smooth, slightly olive skin. A glimmer of light danced across her chestnut brown eyes. "Be that as it may, Mr. Doherty, he's king of the hill around here."

She extended her hand. "I'm Dr. Cohen, Denise Cohen."

As he took her hand in his, she smiled. Warmth enveloped him. It was the first sense he'd had of feeling connected to another human being since he'd left Connecticut. It was as if she'd reached into a deep well and pulled him upward – given him a foothold – an escape from misery and impenetrable darkness.

Shamus watched as she moved about the bed with confidence and efficiency, checking multiple monitors and tubes. Using a small flashlight, she examined Meg's eyes then glanced up at him and smiled as one does patiently with someone staring who intends no offense but is nonetheless offending. He awkwardly looked over her head and then turned his attention to Meg.

Meg looked so small, yet she was at least five-foot-seven. She'd towered over him when he was sixteen and she only twelve. He'd never quite gotten over that. Whenever their mother had taken family photos – and that was often – he'd always positioned himself away from Meg. Now, though, she looked half her former size.

Suddenly, Shamus pulled back, startling Denise.

"God, she moved!" he gasped hopefully.

Denise studied Meg intently for several seconds. "It seems that way sometimes," she said, picking up the chart and making some notations.

"You want so much for her to move that…"

"No!" he interrupted. "I saw her hand move."

For the briefest instant, Denise seemed startled, but then she nodded calmly. She walked around the bed to the side where Shamus was standing. She lifted Meg's hand and dropped it gently back onto the sheets.

"I don't see any change here. I'm sorry." She took a deep breath in and released it. Her lower lip pushed upward and she blinked. It was kindness. Not doubt. She'd seen this reaction before.

Shamus tried to give himself a moment. When he looked up, he found Denise's eyes cradling him in concern. He smiled slightly then nodded. She returned her attention to the chart.

"You know," Shamus offered hesitantly, "I just got here, and that Dr. Michaels wants me to let them pull the plug. He's in an awful rush."

Denise remained quiet for a moment as if deciding what to say. "He knows what he's doing. He's just interpersonally incompetent."

"He acted as if my sister was some kind of experiment," Shamus protested.

Denise regarded Shamus skeptically, as if he'd gone too far. "You must have misunderstood him."

"Isn't this a branch hospital to two bigger ones in Santa Monica?" Shamus asked. "Maybe Meg should be moved."

Defensiveness flashed across the young doctor's face, melting a moment later into understanding. She glanced down at Meg then back at Shamus.

"Maybe we should talk about this outside," she said

"Sure. Of course," Shamus stuttered with embarrassment. It hadn't occurred to him that Meg might be able to hear them.

"I'm not the attending physician," Denise said when they were out of Meg's earshot and she had his full attention. "That's Dr. Michael's role. He runs the show here – chief of staff – so Meg is in good hands. He is on the medical staff at St. John's Hospital in Santa Monica as well. But this is the most up-to-date facility in the area for trauma and coma victims. So Meg is in the right place with the best doctor."

Shamus looked into her confident eyes. Her demeanor and tone of voice were professional now. Should he apologize? Or was he right? Was she defending the new hospital and its chief of staff because she worked there? Her eyes were exploring his, awaiting a reply.

"I'm sorry," Shamus said as sincerely as his fatigue and lingering doubts would allow.

Denise smiled. She patted Shamus' right shoulder. "The truth is that she's very lucky to be alive. If I were you I'd listen to Dr. Michaels. Ask him questions. Delay if you like, but listen to him. He's brilliant. Your sister needs a brilliant doctor, not a friendly one."

"I don't want to appear ungrateful..." Shamus said.

"I know that."

"...I just don't want anything further to happen to her."

"Well, we're doing our best. We were able to save her and the baby, too."

"*The what?*" Shamus' shout sliced through the silence of the ICU.

Denise apologized with her expression to two nurses comforting a restless patient on a gurney only a few yards away. She took Shamus' arm and led him down the hallway away from the spectators.

"I gather from your reaction and ashen look that you didn't know." Denise said. "Your sister was pregnant. We had to deliver the baby. I'm sorry. I wouldn't have blurted it out had I known Meg hadn't told you and that Dr. Michaels hadn't yet mentioned it."

Shamus' eyes closed. He breathed out. Denise pointed to two chairs where they could sit. Shamus followed her, preoccupied with trying to remember Meg even hinting about wanting a baby.

"The baby was delivered by Cesarean. Your sister was only seven months along, so the baby is premature. It's a boy and he's in intensive care. His breathing was erratic and he was jaundiced. Maybe you'll want to wait until tomorrow to see him. He's out of the woods and you've had enough of a shock for one night and on no rest."

Shamus' eyes closed. "He'll be all right? You're sure?"

Denise placed a comforting hand on Shamus' shoulder – this time lingering. "He is a little fighter. He's doing well given his traumatic entry into the world."

Shamus nodded. Meg's baby would be a fighter.

Denise removed her hand and stood. "Do you have some place to stay?" She gently asked. "Where does Meg live? Perhaps you can go there to get some rest."

"Culver City," Shamus muttered. "Her place is somewhere near Sepulveda Boulevard. I've never been there."

"It's too late for you to find it tonight in your condition and you'd likely frighten her neighbors. You'd be better off staying near the hospital. Then perhaps tomorrow we can locate her keys and license. You could rent a car or take a cab to her place in the daylight."

Shamus nodded.

"I'll get you a hotel room. You just wait here."

Perhaps it was fatigue, or perhaps shock. Thoughts did not come. He paced.

Denise returned, smiling. "Constance arranged for a room at the Four Season's Hotel in Marina del Rey. It's a taxi drive straight down Lincoln Boulevard not far from here. It's usually expensive but we do a lot of medical conference business with them so she negotiated a deal." Denise smiled sympathetically. "Here's your confirmation number. There should be a taxi out front. I'll be at the nurses' station if you need me."

Shamus nodded in gratitude. After she left, he slipped from fatigue into a kind of emptiness, floating as if still in flight, meditating without intention. A patient passing by the door startled him. He looked again at Meg. She used to tease him about "zoning out." "You're doing it again, Shamus," she'd say laughing. "What are you thinking?" "Nothing," he'd always replied, embarrassed that such had indeed been the case. "How do you do that?" she'd asked. "I mean, how to do you think nothing while you're awake?" He'd had no answer then and he had none now. "It's a gift," Meg had said affectionately, a sentiment he'd failed to return. Instead, he'd always lapsed into silence, abruptly terminating the conversation, as he had in response to so many of her efforts at sibling rapport.

Had she tried to tell him about the baby? If so, when? Their conversations were largely one-sided. She did most of the talking. He barely listened. "But she should have told her own brother about a baby for Christ's sake," he muttered angrily. "I would have paid attention." He stood, paced, and scratched his head thinking of what his reaction would have been. Likely disapproval. He sat again, spent from losing his own argument, and stared across at a blank white wall as predictable in a hospital as his own lack of understanding must have been to his pregnant sister. There was only one thought left in his mind, one final, feeble defense that would not depart. "She could have at least tried."

CHAPTER THREE

Shamus could barely move when the light peeked through the curtains. The hum of air conditioning, the pervasive smell of starch from the sheets, reminded him that he was not in Ridgefield. By this time of morning, he'd be inching out of his bed and tiptoeing across the cold floor to turn up the heat. He preferred sleeping in a cold room but the trip from the bed to the thermostat was a killer from December through March. He'd usually rush to the kitchen, turn on the electric coffee maker, scoot back to bed, open a good book and listen to the hiss of the radiator and smell the delectable aroma of fresh brewed coffee until he felt the warm air soften the stiffness of his face. On some mornings he'd watch a thin layer of ice on the windowpanes surrender to the insistent heat. With each retreat, the apple tree outside his window became more visible -- its outstretched limbs praying for spring, holding fast against the weight of winter.

He hung his legs over the edge of the bed. Every muscle ached from fatigue, jet lag and tension. Even the cushy hotel bed couldn't rid his body of these insults. A knock on the door and an announcement of his name reminded him he'd ordered breakfast.

"Good morning, Mr. Doherty," the young man said brightly as he swooped into the room. "Did you sleep well?"

"Not too badly," Shamus cordially lied. "Thanks."

The waiter diligently set a table with fresh white linen and removed decorative silver covers from each dish.

"That should do it, Mr. Doherty. If everything is to your liking, I'll ask you to sign here." He held out the bill and with swift, graceful gesticulation removed a plastic pen from his vest pocket and presented it to Shamus.

"Thank you," Shamus replied, somewhat bewildered by the display.

"Your complimentary newspaper is next to the tray, Mr. Doherty. I hope you have a pleasant day." With that the young man backed gracefully to the door, nodded and took his leave. Shamus suspected that he would laugh all the way back to the kitchen, having duped another sucker into a large tip with a few obsequious waves of his hands.

He opened the curtains onto a clear morning and hundreds of boats. Had he been on vacation, it would have been a perfect spot. He watched people sipping coffee and reading newspapers on benches, a far cry from the recycled paper cups he and his construction crew used each morning while sitting on a tree stump or old wall about to be demolished. He watched others cleaning their boats and the scampering children who'd one day own them.

Despite these distractions, his thoughts intermittently focused on Meg, on suicide, and on her now being a mother. None of it seemed real. He was by no means ready to take it all in. He nibbled fussily at the fruits, cereals, eggs and toast. Shaking his head, he turned to the *Los Angeles Times*, which he finished reading in fifteen minutes. "No one can read *The New York Times* in fifteen minutes," he huffed, "not even on a weekday." He took some pride in being among the rabid fans of "the Grey Lady." There was something civilized about reading her every day, especially if you lived in Connecticut. Judge, professor, social worker or construction worker, Shamus thought, you could get on with your day knowing you'd visited the altar of establishment journalism. All were equalized, despite status or salary.

* * *

The hospital looked different in the light of day. People in white coats were scurrying every which way. Others waiting for medical tests sat expectantly or wandered around the lobby. Shamus entered the gift shop looking for something cheery to brighten Meg's stark, white hospital room. He perused the shelves of stuffed animals, knick-knacks, dolls, and artificial flowers, declining all. He noticed some yellow roses in a glass refrigerator. Yellow roses were what their parents had brought her when she completed her doctorate. So, yellow roses it would be this time too. At least he knew that much about his sister.

He stopped at the infant section and inspected the silver objects, frames, stuffed toys and tiny clothes. He began to move away, then changed his mind and selected a blue giraffe.

When he arrived at the intensive care desk juggling his gifts, an amused, elderly lady in pink greeted him

"May I help you, Sir?"

"I'm Shamus Doherty, here to see my sister Meg Doherty."

As the lady examined her patient list, Shamus noticed the wave of her hair. It was like his mother's had been: tight, almost curls, soft yet unrelenting. His mother had been proud of this characteristic. Meg and he had inherited it, much to their shared chagrin in younger years. By age ten, Shamus had adopted the practice of cutting off the tight wave that lined his forehead. His mother had hated that. "Someday you'll be thankful for those waves and some special girl will love running her hand through them," she'd admonished. "Mark my words," she'd always added. The "special girl" part had never quite come to pass. There'd been girls and women in his life, but none truly special. "Fleeting" more accurately described his love life. He wasn't ready, that was how he saw it: not just yet. Women seemed to sense as much after a few months, so he'd seen fewer of them lately, avoiding the inevitable leave-taking scenario complete with desperate soul-searching conversations about his fear of intimacy or stunted maturity. He'd had enough of those to last a lifetime.

"I didn't realize she was here," the greeter said smiling with pleased recognition. She looked up at Shamus. "My grandson was fortunate enough to have her as a professor for his MBA."

Still jet-lagged, Shamus managed an acknowledging smile – a slight raise of the eyebrows to mirror her surprise. She paused, then, undeterred by his silence, continued: "Dr. Doherty's somewhat of a celebrity at this university, especially for a young professor. Hardly a month goes by when you don't read something about her research or teaching in the newspapers."

"She's something special," he managed to say.

"I'm sorry, Mr. Doherty; I didn't mean to go on like that. I was just surprised to see her name here. Professor Doherty is having tests right now. She should return within the half-hour." She pointed toward a small waiting room. "You can have a seat over there if you like. And if there is anything you need, you just let me know."

Shamus sat in a chair in front of the television. "Doctor Doherty," he repeated in his mind. It was odd to hear Meg referred to in that way. Their parents had reveled in her success. A Ph.D. in the family was a sign of having made it. No one else they knew at the time had a daughter or a son who'd reached such heights. The Dohertys of Bridgeport, Connecticut had held their heads a bit higher for it. The entire neighborhood had vicariously reaped the benefit as well. One of theirs had made good.

"Mr. Doherty," The elderly lady called cheerily from her desk. "You can go in now."

* * *

Meg's face had more color. Sunlight from the small window danced across her sandy blonde hair and long, bronzed eyelashes. She remained still. Shamus placed the vase of roses on the bedside table. Already the room felt more comfortable and smelled less antiseptic.

"Meg, it's Shamus – I'm back. I brought you some yellow roses like the ones Mom and Dad gave you on graduation day. They're beautiful. And here is something for the little guy." He placed the blue giraffe next to the flowers. "When you wake up, you'll enjoy them." He looked down at her, waiting, hoping for a reply. None came. "And of course," he said interrupting his disappointment with jaunty optimism unlike himself, "you'll thank your brother for being so uncharacteristically thoughtful." He waited again. Gently moving a strand of hair from her face, he breathed in deeply, closed his eyes and expelled the air slowly.

He opened his eyes, pulled up a chair by her bed and took her needle-bruised hand in his. Words didn't come. He could only sit, feeling useless, watching her face, and wondering how being a professor, so full of promise, had come to this.

People thought they knew Meg and, to some extent, they did; whereas they *knew* they didn't know him. With the exception of his crew, he kept people at a distance. Even strangers opened up to her. She would become close to some of them and then release them like a child lets air slowly, quietly leak from a balloon. Few noticed her gentle exit as anything more than moving on – no hard feelings. Those who took offense, she held onto a little while longer.

Shamus had never seen her reciprocate more openness than required,

31

always just enough for near strangers to feel as if they were her friends. It wasn't the kindest observation a brother could make, and maybe back then, in retrospect, he had been jealous. Compared to him she'd been the extrovert. He wondered now if perhaps that was because she'd had to do the talking for both of them.

Born of the same parents, genetically tied, experientially linked, and equally endowed with their parents' good looks and intelligence, they were very different. Their mother had been slightly harder on Meg. Their father had favored her. That was an understatement. Master of the universe in his own mind, the man was nothing if not cold and distant toward Shamus. Meg and their father talked business strategy even on vacations. She loved the myth of his success and so converted it to reality in her mind. She soaked in his every word — at least that's how it seemed to Shamus. He was sure that her decision to become a business professor was to please their father. And it did. It did immensely.

For his own part, by the time Shamus had turned twelve, nothing he did met his father's impossible standards. Nothing changed the dysfunctional dynamic initiated by a single event — an evening gone awry. They lived like two strangers. His mother tried to establish a bond between them one Christmas by buying two fishing rods. They remained in Shamus' closet, never used. Other times she arranged for his father to take him to school or to a sports event. Few words were spoken. His mother finally gave up. That's how Shamus saw it. She took the path of least resistance, hugging him at times when she'd seen him jealously observing Meg and their father leaving for ice cream without inviting him. His father was the type who made up his mind quickly about people, even his own son. "I like them or I don't," he used to boast, glancing at Shamus — the message clear.

Looking down at Meg lying bruised and unconscious in a hospital bed, knowing they had only been children at the time, he was still unable to completely forgive her for giving their father another option — an easy out from having to find something to like about his son and a reason to forgive.

Denise's entering footsteps interrupted Shamus' thoughts. He smiled gratefully at her.

"Are you rested?"

"I'm better. Thanks."

Denise studied his eyes, smiled skeptically and then checked the medical chart.

"Has Dr. Michaels been in yet?" she asked.

"I've been mentally preparing myself for his entrance," Shamus said, barely veiling the sarcasm.

"You know, he's your sister's best hope."

"I don't see why."

Denise shook her head. Then she looked at Shamus. Her jaw was tight, her eyes fixed. "I was one of Dr. Michael's students. He is an exceptional doctor."

"I suppose then you also think I should take my sister off the respirator."

"I'm sure he was just presenting that as an option, one you are free to accept or reject. Dr. Michaels would not recommend removing the respirator if he wasn't convinced of her ability to breathe on her own."

"Do you agree with him?"

"He is more qualified than I to make that kind of decision. Most people would give their eyeteeth and more to have Dr. Michaels on their case. He does a great deal of research these days, and when he shows up it's only to deal with a special patient."

"What did my lowly assistant professor sister do to deserve such a gift?" He'd gone too far. He knew it. The implication was vague but wrong.

Denise glared at him for a brief moment. She looked down at Meg's chart then back up – more understanding this time. "They served together on some cross-discipline committees and developed a mutual regard. He admires Meg's directness in meetings – her ability to, as he put it, 'cut through the crap' despite her youth."

"I didn't realize he knew her," Shamus said looking at his sister, then back at Denise – apologetically.

Denise smiled. "He is not quick to admire other faculty members."

"He's probably a hard act to follow."

She nodded. "More to the point, he reacts quickly. He says things he should have thought about longer. Gets easily annoyed with people he expects to understand him. A little bit like you, I'm guessing."

She patted Meg on the shoulder. Her eyes raised and held his as if half expecting denial.

"So, I suppose I should be less quick to judge?"

"Cut him some slack. Try managing rather than confronting him."

Leaving Shamus time to consider her proposal, she checked Meg's blood pressure, examined the bruising around her neck and on her right cheek, massaged Meg's forehead briefly, squeezed her hand.

Shamus watched each small move of concern and comfort. She was beautiful.

"Let me just add that Dr. Michaels has experience most doctors can only dream about," Denise said as she continued to tend to Meg. "At fifty-six, he's at the top of his game. If I'm halfway to where he is when I'm that age, I'll be pretty damn important myself." She looked up, her features determined but no longer defensive. She was doing him a favor – declining to be judgmental about him.

"Thanks," Shamus said, his eyes holding hers for another moment – one under other circumstances he would have wanted to extend. "I appreciate the advice."

Denise nodded professionally. She smiled with encouragement. "She'll be fine. You'll see."

Shamus watched Denise leave. Looking back at Meg, he committed to "manage" Dr. Michaels. He wouldn't just hand her care over to him, but he'd try not to confront the physician. Taking Meg off the respirator seemed risky to him, and risk was something he was averse to in most aspects of his life. He'd have to factor that in. Meg, on the other hand, believed in taking calculated risks. She would size up her surroundings, consider the worst thing that could happen and then, if she could live with the outcome, she'd jump. That was what she'd told him when, against his better judgment, she'd moved to Los Angeles.

* * *

"Baby Doherty"

The small sign was taped to the side of the incubator. Inside, the baby, wrapped in soft blue, was pumping his arms and kicking his feet. Shamus leaned over the machine, craning for a glimpse of his nephew's face, wanting to see if he resembled Meg.

"Would you like to hold him?" asked a large-framed nurse in a voice betraying remnants of a Scottish or Irish accent. He always got the two mixed up. Meg would have known instantly given her love for Ireland and her trips there that she'd unsuccessfully invited him to join. He recoiled as the beaming, determined nurse lifted the baby and held it toward him.

"Oh, I don't think so." He stepped back.

"Your nephew needs to be held, Mr. Doherty. Babies need stimulation. You're wearing a mask and robe, so you can't hurt him. Come now. Just put your left hand beneath his head and the other under his body. He'll fit right in there."

Shamus awkwardly followed her instructions. He half expected the foreign creature to start bleating but the baby nestled into Shamus' arms and quickly fell asleep. Shamus breathed deeply, the sweet smell of baby powder tickling his nostrils like the first air of spring, softening every part of his being.

"You're a natural, Mr. Doherty," the nurse declared as if she'd said it many times before. She introduced herself.

Shamus nodded a greeting but quickly returned his eyes to the infant as if he might break.

Nurse Shaughnessy laughed lightly, and then turned to tend to another infant.

"Don't go away," Shamus said, alarmed.

Nurse Shaughnessy turned back. She smiled. None of this was new to her. "You're doing fine. Just rock him a bit. He loves being held. It's been a busy day for him with all the company, but babies can never get enough love. If you need me, just shout Shaughnessy. I knew who you were instantly. Word gets around here. And I always …"

"Someone else was here today?" Shamus interrupted.

"Oh yes. A young woman, Ellen I think is her name. She was going to be your sister's Lamaze coach. She came by this morning and waved furiously from the window. You'd think the little lad was hers."

"There was more company?" Shamus pried, attempting to look pleased at such a prospect.

"Yes, actually, there was a man about your height – maybe a little taller. He was at the window when I came on duty. He had your complexion and seemed to have a gentle nature. Perhaps an uncle?"

"No," Shamus said. "I'm the only family."

"He didn't come inside, but Marilyn held up the baby for him. When I see Marilyn tomorrow, I'll ask her if she knows who he was."

"That would be helpful."

Shamus was rocking somewhat less stiffly now, responding to the infant cuddled against him.

"Your mommy's going to get well soon," he said and immediately felt a bit ridiculous. "And then she'll be holding you."

"I wish that were the case," Nurse Shaughnessy said sympathetically shaking her head.

"Excuse me?" Shamus said.

"We have strict orders to keep the baby away from your sister. A social worker from the Department of Children and Family Services was here earlier. Even if Meg awakens, the baby can't be with her. It was enough to get permission for you to hold him."

Shamus' mouth lowered in disbelief. "I don't understand. I thought all babies are supposed to be held by their mothers as soon as possible."

The nurse's eyes were moist. She closed them for a moment as if not wanting to say what needed to be said. "Not if the mother tried to take the baby's life."

Shamus abruptly rose to his feet. His face was red, angry, and disbelieving. The baby began to cry.

"Let me take him," Nurse Shaughnessy said as she gently removed the infant from Shamus' arms.

"It's the law in California, Mr. Doherty. If it were up to me, he'd be with her now. But it isn't up to me. I'm sorry."

"How can this be?"

"Suicide, Mr. Doherty. When a pregnant woman tries to take her own life, she's taking the life of the infant too."

Shamus, in disbelief, sat back in the chair. He put his elbows on his knees and his two hands over his eyes. Nurse Shaughnessy placed the baby in the incubator.

"The little fellow needs a name," she said, as if Shamus might know it. He shrugged.

"Sorry."

"Sure, your sister will be right as rain soon and then he'll have one."

Shamus looked with sympathy at the baby, fatherless to date with a mother accused of attempting to take her own life and that of her unborn child.

He sighed deeply. He was beginning to feel a kinship with this helpless child; some poorly defined but palpable attachment. Surely Meg would have felt it too, Shamus thought. Wasn't that part of the process? The baby's eyes opened. They were like Meg's. He had her nose, too, one of those slightly turned up ones that aunts like his liked to affectionately grab.

"I'll be back," Shamus whispered awkwardly. "Later today."

"He's a fine young lad," Nurse Shaughnessy assured him. Her eyes blinked away the remaining moisture. "It will all be sorted. You'll see." She managed a smile. "He'll need a bit more time here, some observation and a few tests, but he looks better every hour."

* * *

Shamus was standing next to Meg's bed, holding her hand, when Dr. Michaels walked in. It was 7 a.m. of day three. Meg was no better.

"Good morning," Michaels said, his eyes fixed on the chart.

"Good morning," Shamus replied, civilly he hoped.

"We'll get on with removing the respirator, then. I understand from Nurse Constance that you have agreed."

"You're sure it's the best step?"

"That's my opinion. If you want a second one, we can get it."

Dr. Michael's tone was matter-of-fact, not condescending.

"No. We can proceed."

Dr. Michaels eyed Shamus for a moment; glasses perched nearly on the end of his nose.

"Fine then."

"Can I stay here with her?"

"I don't recommend it – but I'll allow it if you insist."

Did he insist? Shamus wondered. He was putting his sister's life in this doctor's hands. It seemed to him something like flying in an airplane. Even if you could sit in the cockpit, what could you do if the plane took a dive? Nothing. Absolutely nothing.

"I'll wait outside."

Dr. Michaels nodded. "We'll let you know one way or the other."

"*One way or the other*," Shamus thought as he exited the room. "*One way or the other*." He leaned against the wall just outside Meg's door. "*God, please don't let me be wrong here*." Of all things, he didn't expect to find himself praying. He'd given that up years ago. It had been another way to purposely disappoint his father. But, after all, what could it hurt to do so now? Maybe God would be so bowled over by the sound of his voice that "He" would snap into high gear and give Meg a fighting chance – the prodigal son returned.

Shamus felt a gentle hand on his shoulder. It belonged to Denise. "It will only take a few minutes," she said reassuringly. "And he'll put her right back on if there's any problem." This was not one of those times when Shamus' mind was blank, but he simply could not speak. When he failed to reply, Denise nodded in apparent sympathy, and then entered Meg's room. He watched her approach the bedside, where she stood across from Michaels. It was in their hands now. One of the nurses placed a chair next to Shamus and signaled him to be seated. He obeyed. There was nothing else for him to do.

He closed his eyes. The pungent, antiseptic hospital odor he'd managed to ignore now filled his nostrils again and the familiar sick feeling returned. He coughed, before placing his hands over his face, rubbing them up and down, pushing away all but the scent of his skin and the remnant of after-shave on his hands. It smelled foreign, not like his habitual Paco Rabanne, but something he'd grabbed at the hotel where he'd decided to stay longer. A pain shot through his head from ear to ear.

He reminded himself that Meg was the most determined person he knew. He recalled a time when some neighborhood punk had taken a swing at her chest. She had been all of 11 then, an early bloomer, and fully aware that her attacker had aimed straight for her emerging vulnerability. There had been a hush of silence from the onlooking gaggle of children. Meg's eyes had filled with tears of pain. Shamus had begrudgingly stepped forward to fulfill his brotherly protective obligation. That's as far as he'd gotten. He remembered Meg squeezing the tears from her squinted eyes, and then glaring menacingly at the proud victor. Her teeth clenched, her right hand slowly folded, pulled back and with fearsome speed and power found its mark on the twelve-year-old boy's jaw. He'd hit the ground like a huge oak felled by a hurricane, then looked up in astonishment and near panic. With Meg looming powerfully over him, the vanquished, quivering boy clamored to his feet and ran off crying.

The boy's angry mother telephoned the Doherty home early that afternoon. "Meghan!" their father called in that no-nonsense, you're-in-big-trouble-now way he'd mastered. "Why did you do that?" he demanded of her. Meg looked directly into their father's angry eyes. "Because he hit me in the chest. And if he ever does that again, I'll give him twice what he got this time." Their father's anger drained from his face in a way Shamus hadn't seen before. "I see," he said, glancing past his determined daughter to their mother who was suppressing a smile. "Well, let's just call it a draw then. Shall we? Let bygones be bygones." Meg's feet were still planted. "That's up to him, Daddy," she protested. "It's his call." Meg would have stayed in that spot for the rest of the day before saying she'd put the incident behind her and shake the boy's hand. She'd been in the right. That was all there was to it. "Well, I'll pass on that message to his mother, Meghan. Now go wash up for lunch." That was that. Meg had won as she often did by dint of will and invincible conviction. If anyone could fend off the claws of death, she could.

"Breathe, Meg," he said aloud. "For God's sake, breathe."

"She must have heard you."

Shamus looked up to see Denise – smiling. "She's breathing?"

Denise's eyes glimmered with satisfaction.

Shamus stood up. "Can I go in?"

"Absolutely."

He followed her to Meg's bedside. Dr. Michaels was checking Meg's pulse. He raised one of her eyelids then the other.

"Meg?" Dr. Michaels said. "Meg, can you hear me? It's Dr. Michaels." Two nurses, Denise, Dr. Michaels, and Shamus all watched in hopeful anticipation. If this were a movie she'd awaken, Shamus thought. She'd open her eyes, look up at him and say his name. But it was not a movie, and Meg did not stir.

* * *

Pacific Coast University campus was a series of lush greens connected by tree-lined brick walkways. Bell towers and steeples lent an air of historic significance to the Philosophy School. Modern buildings of glass and steel tipped their hats to the future among the science buildings. The center of the art and architecture quad was an oval garden boasting magnificent colors surrounded by sculptures. Adjacent was a checkerboard of grass and concrete squares surrounding a fountain where students sat studying and talking.

Shamus found his way to the business school with the help of a student skateboarding to class. His sister's office was in East Hall, which had little going for it other than some old concrete gargoyles he would have loved to confiscate for a customer back in Connecticut. Otherwise, the red brick building had interesting features but was a disappointment in the midst of impressive architectural planning. Shamus contemplated what could be done to at least spruce the place up – ivy, some sand blasting, and period signage. If he'd owned it, though, given the predictions he'd recently read of a huge earthquake expected in the region within the next twenty years, he would sell it and run like hell. Toying with fate, he nonetheless entered the building and climbed the stairs to the second floor. As he reached the landing, a young, slender woman burst through the stairway door and ran into him.

"I'm so sorry!" she exclaimed, clutching at a rapidly dispersing armful of files. Shamus tried to help her, but only managed to dislodge the papers further, scattering them across the landing. She looked young – early thirties. Her wavy, auburn hair fell across her face as she and Shamus retrieved the files. She looked up and smiled warmly. Her eyes were bluish-green, framed by thick, dark brown lashes and beautiful. Her skin was perfect. Make-up would be an insult.

"My lecture will likely be a bit disjointed today," she said looking down at the disordered files in her hands.

Shamus tucked a particularly errant one farther in. "I hear sometimes those can be the best ones." He smiled.

She laughed appreciatively. "You might be right."

Shamus nodded. "I'd shake your hand and introduce myself but…"

The woman nearly dropped her papers again but managed to catch them. "You're Shamus?" She smiled widely.

"And you are?" he asked.

"I'm Susan Harris."

"Oh, yes. Meg told me about you."

She reached out to shake his hand. Her grip was unexpectedly sturdy for a woman no taller than five-two. He gripped her hand more tightly in return, and then eased off to avoid overdoing it. He'd always found handshakes with women complex – too firm and you were an oaf, too soft and you risked an affront to their equality or your masculinity.

"Meg is a wonderful person. I miss her so much. Can she have visitors yet?"

"Not yet. She's in intensive care."

"My God! They said she was going to be okay."

"Who are 'they'?" Shamus asked.

"Our department chair Bill Wilkins for one."

"The truth is she's anything but okay and I haven't a clue how she got that way."

"The rumor is that she was very stressed about the tenure decision," Susan said with obvious skepticism.

"The rumor?" Shamus queried. "You don't think she was stressed?"

"Women don't get tenure here very easily. It's a known fact. Any woman would be worried – but not beside herself, not Meg anyway."

"Anxious?"

"She'd have to be made of steel to avoid anxiety at tenure time. My sex doesn't get promoted around here unless they pass the 'DOES ANYONE VOUCH FOR THIS WOMAN?' test. Some high-placed guy has to want you to stay. Usually the reason has nothing to do with merit. Meg put the traditional guys on notice that she wasn't going to accept a rejection by putting her tail between her legs and slinking off into oblivion like so many 'good girls' had done. She's a highly regarded young scholar. Why should she kiss anyone's feet? Her work on creativity in organizations is groundbreaking stuff. I wish I'd written it."

"And what about you? Are you tenured? Or vouched for?"

"I'm tenured but my career is permanently stalled. I was involved with someone with real pull, otherwise, stellar record or no I'd be searching the lower-ranked business schools for a job."

"Are you sure you're not just underestimating yourself?"

"Wish I could say you're right. But no," she assured him, "Academia, especially in the higher ranked colleges and universities, is far from bereft of politics."

Shamus could feel his expression belie his doubt. A forced smile proved an inadequate subterfuge.

Susan seemed to note the effort. She smiled with embarrassment. "Actually I'm not sure why I told you all that; I guess I feel as though I know you. Meg adores you. She talks about you so much it makes me wish I had an older brother."

"I don't know what she'd have to say about me beyond a few words. I'm one of those what-you-see-is what-you-get types. No still waters running deep here."

Susan glanced at her watch. "Uh-oh, I'm late for my lecture! Hold this, would you?"

She handed him the files, then reached into her purse.

"Here's my card. My home number is on the back." She headed down the stairs, and then turned back.

"Juan the custodian is upstairs. He found your sister the other night. He was the one who saved her life. I thought you might want to talk with him."

Shamus nodded in appreciation.

"Give Meg a hug for me and let me know when I can see her – and the baby."

Just before disappearing down the stairway, Susan waved. He reciprocated. When she was out of sight, he dropped his hand to his side and began to walk. "Meg adores you," he said aloud. And wondered how he'd come to deserve that.

* * *

A secretary noticed Shamus checking the names on each door and after a thorough vetting showed him to Meg's office. She opened the door with her master key and gestured for him to enter. Meg's office was a disappointment. There were none of the academic trappings he'd anticipated. It was basic and claustrophobic to say nothing of being down a hallway away from most of the other offices. He left the door open to vent the stale air, but it was not about to be coaxed or coerced from its familiar surroundings. His eyes moved across the standard issue gray desk ("vintage" would be a kind description) with its neatly arranged papers. On it was a framed photo of their parents, and another of Meg and Shamus at a Christmas party – they looked tipsy but happy. A clock was face down on the desk; everything else seemed in perfect order. A small flowerpot array along a windowless sill and a new computer stood in stark contradiction to the drab furniture.

"Mr. Doherty?"

A graying man, about Shamus' height but more rounded in the midsection was standing in the doorway.

"I'm Bill Wilkins, *department chair*," he said with emphatic self-congratulation.

The man smelled odd – not the stench of a locker room but the irrefutable intimation of deficient hygiene or truly bad taste in cologne. Shamus nevertheless struggled to avoid premature judgment. It wasn't easy. He reached out to shake hands.

"I won't stay long," Wilkins assured him. " I just came by to say that we're thinking of Meg. Your sister is a brilliant scholar."

"Thank you," Shamus replied.

"She certainly knows that *I* see her that way," Wilkins insisted.

Shamus' brow furrowed. It seemed to him an odd assertion. But he let it pass. "Professor, I was wondering…"

"You can call me Bill," the odd man interjected as if giving Shamus a gift bestowed only on the few worthy.

A momentary silence followed as Shamus considered how to proceed.

"Can you tell me how my sister... I mean how she could...?"

"Stress at tenure time is often acute," Wilkins interrupted, as if describing gastritis rather than attempted suicide. "She obviously fell victim to it. It's not the first time, and certainly won't be the last. According to the *Journal of Higher Education*, tenure is under fire – fewer people are getting it. You can be a superb teacher, I always say, and a marvelous researcher like your sister and still miss it."

Shamus could no longer remain civil. Not after that soliloquy. He did not like this man. He didn't like his manner of speaking, his practiced responses, and his use of the word "obviously."

"You can't be serious," Shamus challenged. "If you're superb and marvelous and you don't get tenure, something is wrong. Something stinks."

Wilkins twitched. He stood more erect as if to offset his discomfort.

"Why would she do what you're suggesting before she even knew whether she'd been declined..."

Wilkins' hazel eyes turned to gray ice.

"...and she was pregnant."

The professor's entire face was now a red, rigid, moist mask. His speech had not worked and he was not pleased.

"I don't know, Mr. Doherty." Wilkins fiddled with his tie.

"Do you have tenure?" Shamus asked, casually.

"Oh yes." Wilkins' chest swelled. "That was some time ago, though."

"And are you a full professor, too?"

"Yes, I am." He stood even taller.

"From your vantage point – *Bill* – what are my sister's chances of being tenured?"

"I couldn't really say. So many factors enter into the tenure decision. *I* support her, of course."

"Of course," Shamus said sarcastically.

"I go to the mat for my people," Wilkins said defensively. "It's part of the job. Some people here don't like it, but when I think highly of someone I'm not about to keep it a secret." He abruptly nodded his head as if to say, "So there!"

"My people," Shamus mulled softly.

"What?" Wilkins asked.

"Oh, nothing," Shamus replied, forcing a smile. "Then I take it she'll be able to count on you when she recovers?"

"Absolutely. She has my vote." The response had been too quick.

"That must have been comforting to her. I mean having the chair of your department pulling for you has to be a real plus, doesn't it? Any assistant professor would feel great about that. Right?"

"I suppose so."

"She'd have to have enemies elsewhere, then, for her to feel less than secure." Shamus pressed. He moved closer to the somewhat shorter Wilkins.

"That isn't necessarily..."

"...I mean look at it this way. Here's her chairman thinking she's the cat's meow and ready to go to the mat for her – and she decides to hang herself. What the hell could she have been thinking? I mean you have to ask yourself." He looked directly into Wilkins' eyes.

The now uncomfortable professor's brow tightened. Small beads of sweat emerged along his hairline. Clearly this time, he hadn't missed the sarcasm in Shamus' tone.

"Tell me, Bill, because you'd know. How is it that a young woman barely thirty years old tries to take her life when her department chair thinks she's wonderful? How is that?" Shamus stepped back as if finished, and then pointed aggressively at Wilkins. "Oh, and before you answer, add to that her credentials and her widespread reputation for brilliance. Now, tell me."

"I don't know." Wilkins said curtly, trembling now with suppressed anger. "She must have been a very upset young woman, perhaps lonely and in deep psychological pain due to the loss of her parents and, I dare say, an absentee brother."

"That's what you social scientists call a theory, isn't it?"

"It's what we call an astute observation. Something an indifferent brother three thousand miles away couldn't possibly make." Wilkins smirked with satisfaction at his riposte.

"You must be a California native then, surrounded by family," Shamus ventured, betting on the rareness of such a breed.

Wilkins' smugness receded, replaced by imperfectly veiled scorn. "I'll bid you farewell. Perhaps our paths will cross again before you leave and all of this will be a bad memory." Without waiting for Shamus' reply, he turned and left abruptly.

As Wilkins' footsteps echoed down the hall, Shamus closed the office door. Had he gone too far, gotten too accusatory with a man in whose hands his sister's tenure surely lay? But this pompous, self-important fool had irked him by both demeanor and words. Denise was right. He didn't know how to manage people, especially ones like Wilkins who thought more of themselves than deserved, who gave vacuous speeches rather than talk to people. It would be hard, but he promised himself he'd do better – try harder – for Meg's sake. And with people like Wilkins for whom disdain was instant, he'd keep a wide berth.

Before leaving Shamus searched for Juan. He needed to thank the man who'd saved his sister's life and to learn as much as possible about how Juan had found Meg and what he'd seen or heard beforehand. But Juan was nowhere to be found.

* * *

Shamus returned to the hospital. It was hard to leave Meg there alone unless he could convince himself that something important had to be accomplished. He doubted that she could sense his presence, but he wasn't taking any chances. So he sat, watching her, reading and then dozing off. His mouth was open wide; his head back against the top of the faux leather chair when the loud echoing of a dropped metal tray jolted him from his slumber. He looked blearily at the clock before retrieving his bearings. Then he turned to his sister.

"Meg!"

She had regained some color in her face. The lids of her blue-gray eyes valiantly struggled to open. She blinked several times before they did.

"Look at you," Shamus beamed at her.

"Shamus?"

"Yes. It's me, Meg."

Her eyes remained on him in disbelief before widening in horror. "Oh, no. Please God no!" she gasped. She looked at her abdomen. "No," she said softly pleading. She placed both hands where her baby had been. Her eyes closed tightly. Her eyelashes were moist. Her mouth turned down in profound emotional pain.

"Meg. Listen to me. The baby is fine." He waited. "Do you hear me? He's fine."

She opened her eyes. Tears rolled down her cheeks as she gazed at her brother.

Shamus smiled gently. He placed his hand on her head and then on her shoulder. "He's fine," he whispered. "I promise."

She smiled warmly and reached to take his hand from her shoulder. She squeezed it.

"Thank God," Meg whispered.

Shamus put his other hand on hers. He watched her as she again looked around the room.

"What happened to me?" she asked – her voice scratchy.

"You had an accident," Meg. "There's no need to talk about it right now."

Meg suddenly grimaced in pain and lifted her head from the pillows.

"What?" Shamus said, alarmed.

"My head," she murmured as she placed one hand on her forehead. "It aches."

"It's all right," Shamus said attempting to assure her. "Don't talk." He searched frantically for the buzzer that had become entwined in the sheets. "There's no need to think about anything now. You just woke up from a coma."

"I can't remember."

"That's normal, Meg. It's amnesia. It happens to people who experience trauma. Don't punish yourself." He untangled the buzzer and pushed hard.

Meg winced again. Shamus took her hand and squeezed it lightly.

A nurse rushed into the room. She looked at Meg in surprise and then signaled that she'd be right back as she turned and exited the room. A few moments later Dr. Michaels was at Meg's bedside. He looked hopefully at Meg and then at Shamus. "Did she speak?"

"Yes," Shamus replied. "Her head is killing her."

Dr. Michaels snapped an order to the nurse. He looked back down at Meg. She was smiling slightly through the pain.

He smiled with tenderness.

The nurse returned and used a syringe to administer pain medication though an intravenous tube leading to Meg's arm.

"That will work shortly. You'll feel groggy but better."

Meg nodded. "Thank you," she whispered.

"You had us very worried," Dr. Michaels said looking to Shamus as if for corroboration.

Shamus nodded.

"Don't try to talk anymore," Dr. Michaels instructed.

Meg opened her mouth as if about to speak.

"You heard me," he insisted. "No talking. And your brother will need to leave now." Dr. Michaels looked over at Shamus inviting him to agree.

Shamus hesitated before his expression turned to acquiescence. "I'll check on you in a few hours, Meg."

Dr. Michaels looked at Meg and smiled. "You just rest. There's nothing that can't wait until tomorrow."

Meg's eyes were closing despite her resistance. Shamus glanced at Dr. Michaels and back at Meg. Would she awaken again? He stood by her bedside watching her sleep. Dr. Michaels had moved to the doorway and was waiting for Shamus to join him. Another look at Meg, a pat on her hand and he reluctantly followed Dr. Michaels from the room.

* * *

Shamus arrived early the next morning. Meg's bed was somewhat raised. Her eyes were closed. He sat in the bedside chair. She opened her eyes and smiled.

"Don't you look good?" Shamus said delighted. He rose from the chair. "I checked with the nurse last night. You were in a deep sleep."

"I'm doing better," Meg said. Her voice was still raspy but stronger.

Shamus smiled. "You're a trooper for sure, Meg."

Meg nodded appreciatively.

"I just saw the baby," Shamus said smiling warmly as if he carried the glow from the nursery just for her. "He's adorable. And he seems quite fond of his uncle."

Meg beamed. "Of course."

"I suppose you were going to eventually tell me about him."

She looked down and then up at Shamus. "I would have."

"Maybe after he was born?" Shamus teased. "Or maybe when he graduated from high school?"

"It was complicated," she said.

"Appears that way."

She coughed and motioned for some water. Shamus placed the cup on the bedside tray and positioned it so the straw nearly met her lips. She took two long sips before sitting back against the pillows.

Meg reached for Shamus' hand and closed her fingers around it. "Is he beautiful?"

"He's a Doherty."

"Surely better looking than that," Meg quipped with effort.

"Impossible."

She sipped more water. Her expression turned earnest. "Shamus, if something happens to me, will you...? I know it's a lot to ask, but..."

"You're going to be fine. All that kid needs is somebody like me trying to figure out which way to pin the diaper."

"They don't use pins anymore," Meg laughed softly.

"You're not going to strap those plastic thingies on him?"

She shook her head in amusement.

"Isn't cloth better? I mean doesn't the kid grow up more stable or something?"

"You're too much."

"I've been told that. Listen, you need to rest now."

"I'm serious. If anything should happen to me..."

"What about his father?"

Meg closed her eyes as if buying time. She looked up at Shamus.

He waited.

She took in a deep breath and let it out slowly. "It was a passing thing. He's not involved."

"Does he know?"

Meg looked annoyed. "Believe me, he's not interested."

"Not *interested?*"

"In either of us." She coughed and sipped more water.

"But…"

"Shamus, you're right. I'm too tired for this. If something happens to me…"

Shamus held up his hand. "He would have to put up with his uncle for the rest of his life…"

"Thank you, Shamus."

"But the thought of *that* should keep you out of a coma."

Meg laughed softly. She said nothing for a moment. Then her eyelids lowered and her mouth bowed upward as if in regret. She looked at Shamus. "There's a lot to tell you."

"It can wait," he said. "Just rest."

"I've *been* resting," she insisted. She coughed again. Her face flushed, red.

Shamus put a hand on Meg's shoulder. "We can get into all of it later."

"It hurts to talk but I have to."

"It can wait until you get more rest," Dr.Michaels announced as he entered the room.

"That's what I tried to tell her," Shamus defended.

Dr. Michaels nodded to Shamus with a modicum of appreciation and then fixed his attention on Meg. "We both know she does as she pleases."

Meg did not smile. "What happened to me? Why was I in a coma? What day is this?"

Shamus took her hand. "Juan found you hanging in your office late Friday night. You were either attacked by someone, or the police think…you…might have…"

Meg looked shocked. "I wouldn't have tried to take my life!" she said to Shamus.

Shamus' lips tightened. He closed his eyes briefly as if pushing away the image she was rejecting.

Meg was looking squarely into her brother's eyes as he opened them. "You know that, Shamus."

"Meg, I believe you," Shamus said softly. "Just rest."

She held his eyes with hers – searching for the truth. "And I would never…"

"I know," Shamus interrupted abruptly. He paused and then forced a smile. "Honestly I do," he said more softly.

Shamus looked at Dr. Michaels. "Mothers-to-be don't try to kill themselves, especially this one," he asserted.

"You two can continue this discussion tomorrow. Right now I'm ordering Meg to rest. That's all there is to it. No more talking. "

"I want to hold Johnny," Meg insisted. "I keep asking."

Shamus' heart jumped in his chest. He looked at the doctor horrified that he'd tell Meg the truth – that she couldn't see him.

Dr. Michaels smiled as he looked down at Meg. "Soon," he comforted. "Very soon. I promise."

Shamus sat down. He contemplated that promise, knowing it to be one of those false but equally necessary ones few people escape making in life. Still he half blamed the doctor. Surely there was something he could do.

Meg began to cough again. Dr. Michaels picked up the cup and brought the straw to her lips. He looked at Shamus. "Perhaps you should go," he said more as an instruction than a suggestion.

"I can't do that. But I'll sit here quietly."

Dr. Michaels returned the cup to the tray. He studied Shamus. He turned his attention back to Meg. "Don't talk to him. He's here for company. We'll be coming in and out – the nurses, Dr. Cohen and I. You'll talk with us only when necessary. That will be enough." He waited.

"And my baby?"

"If you work with me, I'll work with you," Dr. Michael's said emphatically. He waited again.

Meg reluctantly nodded.

Dr. Michaels smiled skeptically. He moved slowly to the door as if thinking of something else to say. Instead, he nodded at Shamus, shot Meg a physician's warning glance, and departed.

Shamus and Meg sat in silence, she looking at the wall, he at the floor. As much as he wanted to reassure her, to tell her the baby would be with her soon, that all of would be sorted out, and he'd make it all go away like a bad dream, the words did not come.

CHAPTER FOUR

Meg could never think straight in a mess. As a teenager she'd kept her closet neat, her bed made and her desk organized, much to Shamus' consternation. His parents had commented often on the slovenly room of their firstborn, denied him allowance, refused him rides to events, but nothing worked for long.

Seated at Meg's office desk, Shamus wondered where to start looking for clues in such orderly surroundings.

"May I help you find something?"

A tall, dark-skinned man with smiling brown eyes, wavy black hair and slight sideburns stood in the doorway. He was jacketless, but his teal blue shirt, top button open, was perfection as if he'd stood all day to avoid creases.

"I'm Meg Doherty's brother," Shamus said, rising to shake hands. "I was looking for the keys to her car and apartment."

"Ah, yes. Shamus. I'm Rashid Singh. I work across the hall." His tone was almost exuberant; his accent seemed Indian. Rashid extended his hand. Shamus grasped the man's large hand with intentional firmness. An amused expression crept across Rashid's face, and Shamus lightened his grip.

"She keeps her purse in the bottom, left-hand drawer under some paper," Rashid detailed to Shamus' surprise. "And her briefcase is behind the far left file drawer. You'll find her green Focus in Parking Structure A near the main entrance to the university, usually on the first or second level against the south wall and close to the stairwell. She comes in early so she has a better choice of spots than we later arrivals."

"I guess you know my sister pretty well."

"Not only are we office neighbors, but I dare say, friends as well."

"You wouldn't happen to know her computer password, would you?"

"Now that's something the police did not ask me," Rashid said, grinning appreciatively. "You are wiser."

"They were here?"

"Here, you say? They've been everywhere on campus. But a detective named Rawlins spent a lot of time with me. Wilkins likely arranged that."

"Did they hint at what they think happened?"

"The detective isn't someone who gives much information. He never smiled. He's very focused."

"I'll need to talk with him."

"Don't expect a warm greeting," Rashid said. "You might try 'GOPC' for your sister's password. It stands for 'Go Pacific Coast.' We were put on a new system recently and many of us haven't changed our departmental codes to personal ones. We're supposed to do it right away for security reasons, but I myself haven't done it yet."

Shamus nodded in appreciation. "You're a professor?"

"I guess you could say that," he smiled as if Shamus had touched upon an in-joke that wasn't entirely amusing. "Not like your sister, though. I'm what you call an adjunct."

"Is that part time?"

"Not in my case. I am full time. I am not a researcher like your sister and so not on a tenure track. 'Adjunct' is a euphemism for 'second class citizen.' One gets the impression that people with such a title are peripheral. I much prefer to be called 'teaching specialist' or something similar to identify that I have a reason for being here and a darned good one at that. However, the powers that be prefer to remind us daily of where we stand. Academia is filled with such subtle distinctions between researchers and simple teachers like myself. Some people, of course, do both well. 'Good for them' is the prevalent attitude, because what really counts around here is research. And I ask you, should everyone at a university be a researcher? What if everyone in a company was an accountant? It makes no sense. But I do have a window in my office. And a rickety fire escape stairwell as an extra extravagance."

"The window must mean something." Shamus said encouragingly.

"I'm the coach of the case competition team. Since visiting coaches come to my office from leading universities around the world, we can't have them visiting me in a dump without a window. Otherwise I'd be in a closet like this one – and I'd be sharing it with two other adjuncts."

"I see," Shamus said – not really seeing at all.

"Meg is in intensive care?" Rashid said, only half asking.

"I thought the word around here, Doctor Singh, was that she's doing okay."

"If I listened to the word around here, I wouldn't still *be* here after ten years – and call me Rashid. When I called the hospital, I was most amazed and distressed."

"She's awake at least."

"Thank God for that."

Shamus reflected appreciatively on Rashid's sincerity.

"I was surprised about the baby," Rashid continued.

"Not as surprised as I was," Shamus said, shaking his head in renewed disbelief. "I had no idea my sister was pregnant."

"Oh, the pregnancy was no surprise to me. My wife and I have had four children. I recognized Meg's condition months ago. What surprised me was that the child made it through such an ordeal."

Shamus felt an uncanny comfort with this man. He had to ask someone the question that had not yet been asked: "Why didn't she tell me she was pregnant?" Shamus watched Rashid's face, hopeful that he'd not expected too much from this kind man.

"That, I am afraid, is something you will have to ask your sister," Rashid said calmly. "All I can say is that she told me she planned to name it after your father if it was a boy and after your mother if it was a girl. I guess this little one will be called Johnny."

"Yes."

"And you've no doubt seen the new addition to your family?"

"I have," Shamus said, relieved he'd not neglected that duty.

"And?"

The question puzzled Shamus momentarily. Rashid raised his eyebrows, as if Shamus should certainly know the answer.

"Oh – Yes! He's adorable."

Rashid smiled. "Of course he is." Then he turned pensive. "Who knows why people choose not to share their inner turmoil?" Rashid said kindly. "Meg is not an open book. From what she has told me of you, the condition seems to run in the family."

Shamus found no hint of insult in Rashid's expression.

"You are an uncle, Shamus. Last week you were a brother only. You now also have a part of your family lying in a crib just a mile from here. It's a good sign – a blessing."

This was a concept with which Shamus could not yet identify, but he nodded appreciatively.

"Have you considered that the baby might be just what Meg needs to give her strength?" Rashid asked, as if he'd somehow read Shamus' mind and found his thoughts wanting. "She is a very tough lady, but we all recover more quickly with a reason beyond ourselves."

There was compassion in every aspect of Rashid's face. No indication of prying or lecturing, just gentle support.

"You're a wise professor, Rashid," Shamus said.

"I am a good teacher – not an adjunct but a very good teaching specialist." Rashid smiled broadly as if sharing a moment of lightness with a very good friend.

* * *

After another fruitless search for Juan, Shamus headed for the police station east of the university on Pico Boulevard. He noticed a small guitar store beckoning him to visit. He wasn't proficient but he dabbled, and rarely passed a guitar store without dropping in. Further along was a diner bustling with people, one he noted for a future breakfast. A few blocks along he noticed an Italian restaurant he surely would have tried given a different reason for his visit. A nice place to take Denise, he thought. The image had crept into his mind without warning. He shook his head and bopped his forehead with the palm of his right hand. "Sure, Shamus," he said. "You and the beautiful doctor. Right. They're always looking for construction foremen to date." He smiled. He laughed. It had been an absurd thought. It had also been a pleasant one.

The police station was a stark place. Unkempt and well-groomed suspects sat on a bench uncomfortably conjoined by circumstances and trepidation. Their now uncertain lives were in juxtaposition to the jaunty goings-on of confident young policemen across the room. Shamus wondered at the small and large decisions that must have occurred, allowing some to be admired and others go on to lives of intermittent or continuous crime. He often pondered such things – how one wrong turn, one year of neglect, a moment or period of abuse could take an otherwise promising young person and set him on the path to which many walking by him were firmly committed. And what of those whose generous families had tried everything only to suffer as their progeny chose to shut them out – to steal or harm? Shamus had been contemplating such whims of fate, such twists of genetics for nearly half an hour when a slender, mid-thirtyish, spit-and-polish, assured officer approached him.

"Who is it you're waiting for?"

"I'm looking for the detective who investigated my sister's case. Four days ago she was found in her office." Shamus paused searching for words to describe her condition that night. None came. "His name is Rawlins."

"Right. I'll see if he's in." The officer pointed a long index finger directly at Shamus, lowered his chin and raised his steel blue eyes. Not a hint of a smile. He held that position for no more than two seconds, but the message was clear. Shamus was to stay put.

He used the time to plan how he'd approach the detective. He would try to be patient and open to the officer's views, not reactive to personality flaws – in short, out of character.

"I'm Rawlins." The gruff voice was the kind that encourages you to state your business and move on. Cut from the same cloth as the young officer.

"Shamus Doherty."

The handshake was the same – all business.

"My sister, Meg Doherty, was found – well – hanging in her office."

"Did that investigation myself. What can I do for you?" Again, the tone bade a quick reply.

"Meg is concerned that you think it was a suicide attempt."

"Yeah, go on."

Somewhat put out by the detective's comfort with the topic, Shamus nonetheless continued: "Well, she's not the type."

"I see where you're going." Rawlins looked away momentarily, barked some orders at an instantly intimidated young cop, then turned back to Shamus. "Where were we? Oh, yeah, well we're waiting for the big shot doctor over there at the university hospital – Michaels, right? He'll tell us when we can talk to your sister."

"Aren't there other people you can talk with while you're waiting?" Shamus said with stifled annoyance.

Rawlins was watching him. His silence was purposeful, inviting of discomfort. The detective waited for a response. Shamus did not move a muscle. Rawlins looked over at the young cop who dropped some papers and rushed off. Rawlins turned back toward Shamus. He looked down at the floor, ran his left index finger along his cheek, held his thumb under his chin, paused, reflected, looked up without eye contact and motioned for Shamus to follow him down a corridor. His office was consistent with its surroundings. Papers were in disarray on the desk, shelves and even the windowsills. A beige mug that had no doubt seen many years of bad guys and infrequent washing was precariously perched on one such pile.

"We've been looking into it, and we have been interviewing people, but I have to tell you that nothing has made us suspicious," Rawlins said, signaling for Shamus to take a seat. "There was no evidence of a struggle, no indication that she fought someone," he reported, kicking a pizza box out of the way as he navigated to his own chair. "We talked to her Department Chair." Rawlins looked upward, searching his mind for the name.

"Wilkins," Shamus offered.

"Yeah, Wilkins." He pointed at Shamus appreciatively. "He blames the stress of tenure."

"And you *believe* him?"

Rawlins sat forward, less willing now to let Shamus' annoyed tone pass. "He knows her."

"He thinks he knows her," Shamus shot back.

Rawlins took a sip from the mug and cringed from the bitterness of the coffee. It smelled stale. He placed the cup down on his desk and nudged it away. "Hey, it can't be easy," he said, somewhat sympathetically. "I mean it being your sister. Wouldn't sit well with me if she were my sister. But people do this a lot, especially in cities. We've got a backlog of cases you wouldn't believe. When men attempt suicide, they usually succeed. Women are more likely to use pills or do what your sister did. If they're lucky, someone finds them before they're dead. Your sister was one of the lucky ones."

"I suppose you could say that." Though it seemed odd to Shamus that luck could be considered a by-product of such a horrific situation.

"No supposing about it. She was lucky. But I'm not the person to talk to here. We have people who talk to families. You can probably tell it's not my strong suit."

"What are you going to do next?" Shamus asked.

"Next?" Rawlins looked confused. "Talk to the doctor. Talk with your sister. But we don't expect this case to be open much longer."

"You've got to be joking."

"Listen," Rawlins said pointing his index finger as the young officer had done only with even more certainty. "Most relatives of attempt suicides and suicides feel just like you do."

They even had a slang term for it, Shamus thought. "Attempt suicide" made it sound distant, like something that didn't happen to a person – to his sister. No wonder they had "people to talk to families," he thought.

Rawlins was watching him, the pointing over, impatiently waiting for a response.

"All I can say is that Meg is a fighter and a devout Catholic at that."

Shamus' tone was even now, not defensive.

"I'm no psychiatrist – and I'm sure no priest – but this happens to people whose relatives think they'd never do it in a million years."

"Pregnant women kill themselves?" Shamus asked, disbelieving.

Rawlins looked directly at Shamus. His deep brown eyes were fixed and stern. "I didn't say that."

"Well, that's what she was – and far along in that pregnancy too." He watched now for Rawlins' reaction.

For a moment Rawlins held his eyes motionless again, as if penetrating Shamus' mind. Then his eyebrows relaxed. He sat back in his chair.

"And she can't even hold that baby now because of some law you guys have here in California. She can't hold her own child. The Department of Children and Family Services will take Johnny soon. And then what will my sister have?"

Rawlins looked down at the floor – thinking. He looked up at Shamus and paused before speaking. "Listen, I'm not trying to be insensitive here, but this is a big city. We don't have time to chase possibilities. I talked to the janitor who found your sister. He said she'd been under stress. There weren't any signs of forced entry or a struggle. There were no signs of foul play and no fibers or blood under her fingernails."

Rawlins looked at his watch. Gray circles under his eyes darkened. He closed his eyes, took in a deep breath and let it out slowly. His eyes opened and he forced a brief smile.

"Listen, give me something to work with and I might put an officer on it. After we talk to your sister, maybe we'll have a reason to look for more than seems to be there. We did a thorough investigation."

"And if I find something?" Shamus offered as if sure he would.

"Then you call me." Rawlins was pointing again.

"I'll do that," Shamus promised curtly as he rose to leave.

"Just make sure you do exactly that," Rawlins said emphatically. His finger now jerking forward and back. "Last thing we need around here is a guy from Connecticut snooping around, looking under every rock by the road."

"Yeah, I know. This isn't Kansas. I've been told."

"It isn't," Rawlins insisted. Shamus rose from the chair to leave. Rawlins got up and came around his desk. He stood facing Shamus – a bit too close to be anything other than an assertion of power. They were about the same height. "If you're so sure your sister didn't try to kill herself, then you should try being a little less flippant and keep your attention focused on her recovery. We do the police work around here. Got me?"

Shamus could have gotten angry. He considered it while he looked steadily at Rawlins. For a moment neither of them moved. But there was something about this detective that stifled Shamus' inclination to argue. At least part of it was the tone Rawlins had taken. It wasn't one of pure superiority but rather a composite of experience and interest in Shamus' well being. He nodded and reached to shake Rawlins' hand. Rawlins' shoulders relaxed. He looked at Shamus' hand. As he reached out to shake it, his eyes rose to give Shamus a warning. Shamus nodded, smiled sheepishly, turned and left the office.

* * *

Shamus returned to campus and headed for parking structure A. He searched the first and second levels, checking the south wall and the opposite side. There was no green Focus. He tried the third level, the fourth and finally the roof. No sign of a car fitting the description she'd so excitedly given him when, months earlier, she'd purchased her first new car. His own advice regarding the purchase had been flatly ignored. He'd told her over and over about the stats on small cars in city traffic. That subject was one that had gotten his attention. Distant as he felt from his sister, he wanted her to be safe. But apparently, he thought, to no avail.

An hour of searching did not produce the car. Had Rashid been wrong? He'd seemed so certain of exactly where Meg would have parked. Had someone stolen it? He could ask Meg, but it might upset her. One more mystery would go unsolved for the moment. She'd need her strength for much worse news. How that would be delivered was beyond him. How do you tell a new mother that she cannot hold her newborn? What words make that palatable?

The guard at the kiosk directed him to a rental car location two blocks up the road. He rented a silver Volvo sedan and headed for the hospital.

CHAPTER FIVE

"Meg, wake up!"

She was writhing and struggling in the bed.

"It's me – Shamus!" He gently shook her right shoulder. He shook it again more firmly.

Meg opened her eyes wide. She was terrified and for a moment, frozen, it seemed, and lost in a way he'd not seen her before.

Meg turned toward him. She took a deep breath. "Shamus! Thank God!"

"What's the matter?"

"I don't know. I had this dream…it was awful. I couldn't awaken. There was someone standing right where you are now. He was hovering, breathing heavily, glancing back at the door and then at me." She took a deep breath in and out slowly. "It sounds ridiculous, doesn't it? But it felt so real."

"With what you've been through, I'm not surprised. They've given you sedatives. It's natural to have reactions to those. Dr. Michaels should know about this. He should pull back on the dose." Shamus' voice was comforting, but the rest of him was clearly agitated. Like the counterfeit intruder, he glanced back at the door and then, forcing a smile, he looked at Meg.

"Sit with me, Shamus. I want to try and piece together what happened the other night. I'll talk to Dr. Michaels. This is more important right now."

Skeptical that she would tell Dr. Michaels, he nevertheless pulled up a chair and sat beside the bed. "I talked with a detective Rawlins at the police station," Shamus said. He took her hand and squeezed it then placed it gently back on the bed. "Not much help from him so far. But he says he'll be coming to see you."

"Thanks," she said softly. Her eyes were studying his and smiling.

Shamus returned the smile, acknowledging her appreciation of a long overdue, clearly more meaningful than he could have anticipated, brotherly display of affection. "Meg," he said tentatively. "I talked to Rashid. He said you always park in Structure A, along the south wall – on level one or two?"

"Rashid knows me very well," Meg said, amused, by the endearing qualities of a truly rare, kind friend.

"Well, I didn't want to upset you with this, but I looked all through the parking garage. I couldn't find it."

"It probably isn't there. When I'm going to stay late I usually move my car from the parking structure to Lot B, near East Hall. It's easier than waiting for a security escort."

With some difficultly, Meg repositioned herself in the bed. "If it's in lot B, then I must have planned to stay late that night." She looked at Shamus. Her brow was furrowed as if her mind was attempting to reach for some remnant of recollection. "I need to remember more. Why is that night so cloudy in my mind? It's driving me crazy. Some student might be dealing with this guy right now."

"The brain has a defensive mechanism, Meg," Shamus said

encouragingly. "Give it time. I'll check on the car." He rose from the chair. "Just promise me you'll get some rest. You've been through a lot. You don't seem to accept the severity of the shock and injury you've experienced. I don't want you relapsing into a coma, or worse."

Meg smiled tenderly at his concern. "Okay. I'll rest. But call me when you find the car. And if you don't see me in this room when you get back, don't worry. They might move me to a regular room today."

"No way!"

"Shamus, I can't take up space in intensive care," she said emphatically. "I don't need it now. This is my call now, Shamus. Trust me. The better I get, the sooner I can be with Johnny."

He looked intently at her. Had someone told her? "What do you mean?"

"I think you know," Meg said as her eyes moistened.

Shamus moved closer to her. He placed his right hand gently on her shoulder.

"They think I tried to kill my baby, Shamus. They won't let me touch him." She covered her eyes with her hands and rocked. "What if they take him from me?"

"Meg. Listen to me. They're wrong. And we'll prove it. He took her other shoulder in his hand and looked directly into her eyes. "Johnny is fine. Nobody is going to take him from you. You'll be able to at least see him soon. I'll make sure of that." He stepped back, his head tilted in sympathy, his own eyes moist.

Meg looked up at the ceiling. She lifted and dropped her arms in maternal defeat – the agony mothers know when they've not measured up to some standard real or imagined. Her eyes still closed, lips quivering, chest heaving from stifled sobs, brow tortured, tears streaming down her raw cheeks, Meg shakily took Shamus' hands in hers and squeezed as he had done to hers moments before.

"Trust me, Meg. You'll hold him soon. You've got to be strong. You've got to get well. He's your child. No one can change that. No one. We won't let them."

Meg nodded once and attempted a smile.

Shamus stayed by her bedside. Just being there beside her seemed to bring her some comfort. He noticed a paperback book from the hospital library on her nightstand – *Persuasion* by Jane Austen. It would do. He read quietly. Finally, just as he was beginning to gain admiration for the writer beloved by women, Meg's emotional pain gave in to rest, then to sleep. He left the room for the university determined to come back to her with better clues about what really happened that night – to bring his sister closer to holding her child.

* * *

The green Focus was in a far corner of lot B. He got in, turned the ignition key and let the motor run as he looked around for a map. A *Thomas Guide* – a beat up, fat book of Los Angeles area street maps – was in the back under the floor mat. He searched the book for Culver City. Denise had been right, he would not have wanted to look for it on little sleep.

Now knowing where Meg's car was, he left it, returned the silver Volvo rental and walked back to the parking structure. He carefully checked all the switches, adjusted the driver's seat to his liking, aligned the rear and side view mirrors and finally inched his way out of the campus parking lot into L.A. traffic.

He considered visiting the baby. The little guy didn't have anyone in the world to hold him except strangers and his uncle. He pushed away the guilt and decided to postpone. He'd held the infant again before seeing Meg the day before – this time more comfortably. Nurse Shaughnessy hadn't known who'd visited Johnny the day Ellen had been there, because no one had signed in. The stranger had just looked at Johnny and left. Shamus assumed it was the father. Maybe Meg was wrong. Maybe he did care, Shamus thought. Or he might have wanted to catch a glimpse of his biological offspring even if he didn't plan to raise a finger to help. In any case, Shamus wanted to catch a glimpse of *him* and share a few words about responsibility.

At two o'clock in the afternoon, he found himself bumper-to-bumper on Interstate 405 heading south. There had to be an easier way. But he was sticking to the main highways as much as possible. Stuck for what seemed an eternity under an overpass, he maintained a lookout for vandals who might dump paint on the car from above and for ones on the ground who, sensing his anxiety, might surround him like a pack of mad dogs setting on a scared rabbit. No doubt they'd know he was from out of town. It was probably written all over his face.

After about twenty minutes, for some unknown reason, the traffic began to move and thin out. He found Meg's apartment building on quiet, tree-lined Keagan Street. There were the usual stucco exterior walls; her building recently painted a light green. Window boxes brimmed with colorful flowers. He parked at the curb in front.

The apartment was on the second floor. A neighbor let him into the lobby. Shamus filed this breach of security for a future discussion with Meg. He fumbled with the keys. The third one was the charm. He opened the door to a room filled with light coming from a French door leading to an exterior balcony. The couches and chairs were upholstered in white. The rug in the center of a gleaming wood floor was a pale blue. Family photos were hung on the far wall and there was a Waterford crystal vase on the fireplace mantel. An open copy of *Fortune* magazine lay on the couch next to a novel he didn't recognize and a copy of David McCullough's *The Great Bridge*. Shelves lined another wall with groupings of hardcover books punctuated by colorful vases.

Shamus went out, retrieved his luggage from the car and took up residence in the guestroom. Sitting on the bed, he picked up the phone, called the hospital and left a message for Meg: "Found car in lot B." Then he let himself collapse backwards on the bed. His brain relented, letting him slip back in sleep to a place and time he'd avoided for years.

If only his homework hadn't been complete. But it was. And so as he'd planned yet never carried out until this night, Shamus hopped on his bicycle to meet his father's train. Even the cold October air and slight mist did not deter the determined eleven-year-old from his plan to surprise his father. He grinned at the thought of the delighted expression his father would have on his face seeing his son, now old enough to make the evening trip, meet him at the station. He pushed out of his mind his father's distaste for surprises. This was different. It was not a birthday surprise party which Shamus' mother, to her misfortune, had given her husband two years earlier. The arguments about that had gone on for months, until finally nothing more was said about it. No time to think about that, Shamus told himself, the joy of surprise once more the focus of his attention. Besides, this was different. This was a son showing his affection to a father home from a long day's work.

Shamus pedaled furiously, careening down the final hill to the Georgetown station. He heard the approaching train's whistle just as he squealed into the parking lot where his father's car, as always, had been parked in the space closest to the platform steps. Shamus scurried up the steps and hid behind a large trash bin. He could feel the cold wind cut through him, but his shivering was one of anticipation. If he timed it right, he could jump out just as his father exited the train.

Through the windows of one of the dimly lit cars he caught a glimpse of his father's black, woolen hat. He ducked back behind the bin – chilled with anticipation. It would be only a few moments now and he didn't want to ruin it by jumping the gun. He wanted his father to feel the full impact of the surprise. He'd imagined it a hundred times.

The train screeched to a stop. For a moment nothing happened. People by the doors stood like obedient soldiers. Then suddenly as if the requisite delay had been accomplished, the doors opened. From his lookout, Shamus could see his father's hat moving up the aisle toward the door right in front of where his excited son hid. It couldn't have been more perfect. His father was talking to someone. Shamus' anticipation welled up within him. One more moment, Shamus told himself. A part of him wanted to leap out, but he waited.

He could see his father's face clearly now. He was talking in an uncharacteristically animated fashion. He threw his head back in laughter. Shamus stretched to get a better look. At first he thought it was a small man, but his final stretch revealed a woman. His father stepped aside at the door to let her exit first. He held her elbow in a chivalrous manner assuring that she would not step into the gap between the train and platform. She was young, pretty, and completely engrossed in his father's words.

Shamus was becoming annoyed. The woman was walking with his father. If she would only move away, his father would have a clear view of him jumping out from behind the bin. If she would just move he could leap into his father's welcoming arms. But she did not move. Instead, she placed her right hand in his father's left. His father smiled again. He watched as this woman and his father descended the station steps. If he hadn't known otherwise, Shamus would not have believed this smiling man was his father. There was something playful about his demeanor and a youthful glow about his face.

Shamus watched carefully as the pair continued down the stairs into the parking lot. His father placed his key in the car door lock. This might be a good time to jump out. He was still only a few yards from his father. The woman walked around to the passenger side of the car. If his father were to give the woman a ride home, the surprise would surely be ruined. "Just go away," he whispered. "Go away NOW!" But the woman lingered as Shamus' father opened the car door and then tossed his briefcase onto the passenger side seat. It was just a matter of time now, Shamus thought. If he were taking her home, he wouldn't have done that. He would have left the seat clear for her. The anticipation surged through him again. Yes, it was just a matter of time now. Shamus congratulated himself for being patient. The surprise wasn't ruined. There was still time.

Suddenly, Shamus realized that he'd left his bike leaning against the station house not five feet from where his father now stood. If he saw the bike, he'd know. It was a unique bike, one with a license plate that read SHAMUS. There'd be no mistaking it. He chastised himself for his lack of foresight. This one small error could mean the downfall of the entire plan. There was no time left. He leapt from the shadows and was about to shout, "DAD," when he saw that his father was no longer standing by the car. The woman was gone as well. Shamus looked about frantically. Under a streetlight not more than thirty feet from the car, his father and the young woman were walking arm and arm. It was not something he'd seen his mother and father do in a long, long time.

Shamus descended the station steps and quietly turned his bicycle in the direction the two had taken. Perhaps, he assured himself, they are going to call a cab for the woman. Perhaps her car had broken down. He considered turning his bike around and heading for home.

But, on the off chance that upon his father's return the surprise might still work, Shamus stayed. They were nearly out of sight when he decided to follow them, trailing far enough back to not be noticed but close enough to avoid losing them. Within two blocks of the station, they turned into an apartment complex, ascended a few steps and stopped outside number 7. Shamus pulled his bike behind a large oak tree and watched. If he stayed there long enough, his father would pass by after delivering the young woman safely home. He could then jump on his bike, take a short cut, and make it back to the station with time to spare.

The woman retrieved a set of keys from her purse. Shamus grew more hopeful. In a moment she'd finally be gone. That was all that mattered. He moved his bike from behind the tree, in full anticipation of a good head start back to the station. It looked as if it would work out. But then his father entered the woman's apartment. Lights were illuminated in the hallway, which Shamus could see through the windowpane of the door his father had closed behind him. He watched them enter the living room and turn on lights there as well. Why was his father inside? What on earth was he doing in this woman's apartment? This could absolutely ruin everything! Several uneventful moments passed. Shamus watched his father help the young woman with her coat. He left the living room to hang it in the hallway closet. Then he removed his own coat and placed it there too.

While his father was closing the coat closet door, a light was turned on upstairs. Through a break in the sheer lace bedroom curtains, Shamus could see that the young woman had blonde, wavy hair. She might have been thirty, but no more. She removed some pins from her hair, letting it fall loosely upon her shoulders and then she moved toward the window. Shamus dropped his bike and pulled back behind the tree. She opened the window slightly before returning to the center of the room. It was then that Shamus saw what a boy of eleven should never see. His father had entered the woman's bedroom. The two were standing very close. Shamus climbed onto one of the lower limbs of the tree to get a clearer view. He watched as the woman leaned her body against his father. She rested her head upon his chest; she gazed up at him. His father smiled tenderly before touching his lips to hers. Shamus' heart pounded. He watched in disbelief. Anger replaced all hope as the woman unbuttoned his father's shirt, removed it and placed it on the bed. He watched, too, as she loosened his father's belt, and reached her hands about his waist. His father closed his eyes and tilted his head back in pleasure. He tenderly kissed the woman's neck and her lips before taking her about the waist and lifting her onto the bed.

Shamus turned. He ran fast, as if the fury of his feet could pummel the image in his mind. But it was too late. He'd seen too much. His father had betrayed his mother and his children. The father he'd known would never have done this. All the baseball games and family outings had been lies. Shamus' world closed about him.

The tears were gone by the time Shamus returned to the oak tree with his bicycle in tow. In their wake were tracks of steeled antipathy stinging his skin. Shamus remained in the shadow of the tree until his father was nearly upon him. He jumped out and stood erect, angrily gazing directly into his father's surprised eyes. They quickly took on a cold, heartless look. No words were spoken. There was no need. His father stood for a few moments seeming to consider his options. Then he passed by Shamus as if he were not even there. "If you tell your mother," he said not looking back, "it will kill her. It might make you feel better, but it will break her heart."

Shamus leaped onto his bicycle, whizzed by his father, elbow out, knocking him to the ground. As he pedaled furiously up the hill his *eyes again filled with tears. Nothing could ever possibly be the same.*

* * *

A tired looking Shamus entered intensive care to the welcoming smell of lavender and roses emanating from a bouquet awaiting delivery at the front counter. Dr. Michaels had left a message on Meg's answering machine earlier that morning while Shamus had been showering, recovering from a restless night. Dr. Michaels wanted to meet. "Nothing urgent," he'd said. "But important." There was no "good-bye," no "I'll see you then," just a click and silence.

As Shamus passed the nurse's station, he noticed two police officers outside a room not far from Meg's room. A middle-aged, brunette woman, disheveled by grief, was seated nearby. A young man beside her pointed in obvious anger and admonishment at the police officers.

"What's going on?" Shamus asked an orderly.

"They brought in a guy who supposedly shot his wife and her brother. Domestic dispute. Both victims are dead. This guy shot himself, but he didn't finish the job."

As Shamus began to walk again toward Meg's room, he saw Dr. Michaels and Denise in a glassed-off area behind the desk. Dr. Michaels, hovering over Denise who was seated at a large table, appeared to be chastising her. She suddenly stood, hands on hips, chin extended, facing off against her much larger adversary. Despite his intimidating stance, she held on to her resolve. Shamus couldn't quite make out what they were saying, but as their voices increased in volume he heard Meg's name. Dr. Michaels extended his right index finger a half-inch from Denise's nose.

"This is not your business. Do you understand me?" he shouted at her. "Am I making myself perfectly clear?"

Denise's arms crossed defensively. Suddenly, she noticed Shamus.

She slowly turned her back to him and said something to Dr. Michaels that Shamus couldn't hear. He glanced at Shamus. He shook his head with annoyance. There seemed to follow some sort of negotiation. Dr. Michaels, frowning, nodded as if in reluctant agreement. He motioned for Denise to follow him into the corridor.

"Good evening, Mr. Doherty," Dr. Michaels said, remnants of anger still evident.

As Denise emerged, her movements were determined yet somewhat embarrassed. She managed a short smile. "Shamus, I have to go now," she said, as if that were not her idea.

"I'd prefer that you stay." Shamus said.

"She has a lot to do," Dr. Michaels insisted.

"I trust her judgment and I'd like her to be here."

Dr. Michaels glowered. The left side of his lower lip twitched. He looked at Denise, waiting for her to leave. She didn't budge.

Dr. Michaels took in a deep breath, closed his eyes, and then opened them as he exhaled with exasperation. "If Dr. Cohen can spare a few minutes, I suppose we can go over Meg's case together." He forced a half smile in Denise's direction. "Is that something you can do, Dr. Cohen?" he asked stiffly.

"Yes, I'd be glad to do that, Dr. Michaels," she replied, repressing a smile of victory. "Let me check on one patient and I'll meet you both in five minutes."

Shamus nodded in gratitude at Denise. "That suits me. I'd like to see my sister for a few minutes anyway." He smiled at Denise, appreciatively, then turned and walked to Meg's room. He could see from the door that she was asleep. Dr. Michaels was already returning from checking on his patient, so Shamus walked toward him. He would visit Meg later.

Dr. Michaels directed Shamus to the conference room, where he took a seat at the head of the six-foot conference table and invited Shamus to choose a more humble one of his own. They sat in silence for several minutes before Denise entered. She took the chair beside Shamus, opened a pad and retrieved a sleek silver pen from her pocket. Clearly it was a special one. Dr. Michaels took note of it. He stiffened awkwardly as if remembering better times when she'd received the pen – a gift, perhaps, from him. The two refused to look at each other.

"I would like to move your sister to the Psychiatric Unit where she'll be carefully watched."

Denise was about to speak when Dr. Michaels interrupted.

"Dr. Cohen is not in complete agreement with me on this."

"I'll side with her," Shamus said, too quickly.

Dr. Michaels looked at Shamus with derision. "It isn't a matter of sides, Mr. Doherty."

"To be honest, I don't know why you're so hell bent on moving my sister. What's in it for you?"

"Shamus," Denise said curtly. "Dr. Michaels isn't in this for himself."

Shamus' eyes darted at her in irritated disbelief. "If you disagree with him then why are you defending him?"

Denise raised her hands in the air, fed up with both of them.

"What Dr. Cohen thinks of me is not the point here."

"The point," Shamus said with increasing agitation, "Is that you want to put my sister at risk so you can spend the hospital's precious resources on people like that guy in the luxury suite who just shot two people. Now there's someone who deserves special care. The point is that you've decided she tried to kill herself and the baby too. No doubt in your mind. Is there doctor? No."

"Your sarcasm won't help here," Dr. Michaels warned.

"Let me just say this Doctor – if you take a single step to have her moved, I swear I'll..."

"What will you do?" Dr. Michaels bristled.

"I'll ask for a peer review, God damn it!" Shamus wasn't sure what that meant exactly but he knew it could delay things. When he and Meg had held vigil by their father's bed, he'd heard a man threaten to do the same if his own father weren't treated with the highest degree of medical and ethical practice. It had caused those doctors to undergo a quick attitude change. It was worth a try now.

Denise looked at Shamus with new regard. She allowed herself a brief smile.

Seething, Dr. Michaels rose from his chair. "I see absolutely no similarity between you and your sister other than some minor physical attributes. She responds to reason in reasonable ways. You are simply arrogant about things you know absolutely nothing about." He strode from the room.

Denise put her face into her hands. When she pulled them away, her expression was not as encouraging as Shamus expected.

"Shamus, I told you that Dr. Michaels is the best. I think he's moving a bit too quickly here and you've every right to challenge him, and the peer review idea was good, but you could be more diplomatic. There's Meg to think about."

"Denise," he said taking his lead from her first name informality, "I'm sorry but he isn't God."

She took a deep breath. "He knows now that you're a worthy adversary. Even prima donnas can have their reputations dented by peer reviews. He'd just as soon not have one of those. Word gets around." Denise paused. She held his eyes with hers. "So you've made your point – now go see him."

"And tell him what?"

"Tell him that while you don't like his bedside manner, you've heard he knows what he's doing. Ask him if you can trust him to keep Meg in ICU at least until you get another opinion about her physical and mental state.

Tell him that if he turns out to be right, you'll accept Meg's transfer then and offer him an apology."

"I won't promise to offer the apology."

"Fine," Denise said emphatically. "Skip that part."

"Tell me, Denise," Shamus said more temperately now. "Is keeping Meg in ICU what you and Dr. Michaels were arguing about when I arrived today?"

She studied Shamus, wondering, it seemed, whether to share what Dr. Michaels would surely consider having been said in confidence. She rolled her eyes. "All right. Yes. He moves on a little too quickly for me. He rarely second-guesses himself. And he's not known for his sensitivity."

"Tell me about it. What a pompous, pretentious ass!"

"Shamus – that pompous, pretentious ass is my father."

Shamus' jaw dropped. "But – but your name…"

"I was married," she said. "I kept the name Cohen after the divorce. That way people aren't always associating me with my father."

"I'm sorry," Shamus said, feeling completely inept. "I had no idea."

"He's an amazing doctor, Shamus. He's not the world's best father, an abrupt communicator, too sure of himself at times, intolerable at others, but an amazing doctor."

Shamus sighed. "Okay, I'll try to talk with him."

"Do it for Meg," Denise said. "And for Johnny. Don't expect him to change his ways. Just work with him. I've become an expert at that strategy and believe me, Shamus, it pays off."

* * *

Following Denise's advice, Shamus presented the second opinion option to Dr. Michaels, minus the apology. As Denise had predicted, the doctor stiffly accepted. Shamus then went to Meg's room, where she was sitting up in bed, pen in hand, taking some sort of notes.

"I see you're on the case," Shamus said smiling. "And could I have expected anything less?"

"Not if you know me."

"Now there's a subject for debate."

Meg smiled slightly but did not take the bait. She chewed on the end of the pen for a moment. "I've been thinking about that night. If I moved the car, whatever caused me to stay was not spontaneous. And given how tired I've been with the pregnancy and the fact that it was the eve before the Personnel Committee was to meet on my tenure decision, I can't think of anything that would have kept me there other than a request from someone I couldn't refuse. I would have gone home and curled up with a book to distract myself if the choice were left to me."

"Who might have kept you there?"

"It could have been Wilkins, though I probably would have put him off. More likely someone with more clout. I keep trying to recall but it's not coming to me. Susan and Ellen might have seen me. And Juan too. Maybe I told one of them where I was going. Ellen would be the likely one. I see more of her. She is always around working on the online classes at night. Wilkins told her if she designed them it would help her with tenure, so she stays late at night doing that. They're just using her like the time Wilkins got her to work nights and weekends on a journal article. She did all the work. He passed the draft around to some of his professor buddies. They were added as authors so she became 4th author. You don't get tenure as 4th author on publications. She was livid. I tried to tell her to focus on her own research and to stop designing online classes. Wilkins gets the credit. The business school gets the bucks and she gets nothing. She didn't listen and now she's in trouble for tenure. She's in a state of panic much of the time. So, I stop by to see her most evenings before I go home"

"They use her like that?"

Meg shrugged. "She trusts too easily."

Shamus shook his head. "What a place."

"Not everyone is like Wilkins."

"We can be thankful for that anyway." Shamus smiled at Meg. Listen, I'll check with Ellen. Juan has somehow been eluding me, but I'll find him. You're looking a bit pale so no more thinking." Shamus poked her arm. "You are a hard nut to crack. Mom and Dad used to say that. People in the neighborhood used to say it. Nobody tells Meghan Doherty what she can and can't do. Nobody."

"Apparently they do," Meg replied.

"You mean you're not a hard nut to crack anymore?"

"I mean somebody got the better of me, so I'm not as intrepid as you might think. And then there's Johnny. She removed a set of photos from under her sheet. They were of Johnny.

"Who gave you…?"

"Dr. Michaels took these," Meg said smiling affectionately at the photos.

Shamus stifled his surprise. "That was thoughtful."

"Yes," Meg said absently.

"I told you he's adorable," Shamus said.

* * *

It was quiet in the corridors and dark in her room when Meg awoke. She wasn't sure how long Shamus had been gone. A throbbing, heavy pain in the right side of her head had repeatedly robbed her of rest. The pain reduced several times in the prior hours, but like an unrecognizable yet clearly dangerous animal it awoke now and then to viciously deprive her of much needed rest. Deep breaths and thoughts of vistas she'd seen and loved on Dingle Peninsula in the west of Ireland, Lake Como in Northern

Italy, Lake Chiemsee in Germany, where she'd vacationed the year before, and of Lucerne followed that same summer by Athens, so bored the petulant animal that it crept away to sleep. A dull pain remained like a mark of ownership, but at least she could think for the moment. She held her head still, not wanting to unsettle the creature.

She moved slightly to the left and tried to relax her neck. The creature stirred but returned to its former state of guarded slumber. She tried to think back. Part of her resisted; the other part was adamant. Having moved the car to lot B, she reasoned, she must have then returned to her office – as she always did when staying late – to place her purse in the drawer. She didn't like carrying it. It seemed a constant reminder to herself, and perhaps to most of her colleagues, of her difference, of her being a woman. She abhorred fumbling through lipsticks and tissues to retrieve a business card. So she'd gone to great lengths to have pockets sewn into her jackets to avoid such ludicrousness. She would have proceeded from her office to the meeting, a pen in her inside breast pocket, a small pad and her cell phone in an exterior one. But where had she gone? What would have kept her late in the office on that night of all nights? And wouldn't she have told someone – Ellen, perhaps?

Ellen would be worrying about her now. She could call, but the fear of awakening the now-docile creature deterred her. It could wait until tomorrow. Meg had come to feel a sense of responsibility for Ellen, who'd spent much of her life in fear of one demon or another, real or contrived. She was only a year younger than Meg but much further behind her in scholarly productivity. She was known in academe as "a borderline case." Meg, by contrast, had been told many times that she was a "slam dunk" for tenure. Of course no one was a "slam dunk" if the powerful wanted it otherwise. Many a borderline case had eked through to associate professor with the help of someone with influence whose need for a grateful and indebted junior colleague was profound enough to warrant intervention.

And the archives of academia were strewn with names of "rising stars" whose inadvertent offense to someone had sealed their ignominious fate.

Ellen had become like a shadow to Meg, an eager follower, tortured and brooding at one time, playful and caring at another. Meg had felt sorry for her. It had been a largely one-sided relationship in terms of support, but Ellen's company – on rare occasions when she was exuberant – was pleasant. Those times made up for the others and convinced Meg that with her help Ellen might become a less frightened, less paranoid, sparkling, bright, witty friend she occasionally revealed. It was probably hoping against hope, Meg realized, but she'd told herself that stranger things had happened. So, she'd let Ellen into her world – not as yet a friend but as a companion.

Her real friend, Rashid, would not have been there that night. Late hours were out of the question for Rashid. His family was too important to him. His wife and children were his first love, teaching his second. Tenure did not interest him. He was far smarter than most of the people with fancier titles, but he would not spend endless hours crunching data and writing papers for conferences and publication when there were students to teach and mentor.

Meg and Rashid had developed a relationship of enduring trust. They shared concerns, even those that revealed their inadequacies, and bolstered each other's spirits by having a good laugh now and then about the antics of one or another pompous, self-proclaimed proprietor of mainstream scholarship. Business school professorial duels for superior status were never-ending, thus she and Rashid did not lack material. Their relationship was the only treasured, reliable one she had in the world. And yet, even with Rashid, about some matters she remained guarded.

Susan was a close second to Rashid on the friendship scale, but not someone with whom Meg felt she could share her deepest thoughts. It wasn't that she distrusted Susan; it was more that Susan didn't care to know very much about people. Unlike Ellen, she wasn't paranoid, and she certainly drew upon her own inner strength rather than sapping Meg's supply. But she'd been burned too often to trust others. So, it was Susan who had dictated the distance and Meg had respected that. Perhaps, she now wondered, too much. She knew it was a personal fault, reading too much into people's expressions, seeing more than she should and turning those expressions over and over in her mind late at night or while driving to work. Rather than probe, she would try to determine their meaning on her own. Susan's hesitancy to arrange lunches or commit to even an occasional movie suggested that she preferred to keep her work and social life separate. Meg honored that.

Then there was Kent Allen. Had they not fallen out, he would surely now be at her bedside, doting on her and smothering her with concern. When she'd first arrived at Pacific Coast University, he'd taken her under his wing. He'd been impressed with her ability to decipher the meaning of obfuscated writings and her keen interest in his own work. Kent had done something few senior professors in their department had done for years – he had taken it upon himself to mentor a lowly assistant professor. They'd spent many hours over coffee discussing and debating the issues he believed to be important to her scholarly development. He'd often stopped by her office to drop off books or articles for her to read. "We'll discuss that one in two days," he'd said each time. Meg was pleased with his attention and the amount she was learning. Somewhere along the line – she couldn't quite remember when – his interest in her had begun to feel oppressive. But there was no distancing oneself from Kent Allen, so she tolerated his frequent interruptions and assignments. She tried to appear pleased and he seemed not to notice her insincerity – at lease not initially.

The creature was awakening. It moved slowly at first, as if the weight of her thoughts had unsettled it. Meg filled her mind with images of verdant fields and waterfalls, but it was no use. The beast would not allow such dismissal. A pain seared across her forehead. She held her head with both hands. She rubbed her temples. "Go away," she ordered, but the creature had risen from its slumber refreshed and determined. Its teeth gnawed at the back of Meg's brain. She pushed the buzzer by her bed. A nurse arrived. Grimacing in pain, Meg pointed to her head. The nurse left and quickly returned with two capsules. "These will do the trick," she said, placing the capsules in Meg's mouth and helping her sip some water. After a few minutes the nurse departed in search of Dr. Michaels, leaving Meg supine, her body shaking and still hostage to the malevolent, irrepressible intruder.

* * *

It was 9 p.m. when Shamus began the drive back to Meg's apartment. He reflected on his conversation with Dr. Michaels. He'd held his temper in check and, though Michaels would remain on the case, Meg would not be moved until all necessary tests had been completed. Denise or no Denise, though, Shamus was going to keep an eye on Michaels. He'd learned from the tragedy of his parents' deaths that doctors aren't gods, even if some of them act that way.

Arriving at the apartment building, he saw an elderly man open the gate to the parking garage by inserting a key in a box beside the driveway. He found the right key on Meg's key ring and parked in space 202. He walked toward the lobby door, checking out the more impressive cars. A sleek, black Mercedes parked by the lobby door caught his full attention for several moments. Only when he had finally convinced himself that the vehicle was an unnecessary extravagance likely owned by someone seeking to impress others did he move to open the lobby door. The door flew open, slamming Shamus in the face and sending him hurling backward with tremendous force. At the blurry edge of his disorientation, Shamus saw a figure rush past him. He staggered from car to car, as if trying to regain his bearings. Another blow came, this time from behind. Pain shot across his shoulders, sharp and upward through his brain. He fell to the ground, unconscious.

Some time later, he regained consciousness to find himself cradled in the arms of a concerned woman.

"Thank God," she gasped. "Can you get up?"

"I don't know," Shamus said.

As his vision cleared, he saw that she was older – likely in her seventies.

"I can help you," the woman said. She firmly grasped his right hand as she slowly rose from the concrete floor. She pulled with impressive strength for one so spindly, and Shamus found himself on wobbly feet.

"I'm your sister's neighbor, Madeline Bryant," she said, studying his head for damage.

Shamus managed a nod.

"I saw you come in the building earlier today. I recognized you instantly from the picture in Meg's apartment," she said, helping Shamus toward the lobby door.

Shamus struggled to stay steady on his feet.

"Those men – they came out of Meg's apartment."

"What?"

The woman didn't respond, but instead guided Shamus to the elevator. As the door closed, she leaned back against the elevator trying to catch her breath.

"I was horrified. There was a terrible racket coming from Meg's apartment. I went onto my balcony to see what was going on. I just know I should have called the police instead. My God! I might have been hurt or killed! What's happening to Los Angeles?"

"Tell me about it," Shamus said, sarcastically.

"What?"

"Nothing. I'm just used to quieter surroundings." Shamus put his hand to his throbbing head. "What was your name again?"

"Madeline. Let's get you some ice for that. Then we should call the police."

"I want to see what they did," Shamus said. He stood erect and began to walk with Madeline, arms outstretched, ready to catch him.

When they reached Meg's apartment, any doubts Shamus may have had that it was a break-in were immediately dispelled. The intruders had left the door ajar. The living room had been torn apart.

"I'll call the police," Madeline said before retreating to her apartment. "Somebody might still be in there. You never know."

Shamus limped into the living room.

Couch pillows were torn and scattered about the room, drawers in a corner hutch had been emptied, pictures had been torn off the walls and a white rug had been pulled up and tossed over by the bay window. The other rooms had fared no better. Meg's bedroom had been completely ransacked. A large white comforter and pillows of various types and sizes had been ripped apart and tossed on the floor amidst the contents of her desk drawers. The bathroom was the only room in the house spared abuse. Nonetheless, Shamus entered it tentatively, recalling the movies he'd seen where victims had died bloody deaths in their bathtubs. He reached for the yellow checked cloth curtain.

Suddenly he jumped back, crashing into the curious Madeline who had been looking over his shoulder. She screamed and ran out of the apartment. There was something behind the curtain. Perhaps a body, he thought. But bodies don't move, not dead ones anyway. He inched toward the tub, hand stretched out to avoid the thrust of a knife. He heard the noise again like the light scratching of fingernails in rapid motion on the tile.

He slowly pushed aside the curtain. Shuddering in the large tub was a little ball of gray fur.

"Mow."

"Oh, God no," Shamus grumbled. "Where the hell did you come from?"

The kitten appeared to be no more than a few months old. It sported a white patch on the left side of its nose. Big green eyes were locked onto Shamus' face. It had nearly the same coloring as a cat they'd owned when Meg and Shamus were kids. Meg was the one who really liked it. He was not a cat person – a condition every feline he'd met had ignored.

"Mow."

"Meow, not mow," Shamus softly admonished.

"Mow."

"What? Are you hungry?"

He led the shivering kitten to the kitchen. Only then did he notice that a pet door had been installed leading to the rear balcony. The plastic was clear, with no evidence of long-term scratching. A search of the cabinets revealed some dry cat food. Shamus put what seemed like a reasonable portion into the kitten's dish. The starving pet was on it before Shamus finished pouring.

"Don't expect me to take care of you. I've got my hands full."

The ravenous kitten ignored Shamus. As he started toward the door, though, it raised its head and uttered a doleful "mow."

"Look, just eat and go do whatever it is you do here. You'll have to take care of yourself. That's all there is to it."

"In here officer." It was Madeline's voice.

The police were bigger than any he'd ever seen. No one in his right mind would mess with these guys, Shamus thought.

"Mr. Doherty, are you all right?" the bigger one asked.

"I think I'll be okay," Shamus replied.

"His sister is in intensive care in Pacific Coast hospital." Madeline added. "She's a professor. He's out here from Connecticut to help her pull through. It's been an awful ordeal for him."

"Mr. Doherty, " the shorter officer said. "Could there be a connection between your sister's condition and this event?"

"My sister is in the hospital. She was found hanging in her office," Shamus replied. The explanation was inadequate. But he ended it there.

The officers looked at him, awaiting more information. Receiving none, the smaller one jotted down something on a pad he retrieved from his jacket pocket.

Margaret looked annoyed. "It wasn't a suicide attempt," she said emphatically. She glowered at Shamus.

The policeman wrote again.

Shamus shrugged his shoulders. Madeline crossed her arms and frowned.

"I can't see any connection," Shamus said. Maybe the robbers found out that she wasn't home and figured they could come in here to take whatever they wanted."

"What's missing?" said the taller officer.

"I don't live here so I can't be sure. I do know she has some Waterford crystal."

Shamus checked the mantle. The vase was still there. When he tried to lift one of the smaller decorative crystal objects, he found it was stuck in place.

"That's blu-tak. It's for earthquakes," Madeline said. "We all do that to keep our crystal and knickknacks from flying off the shelves."

Shamus nodded, thinking of the people of Vesuvius who'd also been warned of impending disaster.

"Can we look around, Mr. Doherty?"

"Sure," Shamus said. He felt something rub his leg. It was the kitten again.

"All right. All right," Shamus relented, petting its tiny head. "Now go play." The kitten rubbed his other leg.

Shamus sighed, and then lifted the nameless fur ball into his arms. It watched his face closely, seeming not to know whether to trust him or to make an escape.

"Mow."

"If only you could speak English," Shamus said patting its head. "But you seem to have enough trouble with cat talk." The kitten relaxed against his chest. He put her down on the sofa. She whined. Shamus noticed that Madeline and the two officers were observing him. He sensed their dismay at his reluctance to cuddle the pathetic animal. He relented and placed her once again in the curl of his arm. This time, she nudged into his side and closed her eyes, relieved and exhausted.

Apparently satisfied, the officers headed toward the kitchen. Madeline began putting the living room back together. The kitten limited Shamus' freedom of movement but he, too, started to retrieve pillows and right furniture.

"I just don't believe it," Madeline said as she picked up a powder blue throw and placed it on the sofa Shamus had just realigned.

"From what I've seen of Los Angeles, Madeline, I'd believe anything."

"You mean like believing your sister tried to take her life?" Madeline looked at him crossly again.

"I don't believe…"

"I've known her for years," Madeline insisted. "She isn't the type. And she wasn't depressed. You could have made that very clear to them."

"I know," Shamus said guiltily. "But sometimes I don't see how she couldn't have done it. She was found hanging in her office with what the police describe as no evidence of foul play."

"I don't care how they found her," Madeline retorted. "She didn't do that to herself. She surely wouldn't do it to the baby. She's working in a messed up place, but she wouldn't have thrown in the towel." She looked at him impatiently. "Surely you know that much about your sister."

"Sure," he said, mustering the conviction he knew Madeline expected.

"Then don't be going around giving people the impression she did it." She ordered. "Because she didn't!"

"Mr. Doherty," one of the policemen said, re-entering the living room. "This may be difficult for you, but was you sister by any chance involved with drugs?"

"Of course not!" Shamus and Madeline asserted in unison.

"Well something is wrong here. The television and stereo haven't been touched. Her jewelry box seems intact from what we can see, and there was even cash on the floor. No one was hurt except you. And why would a thief hit you a second time after knocking you down?"

"To make sure I wouldn't get up and chase them?"

The policeman shrugged. "Seems odd. That's all."

"Seems like a bungled burglary attempt to me," Shamus said.

He patiently answered the officers' remaining questions. Later that night he lay in bed, the kitten nestled contentedly at his side. Sleepless from the pain across his shoulders almost as bad as his headache, he kept trying to push the day's events from his mind. It was no use. Madeline did have a point. Why had he failed to insist that it hadn't been an attempted suicide? Wasn't that a betrayal of his sister? Madeline had been confident in Meg, and rightly angry. Her own brother had wavered.

He decided that he would tell Madeline he'd been thrown off-balance by the burglary – but the real reason he knew had more to do with their past, his resentments, his shutting Meg out, his refusal to forgive her as an adult for once being the child more loved. The truth – he didn't know his sister because he'd wanted it that way.

* * *

"You didn't come back last night," Nurse Shaughnessy reprimanded Shamus as he entered the neonatal ICU.

"I'm sorry," he said, head bowed.

"Don't be tellin' the little one you'll soon be back if you're not really coming. He was fussing all night long – wondering, no doubt, where his no-good uncle had gone off to."

"You're right." He knew she was. "I won't do it again."

Nurse Shaughnessy lifted Johnny out of the incubator and placed him in Shamus' arms. Shamus was starting to feel practiced at this kind of thing. Johnny nuzzled against him.

"Tell me that baby doesn't know his uncle," Nurse Shaughnessy cooed.

Shamus nodded and smiled warmly.

"Maybe it's Meg he really misses," Shamus offered.

"If I were making the laws, she'd be holding him now," Shaughnessy said.

Shamus smiled appreciatively and looked again at Johnny who appeared to be studying his uncle.

"Did you ask Marilyn about the man who was here yesterday?" Shamus asked.

"Goodness! Where's my brain?" she said, striking her forehead with the palm of her hand. "All that time pumping her for information, and I'd nearly forgotten to tell you. The gentleman asked Marilyn not to tell anyone he'd been here so she gave me the cold shoulder – but I pulled rank," Shaughnessy said, with obvious relish.

"Is he the father?"

"Not at all!" Nurse Shaughnessy replied as if there were three of the letter "t" in the phrase. "He's your sister's lawyer!"

"What on earth is Meg doing with an attorney?"

"He handles women's cases – sex discrimination, harassment, and the like. He's a one-stop shop to hear Marilyn tell it. He's not a big shot by any means, but not one to be dismissed either."

"Did Marilyn say why he'd come to see Johnny?"

"That I couldn't pry out of her. I haven't finished with her yet, of course. By tomorrow I might have more." She tickled Johnny under the chin.

Shamus tapped the baby's nose. "That sister of mine is no open book," Shamus said.

"And who is?" Nurse Shaughnessy laughed. "Who indeed?"

CHAPTER SIX

The two policemen from the break-in were sitting on the front steps of the apartment building when Shamus returned.

"We'd like to speak with you for a minute or two, Mr. Doherty," the big one said, as Shamus came in from the garage.

Shamus invited them up, and they sat in the living room. This time he remembered to glance at each man's nametag. R. Smith was the somewhat smaller officer, C. Philips the larger.

"We haven't found anything yet," Philips said.

"Have there been other robberies around here lately?" Shamus inquired.

"Not like this one, I'm afraid."

"Actually, it wasn't even a robbery because nothing was taken," Smith explained. He seemed the more detailed and particular of the two. "It was breaking-and-entering. We don't get many of those by themselves."

"They may have been interrupted by Margaret moving around on the balcony."

"I don't think so, Mr. Doherty," Philips said. "This place was a mess."

They were in here for a while, and they were looking for something. Do you have any idea what it might be?"

"None at all," Shamus said.

"Well, we came by to warn you that you should be cautious. Be sure to put better locks on the doors and windows. Whenever you come home, enter the apartment cautiously. If you notice anything unusual, call us. Whoever these guys are, they may return. And if there is a next time – don't try to be a hero."

"That's kind of overkill, isn't it?"

"We don't think so, Mr. Doherty," said a clearly practiced Philips. His voice was deep with a tone of no nonsense. He didn't smile. Not once. But Shamus didn't take that to mean anything other than professionalism. In fact, he sensed that Philips and Smith were indeed trying to protect him even if he was one of millions. He was their job at this moment in time and they were taking it seriously. Shamus found it unexpectedly admirable for police work in such a large city.

Several minutes after they'd left there was a knock at the door. It was Madeline, but she looked like a different person. She was wearing a light peach pantsuit. Her silver hair was now strawberry blonde and she was wearing light pink lipstick.

"I saw the police outside: big and large," she said smiling.

"Smith is the big one, Philips the large one."

"There's something comforting about sizable police officers," Madeline said.

"As long as you're on their good side."

"Yes indeed," Madeline chuckled. "What did they say?"

"They don't think it was an ordinary robbery."

"I don't think so, either."

"There's something here that somebody wants, but I haven't a clue as to what it might be. Maybe one of her friends knows if Meg had jewelry or something else of value. I don't want to tell Meg yet."

"Start with Ellen," Madeline suggested. "I've seen Ellen here from time to time. I think they were working on a paper together. She seems devoted to Meg, like a puppy to a kind master. I think Meg felt a bit sorry for Ellen, too. Out of need and sympathy they forged a bond. I came by to borrow something. They had spread books all over the living room. Ellen was sitting in the middle of them typing on a laptop computer. They were all business but you could tell they'd been enjoying themselves, too. There were pizza cartons, empty soda cans and popcorn scattered about. It reminded me of study sessions I had years ago with friends. Yes, I'd start with Ellen. I won't utter a word to Meg when I talk with her. It'll be our secret. No need to upset her."

After Madeline left, Shamus used Meg's computer to catch up on e-mails from his crew. They'd be fine for a while without him there, but not for long. The owners of the home they were extending when he left were worried about his absence. Shamus replied with more optimism than the present situation warranted. He'd need to come up with a back-up plan sooner or later. The job would belong to someone else unless he could get back to Connecticut for a few days.

The kitten wandered in from wherever it had been prowling.

"Look who's here," Shamus said. "Back from the wilds of Culver City?"

She leaped onto the desk, over the computer and then up onto a copier where she curled up to watch Shamus work.

"You're lonely, aren't you?"

"Mow."

"We loners in denial need to stick together," he said, petting the kitten.

The kitten nudged affectionately at his hand. Shamus picked her up, rubbed under her chin with his forefinger, tapped her on the nose and walked into the living room to watch television. He set her gently down on a pillow and sat beside her, located the remote, put his feet on the coffee table and petted her as she yawned and he settled in for a much-needed night of brainless entertainment.

* * *

The Faculty Club was a disappointment. Shamus had envisioned a graceful edifice steeped in history, paintings of former university presidents lining the lobby walls, awards in glass cases commencing with Pacific Coast's first year and continuing into the present, retired jerseys from sports heroes long gone, and aging photos of the first faculty. Instead, the building was anonymously modern. A single glass cabinet displayed books that had recently been granted awards from the honor society of Phi Kappa Phi. The overwhelming sense was one of purposeful obsession with the future and disregard for the past.

Susan had suggested they meet at the Faculty Club. She arrived promptly and motioned for Shamus to follow her into the dining room, where she selected an empty table for two in a remote corner. The placemats were made of paper, another disappointment. To Shamus, a restaurant's calling card was its table decor. Paper was déclassé. How could any university expect to become top tier with paper place mats in the faculty club?

"How is Meg?" Susan asked as soon as they were seated.

"She has more color."

"That's good?"

"Yes."

"I'd like to visit her."

"They won't let you in if you aren't family," he said, feeling immediately that he may have sounded ungrateful. "I mean, it's some kind of rule – but I'm sure she'd like to know you stopped by or sent some flowers or something."

Susan smiled appreciatively. He watched as she put the napkin in her lap and straightened her silverware. She looked around the dining room, and then waved to someone. Her blue-green eyes sparkled even more than they had the day they'd met. Her skin was perfection. Definitely beautiful, he thought to himself, and smart as well. The combination reminded Shamus of the slogan on one of Meg's favorite T-shirts: ALL THIS AND BRAINS TOO! Meg had worn that T-shirt when she'd visited their parents the summer before they'd died. It had given their parents a good laugh. It was another one of those little moments of joy she'd shared with them as he'd looked on.

"What did you want to talk about?" Susan asked after they'd ordered.

"Tell me about Meg."

"Me tell *you*?" Susan asked, surprised.

"You know more about her than I do. And it might help me sort out what happened."

"I don't know that much."

"You're friends aren't you?"

"Yes. And I probably know Meg better than most." She paused as if to reflect on her choice of words. "I just don't think anyone really knows Meg. She seems so open, but yet there's a barrier. She tends to change the subject if you get too close. She is always interested in you and she is a master at getting people to talk about themselves, but try returning the favor and she shuts down. She goes no further than friendship requires."

"More of a giver than a receiver?" Shamus speculated aloud.

"Yes. She prefers to help than be helped. A lot of generous people are that way. Let me put it this way," Susan continued. "Meg is generous and caring. She's talkative but not forthcoming. She's just not easy to know."

Susan waited for Shamus to interject his thoughts. He remained silent, waiting for her to continue.

"Yet Meg is willful when it comes to authority. Around here she might even fit into the 'loose cannon' category. She firmly believes that people should be rewarded on the basis of merit, not on the basis of politics. That's all well and good, but it's not the real world. Some departments are politically neutral, but not many."

He barely knew the woman Susan was describing. He'd always envisioned Meg having many friends. Knowing this had kept him from feeling badly about keeping a distance.

"Doesn't sound like the Meg I know," he said.

"But do you really know her?

Shamus shrugged. "Sounds like I know her as well as anyone."

"Maybe not as well as Rashid," Susan said. "She talks with him like he's her brother."

Shamus looked into Susan's eyes for an implication. He found none.

"Oh, that was a stupid thing to say," Susan said reaching for Shamus' forearm and squeezing.

"No. I know what you meant. He does seem to know her well. And I'm glad about that."

Susan squeezed his arm again and sat back grateful for his generosity.

"I thought tenure was an award for promising work," Shamus said in part to change the subject.

"Where have you been?" Susan laughed.

Shamus was about to protest his ignorance when he noticed his coffee cup jiggling. Susan appeared increasingly concerned about the accelerating movement of her own cup.

"Oh no!" Susan grabbed Shamus by the hand. "Come with me quick!"

"What the hell...?" Before he could finish his sentence, Susan had pulled him from his seat. Everyone in the dining hall was heading for the doors.

"Over here!" she shouted above the panic. She nudged two people apart to make room and yanked Shamus next to her in a doorway. People were running now, others were trying to retain some semblance of calm. Two waiters ducked under a table. Within seconds, tables were bobbing and weaving, glasses crashed to the floor, the air seemed suddenly deprived of oxygen, lights flickered and the entire building swayed.

Then, suddenly, with no warning, no steady decrease in power, the shaking stopped. A moment passed. A collective sigh of relief filled the room. Those who'd panicked were now laughing at themselves, relieving their embarrassment at having been huddled at close proximity to total strangers.

"That must have been at least a 5.5," Susan said confidently.

"I'd say 6 or better," observed a man behind her.

For several minutes people debated the intensity of the earthquake while Shamus remained motionless and alone in the doorway.

"Let's sit down," Susan said. "It's probably over."

"Probably?"

"Come on," she said, taking his hand once again and leading him back into the dining room, where they joined other people replacing glasses on tables, righting turned over chairs and relieving their nervousness with chatter about past earthquakes far worse in intensity. The clean up finished at their table, Susan and Shamus took their seats and, surprisingly, not long afterward a waiter arrived with their food. He was the picture of quintessential calm. Shamus' knees were still locked.

"Tell me again why people live here," he said.

"That wasn't too bad," Susan said smiling. "It could have been a lot worse."

Shamus looked around the room. People were taking pleasure in having shared a near-death experience.

"You'll get over it in a few minutes," Susan assured him. "After my first earthquake, I swore I'd be on the next plane home. And many people do leave after one like that. They're the early leavers." She laughed.

"The chickens," Shamus added as if Susan had been thinking this.

"I suppose you could say that. But they might be the smart ones too. In any case, I'm still here, eight years later."

"My hat is off to you," Shamus said gesturing so. His appetite had disappeared. He poked at his salad, considered ordering a stiff drink, but decided against it. He didn't want Susan to think he'd been frightened by something she seemed to consider a fact of life.

Susan smiled reassuringly. "You know, it makes me think of my father."

Shamus looked puzzled.

"Earthquakes, I mean." She took a deep breath in and let it out slowly looking slightly away. She turned back and noticed Shamus waiting for an explanation. "Oh, sorry," she said. "My dad has Parkinson's."

"I'm sorry," Shamus said.

Susan waved her hand as if to brush away the sympathy. "Don't be. He is a fighter." She smiled warmly. "But when I'm in an earthquake, I think that's what it must be like for him. Not the big ones but the tremors that keep you unsteady on your feet, unable to grasp things, uncertain as if your body is not all you thought it was but rather vulnerable. She looked up at Shamus – like we are now."

Shamus looked into her expressive, sensitive eyes, arresting now as they'd been when they first met and felt as if he might fall into them. He sat up and placed his napkin in his lap to buy some time before responding. "You must love him very much."

Susan was slightly embarrassed. "I guess it shows. Yes. And I admire him for the humor he retains even on the bad days. He's very funny." She smiled.

"He must be a very good man."

"The best," she answered picking up her fork as if signaling it was time to return to his life, his concerns. "I do know a few things about Meg that might be helpful."

Shamus waited silently.

"She spent a lot of time on committees over in the medical school and the law school. I'd say she did it to meet some big wigs with political clout, but also because she wanted to make friends outside of the business school. It was a good move. And it may help her get by the politics here. It's always good to have highly regarded people outside of your department or school saying you're terrific."

"Did she become close to anyone?"

"Well, I think there was someone. She never mentioned his name." Susan paused raising her eyes skyward as if reviewing the past. "I could have been a better friend."

"I thought you said she wouldn't allow that."

"Well, it may have been partly me. And I now think she needed someone to push harder to get past whatever that barrier is. I mean she should have had more people to talk to when she got pregnant."

"Hey, listen. My sister is strong. She probably didn't want a fuss. She would have let you know if she did. Don't women have a way of sending each other signals about that kind of stuff?"

Susan laughed. "You mean our intuition?"

"Yeah. Okay. I guess."

"You're funny, Shamus."

"Well now, that's a new one."

"No. You're very amusing."

He could have stayed there all day. How could Meg not have confided in this warm, charming woman? It just didn't make sense.

They spent the remainder of the lunch talking about Southern California, why Susan had left Michigan to live there, what her three-year-old son was up to, and restaurants Shamus should try during his stay. When they finished lunch, Shamus walked Susan back to East Hall. He watched her enter the building, wondering if Meg was as sanguine as she about earthquakes. As he turned to leave, he caught sight of a woman looking down at him from a window in the second story stairwell. His eyes met hers. They were fearful as if his very existence threatened her. She turned abruptly and ran up the steps.

* * *

When Shamus reached the door to Meg's hospital room, he found a group of doctors and nurses crowded around the bed. Dr. Michaels and Denise were leaning over her. Dr. Michaels was barking orders first at one nurse, then at another. Denise was backing up each order with additional ones. Something was terribly wrong.

"Hang in there, Meg," Shamus heard Denise whisper.

Denise noticed Shamus standing in the doorway. Her worried eyes met his. She gave him no reassurance before returning her attention to Meg.

Shamus stood stone still, watching what seemed to be his sister's final moments. Why would so many people be rushing about in near panic if something weren't terribly, terribly wrong?

Dr. Michaels barked another order and everyone dropped what they were doing. Three nurses rushed out into the hall while two others ripped various contraptions from Meg's body. Together, Dr. Michaels, Denise and the nurses swung the bed around and pointed it toward the door.

"Coming through!" Dr. Michaels shouted as they rushed passed Shamus. Within seconds, Meg and her entourage were gone. Shamus followed them to the elevator. They entered it, closed the doors in his face, and Shamus was left to watch the light blink: 3...4...5...6. It stopped.

"Mr. Doherty," a vaguely familiar female voice whispered. He turned and saw that it was Nurse Constance.

"Yes?"

"Your sister's blood pressure dropped suddenly."

"Is she going to be okay?"

"She may have had a cerebral hemorrhage. That's not certain yet, but Dr. Michaels is bringing her to surgery."

Shamus staggered over to the chair into which he'd fallen only three days earlier. Why hadn't he made more of the blow to her head? Insisted on a second opinion? Insisted that Dr. Michaels do more?

"Mr. Doherty, are you all right? Can I get you some water or soda?"

"No. Thank you. I'll be all right," Shamus said distractedly.

"This is a shock. But she is in good hands." She patted him on the shoulder and moved slowly away.

His parents had died this way. There was hope, and then there was none. Why should this time be any different? He'd no sooner had this thought than he admonished himself for it. Here Meg was fighting for what little life she had in her, and he was thinking of himself.

"Typical," he said.

"What?"

Shamus looked up. It was Nurse Shaughnessy. She placed a soda next to his chair. Another cold sting of terror ripped through his chest.

"My God! Is something wrong with Johnny?"

"Johnny is doing fine, Shamus. I came by to see how *you* were doing. We have quite a grapevine here."

Shamus placed his face in his hands, and then pulled them downward.

"She's in superb hands. Dr. Michaels is a true genius. The one to worry about now is you. Your face is the same off-white color as that wall."

"I'm fine," Shamus replied unconvincingly.

"Get up," she ordered, obviously finished with the softer approach. "I'm taking you out to the waiting room, soda and all."

"No. I'll go to the cafeteria."

"You'll go where I tell you, Mr. Doherty," she said with determination and warmth.

He followed her to a small alcove at the end of the hall where they read magazines for what seemed hours.

* * *

Meg was a desperate swimmer making for shore in the midst of a rip tide. The echo of distant voices, encouraged by helpless lifeguards, called her to push on. The tide took her again. She struggled and exhausted lay face down on the sand, breathing heavily.

"Come here. Quick!" A woman's voice pierced through the hubbub. Meg could hear hurried footsteps coming toward her.

"Page Dr. Michaels. She moved her eyelids. Look!"

Is she talking about me? Meg wondered. Am I waking? Where am I? Why are they calling him?

"Can you hear me? If you can hear me, Sweetie, nod your head or lift your finger."

Meg's arms and legs felt heavy. She had no sense of her fingers but by terrific dint of will she moved her head slightly.

"That's it!" The voice was jubilant now. "Dr. Michaels is a genius, an absolute genius."

"Meg, can you open your eyes?"

She struggled, her eyelids fluttering.

"She's coming around, Doctor."

"Meg. Open your eyes. You can do it." Dr. Michael's voice was gentle. "Please open your eyes."

"You had a stroke," Dr. Michaels said softly. He took her left hand in both of his.

Meg's eyes opened slowly.

Dr. Michaels smiled sympathetically. Two of the nurses glanced across the bed at each other, sharing their surprise and pleasure at such tenderness.

"I'll send for Shamus," Dr. Michaels assured. "Don't go to sleep until you talk with him. Poor guy's been through a lot."

"I thought you two hated each other," Meg murmured.

Dr. Michaels laughed. "Probably because we're both so damn stubborn."

"Such introspection for a surgeon."

"I'm not about to spar with someone in your condition. It would put you at too great a disadvantage. Though I must say, it's tempting to be one-up for a change."

Dr. Michaels released Meg's hand slowly. "I'll stop by later," he said, patting the bed rail, his demeanor returning to one of assured professionalism, before he turned and left the room.

CHAPTER SEVEN

Shamus was jarred awake by a light switched on in the waiting room. "I'm sorry," said a startled, tall, black woman in her late forties with a reassuring maternal smile. "I didn't know you were in here."

Shamus blinked to be sure he was not still sleeping and smiled as best he could. "No problem." He struggled to upright himself on the couch. Then he looked up again at the woman, now seated across from him, watching him dutifully, as if she still felt responsible for his evident discomfort. "Can you tell me the time?"

"It's 5:30 a.m." she replied softly.

"I've lost all sense of time," Shamus said. He rubbed his heavy, strained eyes. "Is there someone in your family in intensive care?"

"My sister, Carol." She lowered and shook her head slightly. "She was in a terrible automobile accident." She sighed. She looked at Shamus. "And you?"

"My sister is in there, too. She...," Shamus paused. "She had an accident, too. Not in a car, but in her office. It's a long story."

"Your whole world comes to a halt, doesn't it?" The woman

commiserated.

"Indeed it does. My sister had a baby, too. He's upstairs in an incubator." Shamus immediately realized that this was not information the woman had solicited and wondered for a moment why he'd volunteered it.

The woman's sympathetic eyes met his. "I'll pray for both of them," she said.

"Thank you," Shamus said wanting to return the favor but feeling as if he might belittle the beauty of her gesture by instant reciprocation. "I think I'll get some breakfast."

"My name is Shamus," he said reaching to shake her hand.

"Mine is Martha," she said, rising and returning the gesture.

"Can I bring you something from the cafeteria?"

"I already ate, thank you."

Shamus nodded and again turned toward the door.

"Maybe just a coffee," she said, raising her right forefinger as if the desire had suddenly entered her mind.

He turned back to her. She was smiling a little now, slightly embarrassed by the abruptness of her request.

"Sugar and cream?" Shamus said smiling warmly.

"Both, thanks." Martha nodded and smiled gratefully.

When Shamus returned, Martha's family had arrived. She introduced each one – two girls who Shamus estimated to be 10 and 12 and a small girl of four or five years.

Denise entered the waiting room.

"Meg is awake."

"Thank God. Can I see her?"

"Yes. Dr. Michaels asked the nurses to find you." Denise smiled at Martha.

"He's not that bad, really," Shamus said.

Denise turned to Shamus. She half smiled. "Is that so?"

"Seriously, I'm getting to like the guy."

"He kind of grows on you."

"Apparently so." Her eyebrows were raised, her head tilted, and her smile pursed in shared amusement at his transformation.

Shamus turned to Martha who was evidently pleased for him. "Very good to meet you and your family," he said warmly.

"And you," Martha said. "We'll pray for your sister."

Shamus nodded in appreciation. It had been a long time since his last prayer. "I'll keep your sister in my thoughts too."

"Thank you," Martha said. Her daughters smiled at him. He waved as one does to children, fingers wiggling, to which they reciprocated in kind.

The visit with Meg was abbreviated, per Michaels' instruction. She was pale, fatigued and her speech was halted. Shamus described the kitten's growing affection for him in her absence, generating a sleepy smile from Meg. She muttered the kitten's name – Sunny. Shamus thought it fit the little bright spot of whom he'd become surprisingly fond.

* * *

Dr. Michaels entered the hospital room. He saw that Shamus had left. He walked to Meg's bedside and placed both hands on the metal sidebars. "Do you know who I am, Meg?"

She studied him for a long moment.

"No," she said, quite seriously, until one side of her mouth refused to cooperate in the ruse, tilted up and gave her away.

"Very funny," Dr. Michaels said. "And my name would be?"

"Robert."

He smiled warmly, adjusted her pillow.

This was the side of Robert that Meg wished Shamus could see – the side she admired. She recalled a time when one of her graduate students had fallen into a kind of chronic fatigue. She'd called Robert to ask if he'd see the student. He had been very receptive and concerned. He arranged for a number of specialists, but remained the attending physician. The student was soon diagnosed with a rare but curable form of leukemia. Robert helped her through it and even attended her graduation. The episode had changed Meg's view of him.

"I can barely feel my legs," she said tentatively. "Will I be able to walk?"

"Yes – but it will take time and physical therapy."

Meg willed a smile. Deep down, though, she was worried. What if she had another stroke? What if she didn't live to see Johnny grow up? Her eyes felt hot and moist. Michaels stroked her forehead.

"Robert, please let me hold Johnny. Surely there is something you can do."

"I have a lot of power around here, Meg. But when the DCFS shows up, I'm nobody. I can't change the law."

"But you know. You have to know. I didn't try to take Johnny's life or mine."

"I'll do what I can Meg. I promise. But the law is there for his protection."

"Robert. He's my child." A tear slipped from her left eye down her cheek. The doctor gently wiped it away.

"Meg," he said, pausing until he was sure that she was listening. "Some police officers want to talk with you. Are you able to do that?"

"I suppose so," she relented softly.

"I've held them off for days and I can delay them for a while longer, but they're very persistent."

"I'll talk with them, but I can't remember much. I still don't know what happened. But I do know that I didn't try to kill myself."

Dr. Michaels smile was encouraging but his nod was noncommittal.

* * *

Shamus returned to Meg's apartment. Every muscle in his body was aching. Meg's answering machine light was blinking. He pushed "play."

"Shamus, this is Sharon. We love the work so far. We'd like to talk with you about adding some small windows in the eaves, next to the turret. Hope things are going better. Give us a call when you can."

A second message cut in immediately.

"Shamus, this is Ellen, Meg's friend." The voice was shaky, the words rushed. "I have some information for you that may be helpful. I can see you tomorrow at 3 p.m. if that works for you. Let me know if you'll be there. Just don't tell anyone about this."

The room was taking on an orange tinge. He'd never seen the sun set over Los Angeles. He found the stairwell and ascended to the roof. The orange bulb was reluctantly edging its way downward toward a fringe of ocean just inside Shamus' view. For a moment, just before touching, it paused as if changing its mind. Gold-framed, lavender clouds, providing an escort for the slow descent, gleamed even brighter than they had moments before. Then, as if no longer able to hold its weight, the sun began to sink, peeling away the light from reluctant clouds, slipping, without further protest, into someone else's morning.

* * *

Shamus arrived at the university with considerable time to spare before his meeting with Ellen. As he passed the fountain outside East Hall, he noticed Susan sitting on a concrete bench, reading.

"Now, this is academia as it should be," Shamus said, sitting down next to her. "I mean professors studying by fountains." He lifted her book to check its title.

"Ah, yes," he continued, "*The Effective Executive* by Peter Drucker. Excellent choice."

"And how would you know?" Susan teased.

"I'm not all blueprints and gargoyles, you know."

Susan smiled. "How is Meg?"

"A lot's happened, but the bottom line is that she's doing okay."

"Actually, I'm not supposed to be talking to you."

"What do you mean?"

"Wilkins told me to keep away from you."

"You've got to be kidding."

"Nope. He thinks you're snooping around, trying to pin Meg's condition on the school or the university."

"Snooping around, huh?" Shamus weighed the phrase. "Why is he being so defensive?"

"He was born that way," Susan said, clearly enjoying the chance to denigrate Wilkins. "I wouldn't trust him as far as I could throw him."

"So, are you worried someone will see you with me?"

"No," Susan said convincingly. "I'm tenured. What are they going to do to me? But the only other time I've seen Bill this nervous was when he argued with the dean about what departments would be assigned to the new building. He almost got his marching papers that time."

"I should go see him."

"You won't get anywhere – he lies like a rug. If you want to find out what's going on around here, you need to see Kent Allen. I've never met a professor more observant of university politics. He knows what people are thinking before they do, and how to manage them."

"Where do I find him?"

"At this stage of his career, he only comes to the campus now and then for meetings and teaching. The best place to find him is on the golf course or at his home in Palos Verdes. "

Shamus was sure Meg had mentioned Allen during one of their telephone conversations. Allen must have been one of the more colorful people in her life, Shamus thought, for him to recall the name.

"If you do meet him, be ready for a lecture. He can't help himself."

"Should I do some advance reading?" Shamus asked facetiously.

"I would."

"Tell me you're kidding."

"Okay, I'm kidding." Susan smiled. "But reading one or two of his articles wouldn't hurt if you want to follow what he says to you."

"I think I'll just take my chances."

"Suit yourself. If you change your mind, his area is human capital."

"And that would be what?"

"His specialty is attracting talent to organizations and retaining that talent. You could get your hands on a book or two, preferably one of his, on the topic and familiarize yourself. That would dazzle Kent."

"Probably over my head. Besides, I thought you just give talented employees big bonuses and they love you."

"Don't tell him it's that easy," Susan joked. "He has a passion about his chosen field – an obsession, actually. He has a lot to say regularly about academia misguidedly discarding its senior professors in favor of younger ones who supposedly have new ideas and cost less. That, he argues vehemently, is a waste. He's right in a way, but he carries such a torch on this issue that most people turn a deaf ear when he starts regaling them with his diatribe. He resents young scholars – that is, unless they're sufficiently impressed with him. So the best way to deal with Kent is to show a profound interest in his work. Meg does that; I always do, too. But with Meg it's real."

"She likes him?"

Susan squinted. "I wouldn't say she *likes* him. He never makes that easy for long. But she respects him. Or at least she did."

"Something changed?"

"Let's just say I haven't seen him dropping by her office as much. So, he may not be as helpful as he would have been. But if you get him on a roll talking about things he finds interesting, he may just tell you what you want to know."

"I'll do that. Thanks."

"I'm sure Kent doesn't know what happened to Meg that night, but he can tell you what it's like here. I can give you insights but he has the big picture. Just give him some time. Let him warm up to you. And it wouldn't hurt to talk about golf if you play."

"I dabble."

"That's good enough. You wouldn't want to be better than he is."

"I gather he doesn't like being upstaged there, either."

"You gather right. Oh, and he has quite a temper. I've never been the target of it, but I've heard enough to know it's better to let him be king of the hill."

Susan examined her manicured, clear polished fingernails for a long moment.

"I was there that night."

"You mean the night of Meg's accident?"

She looked at Shamus. Apologetic. "I suppose I should have told you earlier. I didn't know she was still there when I left. I often stopped by her office before leaving, but I was in a rush that night."

"So you didn't see her?"

"Actually, I did – but only for a second. She hurried past my office sometime around 9 o'clock. She would usually stop by and say hello, but not that time. I wish now that I'd checked to see if she was okay but I needed to get home to my son."

"Meg never mentioned having a meeting with someone that night?"

"No, but she's seemed out of sorts lately. That's all I know."

"Do you suppose someone, maybe Wilkins, told her that night that she wasn't going to be promoted?"

"Not likely. It's only March and no one would have known that for sure until May or June. The worst he could have said at that point was her tenure chances weren't good."

"Would that have been devastating to her?"

"It sure would have been upsetting."

"You said women don't get promoted here unless they pass some kind of macho test. What did you call it?"

"You mean the '*Does anyone vouch for this woman*' test?"

"So why would she expect things to go smoothly? Maybe she wasn't vouched for."

"Well, Allen would be the one to know. Though he would deny the existence of such a test. He'd put it in the female angst or sour grapes category."

"He'd say that?"

"Maybe to you. You know, to a man. But he knows it exists. Trust me. He's too observant for it to be any other way."

They reached the door of East Hall just as Bill Wilkins was exiting. He passed them, momentarily glaring darkly at Susan and then nodding marginally to Shamus.

"Looks like you're in deep trouble now," Shamus said.

"He's small potatoes. As I said, the most he can do is give me an even smaller pittance for a raise than I got last year or make another attempt to belittle me in front of my colleagues. In either case, he's the one who will look pathetic."

"None of what you tell me about this place jives with my image of academia."

"Oh, there are a lot of good things about it. I love teaching. And it's rewarding to publish. If you keep under the radar, it's a great place to work. Few academic departments are political snake pits, but that kind of situation is more common than most people suspect where the competition is stiff."

Susan lightly touched Shamus' arm. "Gotta run," she said smiling.

"Thanks, Susan."

"Anytime."

As Susan hurried off to class, Shamus headed for Meg's office. While he climbed the stairs to her office. His thoughts were on his own naïveté about bucolic university campuses. He wondered if, as a professor, he could "stay under the radar" and whether Meg had failed to do so. But how could that kind of political pettiness have anything to do with her near demise? It just didn't make sense.

As he entered the lobby of East Hall, he saw that the elevator had been cordoned off with yellow caution tape. A sign had been posted on one of the doors:

ELEVATOR UNDER REPAIR
PLEASE USE STAIRS
OR CONTACT THE FACILITIES
OFFICE FOR ASSISTANCE
EXT: 2256

Upon reaching the third floor stairwell landing, Shamus noticed a crack in the wall that ran from the floor to the ceiling on the left side of the door. He couldn't recall having seen it on his last visit. He trailed his hand along the crevice. It was deep.

Once in Meg's office, Shamus turned on the computer, intending to e-mail his clients before he found himself out of a job. As he waited for the PC to load the programs, he noticed another crack, this one in the wall right above the computer. It looked to have been filled and painted just recently. He followed the crack from a point just above the computer monitor up to the ceiling – some six feet at least.

"What a dump," Shamus said to himself, scanning the office.

He found another crack along the baseboard on the opposite side of the office. This crack was wider than the one behind the computer and it ran from the corner to the doorway, then along the doorframe, finally terminating midway across the top.

Rashid appeared at the threshold to the office.

"Hello again," Rashid said, seeming bemused by Shamus' intense expression. He was wearing a navy blue jacket, yellow dress shirt and a tie this time. The pants were still casual, as were his shoes, but he looked very dapper. There was a hint of Old Spice in the air.

"Oh, I see you've noticed my impressive garb." Rashid beamed.

"I did," Shamus admitted.

"I am on my way to teach. And then I'm having lunch with students on the case competition team. I must dress the part." Rashid smiled broadly. "I am a role model."

"You are indeed," Shamus said laughing.

"And what are you doing with your time today?" Rashid asked.

"I was just checking out these cracks in the ceiling and walls."

"I've gotten so used to them I don't even notice anymore," Rashid said waving them off. "If you ask me, this whole university should be red-tagged. We're sitting right on a fault. It's another Pompeii waiting to happen. You'd think in more than two thousand years we would have learned to not frolic about on unstable ground."

"I wouldn't live here. I don't know how you do."

Rashid chuckled. "Where is it safe?"

"Somewhere other than here," Shamus replied quickly.

"I suppose. But you know, life has it's own earthquakes. You cannot hide. They find you. I believe it's what we do afterward, how we handle aftershocks that determines if such events eat away at our lives by causing us to live in constant fear. Do you not think so?"

Shamus looked into Rashid's brown, intelligent, caring eyes. Was he speaking of him? "I suppose that's true."

Rashid paused as if deciding whether to question Shamus' conviction. "Yes, I think it is true. And it's wise of us both to think so too while we're here."

Shamus nodded. He sidestepped a conversation he did not want to have. And yet, Rashid was right. He knew it. There is no place to hide from adversity in life. How we handle the cards we're dealt, as his mother had framed it, defines our lives.

"Tell me, Rashid. Don't they inspect these buildings regularly?"

"Oh, yes. Indeed, each department has an earthquake representative. It's usually one of the secretaries. She makes sure people don't have heavy or sharp objects on their shelves. She – as all of our secretaries are women – then reports to the powers that be any large cracks or loose ceiling fixtures. It's all taken very seriously."

"You would never know," Shamus said.

"The building was retrofitted quite recently, while we were on summer break."

"Do you have cracks in your office, too?" Shamus asked.

"Oh, yes," Rashid said. "I have come to think of the older ones as historical markings, like the rings of a tree. When I observe them, I wonder who before me did the same thing. It's a way of connecting to the past."

Shamus laughed.

Rashid smiled. "We have newer surface cracks remaining from the retrofit, as well. We were assured that they would fix them, but I'll believe it when I see it. You're welcome to come and inspect them."

"That's okay," Shamus said. "I just wondered if there are a lot of them."

"Yes they are bountiful. If they weren't surface cracks, I'd be worried."

Shamus didn't want to alarm Rashid, but there was nothing "surface" about the crack above Meg's computer or around her doorway.

"I'll leave you to your work," Rashid said.

"Thank you for brightening my day. Your students must enjoy your subtle humor."

"They enjoy high grades more." Rashid smiled broadly.

"But they'll remember you more," Shamus replied.

Rashid nodded in appreciation and headed down the corridor.

Shamus sat thinking about Rashid's analogy. He'd let a traumatic event in his childhood infect the rest of his life and Meg's life as well. His father had been the adult. So surely he deserved part of the blame. But wasn't it Shamus who had served as a host carrying the contagion of the distance between himself and his father to his relationship with his sister? He wondered now if that could be undone, redirected. Could he keep an event that should be a distant memory from infecting Johnny's life by depriving him of an uncle?

He placed his hand on the computer mouse. It was very sensitive. Even the slightest movement of his finger sent the arrow careening out of sight. When he finally gained some control, he accessed the Internet search engine. When the query box appeared, Shamus typed:

S-E-I-S-M-O-L-O-G-Y.

* * *

At 3 p.m. Shamus realized he had spent two hours brushing up on retrofitting for earthquake protection. It was time to meet with Ellen. He looked up her office number in Meg's faculty telephone directory, and then went out into the hallway.

As he passed the mailroom, a strong odor of popcorn was wafting into the corridor. He always considered making popcorn a significant breach of office etiquette. One person fills the entire floor with the smell of popcorn, making everyone hungry, but doesn't share it. When he got to office 308, the nameplate on the door read 'ELLEN NELSON.' The door was slightly ajar.

"Hi" he said cheerily as he slowly pushed the door open. "I'm Shamus Doherty."

Ellen looked up from her desk. She was about Meg's height – average for a woman but slighter of build, blonde, probably not naturally so, with large, brown eyes. sad like an affection-starved St. Bernard. Her hair needed combing. In fact, Shamus thought, she could use a makeover. Her office and desk were cluttered. There were no windows and no plants, which would have been tolerable had she decorated. The walls were barren as if meant for drop-by professors rather than someone intending to stay. Shamus felt immediately claustrophobic.

"I can't talk now," Ellen said, hurriedly gathering up her briefcase and several books. "I've got to get to a meeting. I … I'd forgotten about the meeting. I just stayed here to let you know. I have to go."

"Are you going to leave your computer on?" Shamus said evenly. "That wouldn't be very green, would it?"

"Oh, yes. Of course not," Ellen replied nervously. As she fumbled with the computer, Shamus came into the office and shut the door behind him.

"Don't do that!" she snapped. Her eyes were those of an angry Doberman now. She glanced toward the door and back at Shamus. "I can't meet with you now," she whispered.

"You don't have a meeting, Ellen," Shamus said. He sat in the chair by her desk. "You just have orders from Bill Wilkins not to talk to me."

Ellen glared at him. She took a deep breath and slowly let it out before sinking – defeated – into her chair.

"Listen. Meg is my friend. She's done a lot for me, but this is my career. If they tell me not to talk to you then I have no choice."

"But Meg would help you, wouldn't she?"

"Meg has a record superior to mine. I'm a borderline case. Wilkins told me that."

"From what I hear, Wilkins is the one who's borderline."

The fear in Ellen's eyes dissolved for a brief moment, then quickly returned. "Be that as it may, I've got to give it my best shot. I don't have a husband or partner. It's just me supporting me. So please, please, leave me alone."

This woman struck Shamus as one of the frightened people of the world, lurking about in the shadows, making little difference. "Negligible" was the word that came to mind. Yes, she had that way about her of people who are convinced they don't count and then proceed to convince everyone else as well.

"I'll be out of here in no time. Just tell me one thing," Shamus bargained.

"What?"

"Who did Meg meet with the night they found her?"

"I don't know," Ellen said abruptly.

"Okay, then were you here that night? You can at least tell me that."

Ellen looked down at the floor. She raised her head, placed her elbows on her desk and her face in her hands. Shamus waited patiently for a reply.

"Ellen, your friend and my sister is lying in intensive care. She cannot see or hold her baby. Do you understand me? She is a mother now and because people with power believe she tried to take her life, and thereby the baby's life too, she cannot touch her newborn. Do you know what that must be like? Ellen, can you imagine how painful that must be?"

She looked directly at him. There were tears in her eyes. "I was here.

I heard Meg hurry by some time around 9. I knew it was Meg because she ever so slightly drags one of her feet. We tease her about that."

Shamus thought back to the way he had teased her about it himself. When they were children, he'd playfully called her "lead foot." Whenever they played hide-and-go-seek indoors on rainy days, that telltale foot gave her away.

"I would have opened my door to talk with her, but I was trying to make a journal deadline. The paper was almost complete. I knew if I stopped to talk I'd lose my train of thought and never finish on time."

"Where did she go?"

"To the mail room."

"Did you hear anything after that?"

"I heard her rushing back to her office."

"And after that?"

"I went downstairs to the restroom. When I got back, Susan's light was out. She'd been in her office late, too. I thought she and Meg had probably left with Juan, the janitor. He walks us to our cars at night. He has daughters of his own and doesn't like them walking alone at night. He's the one who found your sister. You should talk to him. He knows more than I do."

She glanced furtively past Shamus to the door, her eyes wide.

"Don't worry, Ellen. I'm going to leave now."

Ellen sighed with relief. She walked to the door, opened it slightly and peeked out.

"I don't see anyone," she whispered. "Please go."

Shamus slinked out. He passed another office and slipped into the mailroom. It was just outside the department office, accessible to anyone. He found Meg's mailbox. It was full. He removed the mail and started toward the door.

"You're not supposed to be in here."

It was Bill Wilkins, standing in the doorway again. Shamus wondered for a moment if that is how he maintained his power over people, blocking them from wherever they wanted to go. It surely wasn't his impressive demeanor that held sway over them. Doorway dominance was a paltry device, but likely worked with people like Ellen.

"This room is only for faculty and staff. It's not for visitors."

"I know," Shamus said, walking toward Wilkins. He stopped with a mere six inches remaining between them, and stared into Wilkins' eyes. Wilkins twitched.

"I'm not visiting. I'm staying as long as it takes to find out what happened to my sister."

"I told you what happened," Wilkins said, more agitated now. "She was under stress."

"You told me *your* version," Shamus asserted, their eyes locked. "That's just not good enough."

Wilkins backed away slightly. There was no doubt in Shamus' mind – whatever had happened to Meg, this man was somehow involved. He refrained from provoking his sister's boss with the insults pulsing through his mind. His free hand clenched, then released. He stepped back, pointed in warning at Wilkins, then turned and headed down the hallway, down the stairs and outside into the warm, arid southern California night.

* * *

Shamus ate dinner in a campus fast food joint filled with students, then returned to Meg's office. Rashid had been right: the GOPC code worked. Despite her penchant for organization, Meg was apparently one of those people indifferent to computer security warnings. Shamus created a new pass code for her. He then located her file of read mail. There were hundreds of opened e-mails that hadn't been erased.

After an hour of searching, none of the e-mails had given a clue of a scheduled meeting on the date in question. Frustrated and tired, Shamus decided to go to the hospital. He wouldn't have anything to report to Meg, but his meetings with Susan and Ellen had generated some questions in his mind. Besides, he needed to see Dr. Michaels. Meg needed to be with Johnny. Surely something could be done.

It was dark when he exited East Hall. Students were gathered in groups under bright lights, some holding coffee they'd purchased at a nearby snack wagon. Other students passed by on bicycles and skateboards. They seemed so carefree. As he walked toward Structure A, Shamus imagined how it would be to return to school. It was an appealing thought. No more testy clients to deal with. He could go to Fairfield University or perhaps Yale. He wasn't too old yet. Criminology could be his major, psychology his minor. At least then if he found himself solving a mystery, he'd know what steps to take.

He entered parking structure at the south stairwell. A young couple climbed the steps just ahead of him. They opened the door marked Level 2 and exited. Shamus pushed on slowly. Normally he would run up steps, but now he was tired. Jet lag had not yet completely subsided and dealing with his sister's near demise had taken a toll. The heavy, metal door to Level 4 was ajar. Shamus pushed it open, then glanced around. The few lights were old and nearly useless. Several were flickering with indecision. The silence was eerie. No wonder Meg always moved her car to lot B if she planned to stay late, Shamus thought. As he walked toward her car, the only sound was the echo of his own footsteps. He glanced around, quickened his pace, sticking to the center of the traffic lane. As he approached the Ford Focus, a black Lexus sped down the ramp from Level 5 and careened around the corner, heading straight at him. Shamus' legs felt as if they were stuck in quicksand. He lurched his body forward, falling, between two parked cars. The Lexus came to a sudden, break-squealing stop. Shamus lay in the shadows, shivering on the cold cement. The Lexus was slowly backing up. He tried to stand, but his head was spinning. He lay there listening, expecting to hear someone come out of the car to look for him. Instead, the Lexus reversed direction, edged slowly away, then sped up and screeched down the ramps of the lower levels.

Shamus sat up. He leaned breathless against one of the cars that had sheltered him. After few minutes, he got to his feet and stumbled to Meg's car. He unlocked the door and fell into the driver's seat. He locked the doors, rested his head on the steering wheel and shakily placed and turned the key in the ignition. "Shit!" he sputtered then shouted it at the top of his lungs: "SHIT!" He slammed his fists on the steering wheel. Had he been in Ridgefield, he would have tried to tail the moron. But this was Los Angeles and he was lucky to be alive.

CHAPTER EIGHT

Get-well cards pinned up by the nursing staff adorned two large poster boards by Meg's bed. Her head was still bandaged. Her skin now had a promising hint of pink.

Waiting for Meg to awaken, Shamus sat in an upholstered chair provided by Nurse Constance, reminding him that first impressions are not always good predictors of the goodness of people. He watched Meg's pulse and blood pressure readings fluctuate on the ever-present monitor by her bed. He was still agitated from the incident in the parking structure. He nudged it from his mind.

A nurse came into the room, perfunctorily greeted Shamus, jotted some notes on a clipboard and abruptly left. Meg stirred, opened her eyes and smiled.

"Where have you been? I mean other than insistently trying to get someone in charge to let Johnny be with me?"

Shamus smiled. "Guilty as charged. And I'm making progress. I can sense it."

Meg smiled. "Thank you."

Shamus patted Meg's hand. "I was actually sitting here while you were sleeping, growing increasingly envious of your low blood pressure and your popularity. There must be fifty get-well cards on your wall."

"They're mostly from students – and a few faculty."

"I don't even know that many people."

"You know, Shamus," Meg struggled to play. "There is a prerequisite to knowing people."

"And that would be?"

"Going out."

"Very funny."

"I mean it. You can't meet people if you don't go out."

"I go out," Shamus sparred.

"You need to put yourself where you'll meet new people. You live in a box."

"I like it."

"Someday you'll have to deal with your introversion."

"It doesn't have to be today, does it?" Shamus taunted.

"I suppose not."

"Good."

"So, what have you been up to?" Meg asked, pressing a button to raise the head of her bed.

"I talked to Ellen and Susan. They both remember you rushing past their offices. That's all."

"There is someone else who might be able to help," Meg said.

"Who?"

"Most evenings the graduate students congregate outside of East Hall. They drink coffee and socialize."

"I've seen them."

"If I went to a meeting that night, I would have had to pass by them. There's one student who I try to dodge, but he invariably notices me and comes over. He's walked me to my car on several occasions."

"If you don't like this guy, why do you let him walk you to your car?"

"I don't dislike him. I'm just a little uncomfortable with him. He's around too much. I turn a corner and there he is. Must be a crush."

"How old is he?"

"Early twenties."

"A bit old for a crush, Meg."

She nodded. "I figured it was better than walking alone to the parking structure."

"So any old serial killer will do?"

"Very funny."

"His name?"

"Bill Savage."

"Beast of a guy, huh?"

"You're knocking me out here, Shamus."

Shamus chuckled.

"I'll check it out."

* * *

Shamus arranged to meet with Kent Allen at his home in the Palos Verdes peninsula, a promontory south of Los Angeles, overlooking the ocean and the island of Santa Catalina.

The first stop sign Shamus encountered in Palos Verdes was at Malaga Cove. A line of shops, banks and real estate offices were set back from the main road. A large and beautiful marble fountain graced the plaza. Shamus had read about the exclusive city of Palos Verdes Estates and its famous fountain during one of his sojourns to the Ridgefield Library. He enjoyed taking a few hours, especially on Sunday afternoons to learn about architecture. It always gave him ideas to share with his clients. Palos

Verdes had been the brainchild of a community of architectural and financial visionaries. The fountain itself was a replica of a larger bronze one in Bologna, Italy.

Shamus parked the car nearby and walked around the fountain's perimeter, admiring what he remembered as its baroque or maybe late renaissance features. Mermaids atop dolphins leaned back contentedly against each of the fountain's four pedestals. They held their naked breasts in their hands indifferently as water spurted up and outward in thin streams from their nipples. Above them figures of cupids, dolphins, and seahorses worked their way up toward a muscular Neptune, Roman king of the sea, who gazed with apparent pleasure and protective purpose across the verdant lawns and eucalyptus groves to the ocean beyond.

A red brick walkway stretched from either side of the fountain down the middle of the parking lot. There was a flavor of small town utopia. Even the police and fire stations on the periphery of the plaza blended in gracefully with the peaceful surroundings. Shamus vaguely remembered reading that this plaza had been the talk of the architectural community in the 1920s. The Olmstead brothers, whose father had designed New York's Central Park, had a major hand in designing Palos Verdes. They were fulfilling the vision of thousands of underwriters who had bought shares in the future seaside paradise. Thousands of acres were set aside for parks and recreation. Consistency in architectural style was to conjoin with disciplined variation in trees and flowers to create a dreamlike oasis. As Shamus returned to the car and drove through Palos Verdes, he estimated that Kent Allen must do fairly well for a professor to live in such surroundings.

Like many homes in Palos Verdes, Allen's house was perched on a hill overlooking the ocean. When Shamus pulled into the driveway, he saw two large peacocks perched on the rooftop. Both birds were screeching as if they were lost. Shamus assumed they must have escaped from a neighboring zoo.

As he emerged from the car, a smaller, less colorful peacock landed on the front lawn of Allen's house. The larger birds on the roof seemed now to be calling to this one, warning it of Shamus' intrusion.

"Welcome!" he heard a resonant voice call as the door opened to the opulent home. "Welcome!"

"Professor Allen?" Shamus said as he extended his hand to a tall, graying man whose face was youthful for his years.

"Indeed I am. You found me," the man said jovially. "And, please, call me Kent."

"Are those your peacocks?"

"They're a pain in the ass is what they are," Kent scoffed with a sudden disdainfulness that took Shamus aback.

"They're beautiful."

"Beauty, my friend, is in the eyes of the beholder. Someone in his infinite wisdom decided years ago that these yelping trespassers would add to the charm of Palos Verdes. They add all right – to the cost of fixing my roof!" Kent had raised his voice to a shout as if lecturing his neighbors.

He stepped past Shamus to the front step, picked up a rock from the adjacent garden and flung it at the strutting peacock that had alighted on his lawn.

"That'll teach you!" he shouted victoriously as the bird fluttered in fright toward a neighboring yard. "Are you bird-loving ignoramuses listening?"

Kent turned around and started, as if he'd momentarily forgotten Shamus' presence.

"Do come in," he recovered, smiling broadly and gesturing with earnest hospitality. They entered a luxurious entrance hall. "Come in and be welcome."

Like many of the homes Shamus had passed on his way, Allen's house resembled the Italian villas the Olmstead firm had envisioned. Three large vases of luscious purple delphiniums and pink roses competed in fragrance for Shamus' attention. "Would you like a little tour before we start?" Kent asked, basking in his guest's admiration for his home.

"Yes, indeed."

"Let's do it then." He wrapped one arm around Shamus' shoulders and gallantly extended his other, directing his awestruck guest onward.

The vaulted ceiling entrance hall led into a large living room lavishly furnished with antiques and exquisite, obviously expensive art. An ornate ceiling, flame candle fixtures, Persian rugs, polished wooden floors, plush chairs and a marble fireplace all beckoned the visitor to linger. Nonetheless, they pushed on through a portico and encountered what Kent's expression revealed to be his favorite aspect, a garden fountain modeled on one in a palatial home he'd visited in the Lake Como region of Italy. The surrounding patio was framed by yellow-flowered cassias, acacias, pink and scarlet passionflowers, red geraniums and heather. A sweet, harmonic scent lofted on the ocean breeze as it traversed the terraced stone patio.

"That's a wonderful aroma," Shamus exclaimed.

"It comes largely from wild currents and gooseberries actually," Kent explained with obvious delight. "Someone should capture that combination in a perfume. They'd make a bundle."

Kent's contented smile had erased Shamus' memory of the violent peacock episode. This man was at one with nature. Just not with peacocks. As they proceeded through the house, the bedrooms proved anything but disappointing. There were six of them and each had its own marble fireplace. Several had beamed ceilings. Built-in bookshelves covered at least one wall in each room – several with French doors opening out to the sea or the lush garden.

"Marvelous, isn't it?" Kent said proudly.

"Why would someone live anywhere else?" Shamus replied, dazzled.

"My sentiments exactly."

"I have a visit to the Wayfarers Chapel on my itinerary today," Shamus said. "I understand that is beautiful as well."

Kent's eyes widened with heightened regard. "Now there's a case of a son living up to his father's expectations – a magnificent tree-chapel of glass overlooking the ocean."

"Organic architecture, as I recall."

Kent was pleased. "That's right: an experience not to be missed. Lloyd Wright was quite an architect," he said reverently. "He built houses all over Los Angeles. He was more popular than his father, Frank. He and his brother John came out to Los Angeles and prospered. With all the comings and goings here, they would build houses for clients and then remodel them two or three times for subsequent owners."

"You seem to know the local architecture quite well," Shamus complimented.

"I have taken greater notice of my surroundings now that I'm not a young professor rushing hither and yon proving myself. Besides, the Wrights interest me. Come with me and I'll show you why."

As Shamus followed Kent through one of the bedrooms to another garden patio, they stopped to admire a rippled stone bordering the doorway.

"This section of the house was modeled on Lloyd's work with precast concrete block and glass," Kent boasted.

"It's magnificent."

"I can't tell you what a joy it is to meet someone who understands the architectural beauty and integrity of this part of the house."

"With all this concrete and stonework don't you worry about earthquakes wrecking the house?"

"My dear Shamus, we're in Palos Verdes!" Kent said as if everyone there knew something Shamus didn't. "Much of this peninsula is on bedrock. It has survived a number of powerful earthquakes while remaining relatively unscathed."

"I see. And what about the university?"

"Now there's a travesty waiting to happen," Kent said casually, as he plucked a drooping petal from a rich blue flower.

"What do you mean?"

"The administrator who decides what buildings should be retrofitted is a tight-fisted, penny-pinching team player – that's what I mean!"

"I see."

"When Small – that's his name – took office some fifteen years ago, the university was sitting on a threadbare endowment of $6 million. Now, even after the financial crisis, it's up to $150 million. You don't do that by being a – *spendthrift*," Kent said.

"How safe is East Hall?"

"Retrofitted last summer," Kent said as if he'd expected the question.

"So between living on bedrock and working at the business school, you're probably pretty earthquake resistant."

Kent turned away from his flower pruning, brushed some imaginary dirt from his hands, and smiled at Shamus. "I guess you could say that." He appeared to be growing tired of the subject. "Can I get you some tea or coffee?" He asked graciously.

"No thank you," Shamus replied. "I'd just like to ask you a few questions."

They returned to the sitting room, and Shamus took a seat on one of the plush, white sofas. Kent sat across from him in an antique dark oak chair.

"Okay. Shoot."

"My sister is up for promotion."

"Yes, that's right. I was sorry to hear about Meg," Kent said. "Can't say I would have believed it of her. Then again, academia is not as peaceful as it appears."

"I'm learning that. Do you think her chances for promotion are good?"

Kent rubbed his right palm thoughtfully against his cheek, revealing an impeccable manicure that Shamus would not have associated with a professor.

"I'd say she has what it takes in terms of her curriculum vitae."

"In academe, that would mean she has enough quality publications and good teacher ratings?" Shamus added.

"Precisely."

"But that isn't enough, though, is it?"

"It's a damn good start," Kent assured him. "But is it enough?" he asked, addressing himself and pausing to reflect.

Shamus waited. Surely this man knew the answer.

"I'd say it's not enough. No, to be honest, it isn't. Not in Pacific Coast's political climate."

"And Meg knew this?" Shamus asked.

"Perhaps."

"It wouldn't have come as a surprise to her, then?"

"What do you mean?"

"If she discovered that her candidacy was in trouble – that maybe despite her record she wouldn't be getting promotion and tenure. That wouldn't have surprised her?"

Kent studied Shamus' expression.

"Where would she have found out something like that?" he said. "Her package hasn't even gone up before a formal meeting of the Promotion Committee."

"Her package?"

"Every tenure candidate compiles a package. It contains a CV that provides evidence of scholarship, teacher ratings, letters of recommendation from outside reviewers and a letter from her chair, among other odds and ends. Meg's package was about to be considered by the business school promotion committee when she...well. I mean." Kent paused, seeming to search for the right words. "Well, when she tried to take her life."

"I don't believe it," Shamus said emphatically. He watched Kent to see if he would bristle, as Wilkins had.

"I see," Kent said. He looked sympathetic now. "And your reason for this?"

"My sister is very strong. She's sensitive, yes, but very strong. I just can't believe she would do this over anything, let alone a tenure decision." Shamus was about to protest, too, that surely he knew Meg well enough to realize she would not kill her own unborn child. But he held back, reminding himself of his reason for being there – to learn, not to argue.

"It wouldn't be the first time," Kent offered.

"You mean other people have hung themselves here at Pacific Coast?"

"I don't know of it happening at our university, but something like it probably has. Tenure is a precious objective to aspiring professors. It's the gold ring for junior people. Many become so transfixed on getting tenure that they lose sight of the reason for getting it."

"And that would be?" Shamus asked, intentionally mimicking Kent's professorial style of inquiry.

"To stay at the university or college where they work. Sometimes they fail to realize that is precisely where they do not belong. They're too busy struggling for tenure to consider whether they'd be happier or more productive somewhere else."

"Did you ask yourself that, when you were where Meg is in her career?"

"Can't say I did. I was at Harvard then. Tenure meant everything to me. At least that's the way it seemed."

"Did you get tenure?"

"I did."

"If you hadn't, would you have hung yourself?"

"I wasn't a young girl alone."

"And Pacific Coast isn't Harvard," Shamus countered with barely veiled sarcasm. "It isn't even one-half the size of the leading universities here."

Kent's eyes narrowed defensively. "Pacific Coast is not USC or UCLA in size, my friend, and it may have been a feeder school to them fifteen years ago, but it is arguably above both of them in quality now. It has a long history, a sizable endowment, top-notch faculty, brings in enviable research grants, and a good number of its graduates are Rhodes Scholars. Faculty teach classes here, not graduate assistants, and our faculty-student ratio is and impressive 12 to 1. Our average class size 15."

"I just meant she could have gone elsewhere – one of a host of Los Angeles colleges," Shamus said, awkwardly attempting to right their conversational path.

Kent was not satisfied. He continued: "Pacific Coast has all the benefits of a small college. People know each other. We know our students and we're available to them after hours. There's none of the indifference of a large university. We're like a family. We may not be sitting in Malibu, but ask any faculty member if they'd rather be at Pepperdine and you won't get a 'yes' from anyone who can make the grade. Faculty at USC and UCLA would give their right arms to teach at Pacific Coast – a lot from Harvard too."

Shamus tried to look convinced.

"With all the benefits – you know, the lack of indifference, the family bit, why wouldn't Meg have felt supported, even confident? She seems to have friends. You, for one."

Kent rose from his chair and walked over to the window overlooking the sea – on this day a vast, undulating mosaic of light blues and greens. He seemed to be giving himself some time to think again.

"I like your sister," he said after a nearly a minute had passed. "She's bright, determined – and charming, I might add." He turned back toward Shamus. "But, to be perfectly honest, she's not considered a good fit."

"You mean she doesn't belong here."

"In the eyes of some," Kent replied. "Fit is very important, especially at smaller, elite universities.

"In what way doesn't she fit?"

"She doesn't play the game. And at a smaller college that's even more noticeable."

"She doesn't kiss up, you mean?"

"It's not so much that – although she doesn't do that either. She gets on people's nerves – the wrong people."

Shamus got up from his chair and joined Kent at the window.

"Would one of these people be Bill Wilkins?"

"One of them," Allen acknowledged. "His main problem is that he can't stand it when a woman challenges him. None of us likes it, truth be told, but it makes him crazy."

"Sexist, huh?" Shamus suggested.

"Not in the common sense of the word. I'd say insecure is the better description. He has hardly published over the years. That was fine years ago, but not now. His only lifeline is the department chair position, so he takes it very seriously. He does what he's told for the most part, and that plays well upstairs. Lately there's been pressure to tenure people who do what we call 'mainstream' research. If Aristotle were alive today, he wouldn't get tenure at Pacific Coast because he'd be considered too eclectic, too non-mainstream."

"And that's a good thing?" Shamus asked skeptically.

"Not necessarily," Kent replied. "But it is how it is."

Shamus was seeing in Kent exactly what Susan had described. He was a straight shooter. Susan would, no doubt, disagree with some of Kent's views, but this man believed what he was saying to Shamus.

"I hear your area of study is human capital."

"Ah, a man who does his homework. I like that."

Shamus smiled appreciatively, trying not to appear content with the success of his preparation.

"Let me tell you, Shamus. There is too much talent out there being wasted by idiots who call themselves leaders. They are deluded. If something isn't new, they don't want it. It's a product of our culture. Thinking outside of the box and creativity are fine, but they do not work in the absence of experience. I've argued with your sister about this on many occasions."

"Would you say that she values the new over the old?"

"More than she should." Kent said. "But, as you no doubt know, your sister is too intelligent to categorize that easily. Let's just say she is more taken with novelty than I am. Her focus is on creativity, so that is not really surprising."

"No, I suppose not."

"What is surprising is that a young woman so well read does not place more value on history, experience, acquired knowledge. It is perhaps her only weakness." Kent paused. "As a scholar, I mean."

"You also mean that had she been more appreciative of history, the culture of the school perhaps, she wouldn't have gotten pregnant right before tenure and without being married?"

Allen looked hard at Shamus. It was as if a line of propriety had been crossed – an unsuitable subject raised. But his eyes softened somewhat. He walked over to a landscape painting, studied the frame before removing a speck of dust. He turned back to look at Shamus. He smiled as if he'd remembered the need for sympathy for a brother desperate to believe his sister had not tried to take her life.

"Let's just say it wasn't good timing. Some likely saw it as the last straw – a final slap in the face and an embarrassment at such a public time. She is not the only professor who has had a child without being married and surely is not the last. But her timing provided another indication of her disdain for what is expected."

"I see," Shamus said.

"Do you?" Kent asked as if for an outsider to truly comprehend academia was not possible.

"A bit old fashioned, wouldn't you say?"

"As I said, Shamus, experience matters. People who have a sense of history know when new ideas are fully accepted and when people in power are merely acting as if they have been."

Allen would say no more; that much was clear. He looked at his watch.

Shamus rose to leave. "I hear you play golf," he said as the two walked to the front porch.

"If you want to call it that," Kent said.

"I'm a golf novice myself."

"Aren't we all?" Kent smiled. He reached to shake Shamus' hand.

"Thank you," Shamus said.

Kent nodded. "My pleasure. And please give my best to Meg."

Shamus drove along the coast toward San Pedro. He stopped at Wayfarer's Chapel as his personal tribute to Frank Lloyd Wright's genius. It was well worth the stop. The glass chapel framed by trees, sky, and sea was captivatingly beautiful. As he walked through the wooded path back to his car, he reviewed Kent Allen's comment about Meg's lack of "fit" and rubbing people the wrong way. He weighed the professor's elitism and belief that his colleagues from major universities would want to be at Pacific Coast given half a chance – a perspective Shamus found a bit hard to swallow. And yet, in balance, he'd learned a good deal from the peacock-hating professor.

* * *

From the chapel, Shamus drove to the hospital. He continued to mull over Kent's observations. He always thought Meg could get along with anyone – anyone that is who didn't exceed her threshold. Once that happened, she'd set them straight. But it took some pretty nasty behavior to exceed Meg's threshold.

Then again, Shamus thought, perhaps he didn't know his sister. She had managed to get pregnant and nearly be killed, two things Shamus would never have considered possible.

He wanted to close his eyes, wake up and find everything back the way it was – she the perfect daughter doing well and he back in Ridgefield building houses. Given a chance to do it over, though, he'd surely be in touch with Meg more. He'd remember her birthday and call her on Sundays.

When he arrived and went to Meg's room, he was pleased to find Denise with her.

"How's my favorite sister today?"

"She is coming along nicely," Denise smiled reassuringly at Meg.

"If I'm coming along so nicely why am I still in this bed while my brother does all of the detective work?"

"I'm not doing all of it. You gave me several leads."

Denise looked puzzled. "What detective work?"

"Shamus is helping me piece together what happened to me that night. If only I could get out of this bed. If I were to put myself back on campus, maybe I'd remember something."

"It'll come to you," Denise said.

"You'll just have to be patient," Shamus said. "Not one of your strong suits."

"My strong suits?"

"I hate to break into this enchanting sibling rivalry but I need to go now. I'll check in on you later, Meg." As Denise left the room, Meg stared at Shamus like a twelve-year-old who's picked up on something that was supposed to be over her head.

"What?" Shamus defended.

"Nothing. I just thought I saw a sparkle in your eye. Hers too. If I didn't know how much you avoid women, I'd say you're taking an interest in this one and she's reciprocating."

Shamus was about to launch into denial, but then he saw that Meg was smiling, truly enjoying the moment. With the stress of not seeing Johnny, he wanted to let this moment last.

"You really think she's reciprocating?"

Meg rolled her eyes.

"What?" Shamus protested, shrugging his shoulders for added effect.

"Cute, Shamus," she said, enjoying the game.

Shamus dropped his hands. "She's pretty."

"Beautiful, you mean."

He looked toward the door as if Denise might still be there. When he looked back, Meg was still smiling as she rearranged her blanket.

"So tell me what you've been up to."

Shamus remained silent for a moment, considering how much to tell her.

"Susan suggested that I meet with Kent Allen so I did."

Meg's smile vanished. "Why?"

"He knows the system."

"You didn't tell me before going?"

"I didn't want to upset you."

"Why would that upset me?"

"I heard you two had a falling out."

Meg looked surprised at first. "I suppose you could call it that." She nodded and paused before continuing. "So what did the imperious Dr. Allen have to say?"

"He says you're way off track on that creativity stuff you study."

Meg laughed. "I bet he did."

"He also thinks you were under a lot of pressure given how hard it is to get tenure here – and that you are perceived as not being a 'good fit.'"

"I see."

"He thinks you're brilliant."

Meg smiled. "But not as brilliant as he is, right?"

"That goes without saying."

"Kent and I used to get along famously. He loved talking with me and I with him. He is very bright, but he can't abide people disagreeing with him, especially people younger than himself."

"That's most people."

Meg laughed. "I guess you're right. What I mean is that assistant professors aren't supposed to disagree with him, especially publicly."

"And you did that?"

"In a way. I got tired of him smothering me, dropping off books for me to read as if I were a graduate student and insisting I read them and meet with him to discuss my thoughts. I finally told him I couldn't keep reading things whenever the spirit moved him. Now when I pass him in the halls, he nods but doesn't stop to talk. At meetings he takes every opportunity to dismiss my comments. He doesn't attack my views directly, but he talks right after I do as if what I said had no merit. He knows I don't need him as an enemy right now. If Kent isn't on your side, you don't get tenure. It's as simple as that."

"Is it that bad?"

"Like many senior professors, he expects a certain amount of obsequiousness from assistant professors. He wants to debate issues, but only so far. You can't make him feel as if he's wrong, only that there might be another way of looking at the issue."

"Meg, you might have tip-toed around him for a while longer given you were coming up for tenure?"

"It's too late now. To make matters worse, that same night I also hit a nerve. I sort of told him that his disdain for creative ideas is his fear of becoming obsolete."

"God damn! You didn't say it that way, did you?"

"Not exactly, but that's how he took it. I simply said, 'I think we're all afraid of not being valued someday.' I didn't mean now. I didn't even mean him so much as all of us, as we get older. The truth is that he's well regarded. He's a white-haired eminence. He struts around conferences with an entourage of mid-career and new professors at his heels. They want to be with him and want to be seen with him. In his mind, though, upstarts like me can take all of this admiration away in a heartbeat. It's unnerving for him. I know him well enough now to be sure I'm right about this. My error was in telling him so."

"What were you thinking?"

"I'd had a couple of glasses of wine. We were laughing and very relaxed. I went too far. I told him he was too defensive and he asked me why I thought that. Unfortunately, I told him. He sat up and asked for the check."

"He left you at the table?"

"No. He's too chivalrous for that. He walked me to my car but said nothing."

"So, maybe you were going to meet with him that night? You might have wanted to apologize? Could that be?"

"Not likely."

"Why?"

"I knew he wanted me to suffer. He wanted me to worry, too, and I did. I knew that were I to lose his support, I'd be in very deep trouble in terms of tenure. But if I were to lose his respect by becoming obsequious, I'd be in an even worse bind. It was and still is a Catch-22."

"Nevertheless, it's a possibility."

"I suppose there's a chance that I wanted to soften the blow of what I'd said."

"Kent thinks you tried to take your life because you were, well, alone."

"He just wants you to feel badly for living 3000 miles away. Next time he tries that line, ask him if perhaps he drove me to it by shutting me out of his circle. That will send him into a rage but it will shut him up, too."

"I'll do that."

Meg slapped at Shamus' arm. "No. Don't do that. I'm kidding."

Shamus smiled.

Meg sat up a bit higher in the bed. "I know you don't know me very well, Shamus – not the adult me anyway – but you should know me well enough to know that I would not take my life. And most of all I would not take my child's life."

He looked into her eyes. "OK," he said. He touched her hand. "Got it."

"No, I don't think you do. After our parents died and I couldn't connect with you, I went through a period of depression."

Shamus' eyes widened. "But …"

"Let me finish," she said firmly. "It didn't last long. I took medication for a while. I went to group therapy. And I pulled out of it. It was a dark time."

Shamus walked across the room and back. "You didn't tell me."

"Come on, Shamus. What would I have said? And what would you have done?"

"I would have listened."

She looked at him as if he were giving himself more credit than he deserved.

"Okay. Maybe I wouldn't have understood."

"Maybe you wouldn't have cared and I couldn't take that risk."

"I'm that bad a brother, huh?"

"Apparently not," Meg said with a slight smile. "But back then I wasn't sure."

Shamus thought for a moment. "So did you think about suicide?"

"Once."

"What!"

"Nearly everyone does at some time, Shamus."

"No they don't!"

"Yes, they do!" she said emphatically. "Read about it."

Shamus shook his head.

"Fine. But it's not uncommon among young people. And in any case, I got through it."

"I don't know what to say."

"There's nothing to say. It's in the past. I just wanted to be completely honest with you so you'd believe me."

"But if you thought of it before..."

"Shamus, we'd just lost both our parents. It was tough. Robert knows I went through that and he helped me."

"And that's why he thinks you tried to take your life?"

"Yes."

"A relapse?"

She nodded. A tear ran down her cheek. She wiped in away, clearly annoyed by her emotions.

"And so we can't really blame him for that?"

"No."

"But he's wrong?"

"Yes."

Shamus looked at Meg – her sincere expression, her obvious desire for him to believe that she hadn't tried to take her life. "Okay, Meg," Shamus said softly. "I believe you."

Meg scrutinized his expression for contradiction before sighing and lying back on the pillow. "I'm sorry for doubting you. It's just so frustrating. My baby is in this hospital and I can't be with him. And whoever did this is out there – somewhere. I can't get out of this bed. And my doctor doesn't believe me."

"I know," he assured her. He waited a moment in silence. "But you're safe here. And Johnny is safe. Furthermore, you've convinced your brother that he is an ass if he thinks you would take your life, especially while pregnant." He squeezed her hand and smiled. "And now you could use some rest."

"You're the one who could use some rest," she said affectionately.

"I'm fine."

He kissed her on the forehead.

She smiled.

"I'm fine and you're fine," he insisted. We'll get Johnny back. And we'll get whoever did this. I promise."

CHAPTER NINE

When Shamus returned to the apartment, Sunny was waiting at the door. The kitten appeared to have gotten into a scuffle. Her fur was ragtag and she insisted on following Shamus from room to room, mewing for him to pet her. He obliged, picking her up and sitting with her at Meg's desk. She snuggled against him, Shamus thought, the way Meg and Johnny should be now.

His thoughts turned to Meg's admission about having been depressed. He'd lied to her. Despite her sincerity, knowing she'd thought of taking her life even once, he could understand why Dr. Michaels was so adamant about her having tried to take her life. If she experienced that level of depression not all that long ago, wouldn't the looming loss of tenure be enough for a relapse? He felt guilty for thinking this way. But he couldn't help it.

He logged onto the computer and began to peruse the holdings in the university architecture library. He spent hours reviewing the state of the art for earthquake-resistant building designs and studying retrofitting procedures for existing buildings. Without flexible bases or substantial reinforcement, boxy rectangular buildings like so many on Pacific Coast's campus could literally convert to parallelograms in seconds in the event of a severe earthquake. The results would be catastrophic.

His eyes began to blur from fatigue. Carrying the kitten into the living room, he sat on the couch and stared blankly into space for a few moments before he noticed Meg's purse on a nearby table. He'd opened it once to find her keys but had otherwise left it untouched as, apparently, had the "burglars." It wouldn't hurt, he thought to himself, just to see if it held anything that might help him understand how she'd almost died that night. Gingerly opening the purse, his first find was an iPhone. He turned it on and fiddled with it until he figured out how to access the appointment program. He came to the day he was looking for. There it was: "6 p.m.: Meet w/Jake."

"Who is Jake?" Shamus asked himself aloud, waking Sunny from her peaceful slumber and causing her to scamper away. He opened the central zipper section of her purse and searching among lipstick, eyeliner, a nail clipper and other sundries, he found a folded sheet of paper. He opened it. The hand written message read:

> *Meg, meet me at 6 tonight. Got a*
> *real opportunity for you. Let's talk about*
> *tomorrow's vote too. I have some ideas.*
>
> *Jake*

Shamus picked up the telephone and dialed Susan's number.
"It's Shamus."
"Well, hello there."
"Can you tell me who 'Jake' is?"
"Jake Winhurst?"

"Maybe."

"He's head of the promotion committee. At the age of forty-five, he could work at any leading college or university yet he chooses to stay here. So, he's paid a lot. He runs a thriving program called CIM – The Center for Innovative Management. The promotion committee is another of his claims to fame and power. And I wouldn't be surprised if he has his eye on the dean's position."

"Why would he ask to meet with Meg the night before the tenure vote?"

"Wow! That's a hot one!" Susan replied. "In his defense though, professors work all kinds of hours, especially if they run centers like CIM. But the night before the committee was to vote on her tenure is not just any old night. Then again, Jake does what Jake wants to do."

"He was taking some risk, though?"

Susan thought about it for a moment. "Yes, but not enough to deter him if he needed her for something. And it just occurred to me that he has been looking for somebody to run the center, sort of under him, like an associate director. I've been praying he won't ask me. But if he does, I'll probably have to take the job. Jake Winhurst is not the kind who takes rejection lightly."

"Would he have the temerity to ask Meg to take that job the night before the promotion committee vote?"

"Temerity is his forte. If he could use the pressure of an impending vote to get her to accept the position, it wouldn't be the first time he'd used power to get his way. Jake does what's good for Jake. And Meg would have known that he could influence the committee tenure vote."

"Would he have threatened to not vote for her if she refused to cooperate?"

"That kind of directness doesn't sound like Jake. He uses hint, not combat. That would especially be his style with a woman Meg's age."

"Why? What does her age have to do with it?"

"A young professor would be *expected* to cooperate. Now as I recall he told Meg he was going to vote for her, so if she had some opposition on the committee I'd be surprised if it was from Jake Winhurst. If he did ask her to take on that job, though, she wouldn't need any incentive other than the knowledge that at an early stage of your career you don't cross a guy like Winhurst and get promoted."

"These guys sure lord it over the defenseless."

"You don't know the half of it."

After hanging up, Shamus' first thought was of calling Meg right away. This information from Susan might be just the jolt she needed to remember that night. Then he changed his mind, deciding he wanted to be there if that happened.

* * *

The building where Winhurst's office was located stood in stark contradiction to East Hall. It was newer, dark pink stucco, the front lined with a series of arched openings to a beautifully maintained, long, orange and tan slate patio. It reminded him of photos he'd seen of Stanford University. The interior had been freshly remodeled. The lobby was impressive, almost overly so for its size. The walls were lined with photos, plaques and lists of donors. The building itself had been named after the largest benefactor, whose likeness had been captured in an imposingly large painting on the wall facing the lobby entrance. The silver-haired, blue-eyed benefactor looked to be in his late sixties. Everything about him indicated great wealth and superiority. His chin rested on his curled right forefinger and extended thumb, he looked pensively off to one side. The cufflink on his visible wrist was unlike any Shamus had seen before. Seemingly 24-carat gold, the lion's head with diamond eyes protruded angrily outward half an inch or so from the shirtsleeve. On a younger man it would have been a presumptuous display of affluence. On Mr. Sherwin Atleswood, however, it seemed an indicator of distinction with which he was quite comfortable. This, after all, was his building. He'd paid for it and likely a few more of its kind as well.

Shamus entered the elevator and took it to the second floor. He proceeded to look for room number 201.

"You must be Shamus Doherty," a man's voice called from an office Shamus had just passed.

Shamus walked back. "Jake?" he asked, peeking into a well-furnished room.

"Come on in," Winhurst said, rising. "I want you to know how distressed I've been about Meg. She is a wonderful colleague. So smart and with such great potential."

Winhurst shook Shamus' hand in both of his, as if they'd known each other for years. He was a tall man; Shamus estimated his height at 6'4". His dark hair was graying along the sides. There was something disingenuous about his smile – too much for the occasion. His cologne was too intense.

Shamus sat in a burgundy-cushioned mahogany chair and glanced around the office. The walls were full of framed degrees, awards, and photos with politicians and a few celebrities. Winhurst had graduated summa cum laude from Yale and had received his Ph.D. with distinction from Princeton. A faculty robe hung from a hook on the back of the door. Over it was draped a Pacific Coast school tie.

"This office is a far cry from Meg's closet," Shamus said, realizing immediately that he hadn't offered one of his best openers.

"I served my time," Winhurst said defensively.

"No offense intended."

"None taken," Winhurst said, though he appeared perturbed.

"I was just thinking that Meg must have been quite impressed with you."

Winhurst peered over the top of his wire rim glasses to assess Shamus' meaning. His eyes were dark, judgmental and penetrating.

"I don't know whether she was or not. She never said one way or the other. A lot of professors display accolades in their offices. It's good public relations when we have visitors from outside the university. Not really so out of the ordinary."

"You're modest."

"Just honest."

The phone rang. Winhurst excused himself as he reached for the receiver. Shamus started to get up from his chair in order to wait in the hall but Winhurst shook his head and waved him back, indicating that it wasn't a private call.

As he spoke on the phone, Shamus took the opportunity to examine him. Jake Winhurst was heavy-set. The wire-rimmed glasses added an air of sophistication to what would otherwise be a rather nondescript, pudgy face. The initials JRS were embroidered on his cuffs and shirt pocket from which a Mont Blanc pen protruded. He was sporting a solid gold Rolex watch. On the desk next to the phone was a photo of Winhurst standing next to a Jaguar and another of him seated in a vintage Rolls Royce.

"Sorry about that," Winhurst said placing the receiver back on the console.

"No problem," Shamus replied absently. "Are those your cars?"

Winhurst beamed. "I'm an amateur collector. Nothing big. Just whatever I can get my hands on."

"And I see you're a golfer," Shamus said, nodding toward another photo.

"Not a good one, but I give it a whirl," Winhurst said as if he'd already tired of being examined. "Now – let me help you any way I can."

"My sister was here last Thursday night, and she..."

"I wouldn't call it night," Winhurst quickly interrupted. "It was about six o'clock."

"Around sundown?"

"About then, yes." Winhurst searched Shamus' face for intent.

"Any particular reason why she'd meet you at that hour?"

"I wanted to offer her the associate director position here at the center. It would have been an excellent opportunity for her – very prestigious."

"Did she take the job?"

"She wanted to think about it, but I'd say she looked pleased. And why wouldn't she? After all, it's quite a compliment for a junior professor to be offered such a high position. It would have meant release time from teaching and more money."

"She was about to be voted on for associate professor?"

"Yes she was. In fact I'd hoped to be able to tell her the next day that she had been given a positive vote by the promotion committee. She had my unequivocal support and I believe she had that of at least three of the other five members. There are a few hurdles in promotion from assistant to associate professor. The candidate has to have excellent teacher ratings, an impressive publication record in leading journals, letters of recommendation from highly regarded professors at prestigious universities, and other indications in the promotion file of excellence and promise. We all review these and meet together as we'd planned to do to discuss the candidate and make the final decision."

"Sounds like there is a lot of room for subjectivity in the process. I don't see how she could have risked turning you down the night before the vote?"

"Of course she could have! Well, in hindsight certainly my timing might have been better, but the dean had been on my back to fill the position. He still is."

Shamus was silent.

"I'll be honest. Meg was sometimes irascible and her work was not always mainstream, meaning her subject areas were not the ones prized by most professors here. Some of the ones on the committee might have held those two things against her. I was helping her out. They'd see her allied with me and they'd think twice about preventing her promotion. Just a bit of academic politics – nothing harmful. I'd be happy, the dean would be happy and Meg would be too."

"Irascible is not a word I've ever heard anyone use to describe Meg."

"Perhaps she's different at home," Winhurst said with evident annoyance. He smiled as if composing himself again. "Anyway, this academic minutia may be tedious for you, but some of her letters of recommendation from professors at other universities weren't stellar. Two of the committee members wanted to go out for more of them – better ones."

"How many letters did she have in her package?" Shamus asked, feeling smug at learning the lingo.

"Eleven or so. Maybe a dozen."

"Is that usually enough?"

"Yes. That's the normal amount. But committee members have the right to ask for more. They might want a letter from a professor at a particular prestigious school or ones giving evidence of international recognition. Such letters indicate standing in the field. They're considered very important. It's all very complicated. The bottom line is that we were looking at some possible delays and I thought Meg might be able to persuade the naysayers to overlook the letters issue. I was advising her on how to do so that evening."

"Did she plan to attend the committee meeting?"

"It's not often done, but I advised her to consider it. As I recall, she said she'd think about it and get back to me later that evening. But, of course, she never did."

"Instead, you think she tried to kill herself?" Shamus offered abruptly. "And it's hard for me to figure why she'd do that after you had just offered her the associate director position."

Winhurst did not reply. His expression was one of barely veiled contempt.

"What time did she leave?" Shamus asked, as if he hadn't noticed Winhurst' reaction.

"She left here around seven o'clock, I'd say. Maybe it was a little after." Winhurst looked up at the clock over his desk, as if to visually recollect the time Meg had departed.

"Was she upset?"

"Quite the contrary. She was concerned about the vote, but she knew she had my support and that I could exert influence on her behalf."

"Could or would?" Shamus asked.

"Both."

"And she was convinced of that?"

"Yes."

"And she was aware of this letter business?"

"I hadn't told her all the details. I only told you so you'd understand the situation. She wasn't a perfect fit. She knew that."

"I hear most women aren't."

"That's feminist angst, not reality," Winhurst shot back. "It's an easy excuse for not measuring up. It doesn't matter here whether you're male or female, gay or straight, white or black, or green for that matter. If you have the credentials, you get tenure."

"I thought you just said the committee members have biases," Shamus said.

"About the letters."

"I see," Shamus said sarcastically. "Only about the letters. Otherwise they're completely objective."

"I'd say they strive to be."

"And you mentioned that you can... what was it you said?" Shamus looked directly into Winhurst's infuriated eyes. "Oh yes – you can exert influence."

"Look, picking apart the tenure system isn't going to get you anywhere. Something must have been upsetting Meg. Maybe it was the loss of her parents and the stress of the tenure process. Maybe it was the pregnancy."

"Why would she be upset about that?"

"Because it might hurt her chances. This is a highly moral, conservative university community even if it is in Los Angeles."

Shamus smiled slightly. "But you just said male or female, gay or straight, one color or another, if you have the credentials all is well."

Winhurst waited to reply. His eyes were squinted now. The corners of his mouth had taken a downward turn. "A woman having a baby without a husband isn't quite acceptable around here," Winhurst continued. "It hurts the image we've carefully crafted. No one would say that, but they'd think it."

"They'd treat a man the same I imagine?" Shamus said knowing the answer. "I mean if one of you had a child without being married."

Winhurst looked away, preferring not to go down that path. Then he turned back to Shamus. "It doesn't influence my view of her competence."

"Is there any other reason you can think of why my sister would have left this office and gone to her own with the intention to kill herself and her unborn child?"

"I am not a psychologist. She was fine when she left here. We're all in shock." Winhurst looked at his watch. "My apologies but I need to get to a meeting."

They walked into the hallway and stopped just outside the main office. Several women were scurrying about with papers as if suddenly trying to look busy for the boss; others were working away at computers. No one looked up.

"If there's anything I can do, absolutely anything, please call Anne here and she'll get in touch with me right away."

Anne ceased her word processing to smile at Shamus. She looked to be about forty, slight build, brown hair and glasses. Shamus nodded and returned the smile.

"She's my right hand person." Winhurst looked over at Anne.

"I'll call you, Anne, if there's anything Jake can do."

Catching Shamus' sarcasm, she stifled a smile, nodded and returned to her work.

"Once again," Winhurst said, "I want you to know how very concerned we are. Things like this just don't happen at Pacific Coast University. I can't remember anything like this occurring and I've been here for ten years."

"It's a pretty tranquil place most of the time," Anne interjected. "Harry's death was the only other shock of this nature that I can remember."

Winhurst glared at Anne as if she'd overstepped her bounds. She took tranquil note of the nonverbal reprimand and returned to her paper work.

"Who was Harry?" Shamus asked Jake.

"An engineer who worked here. He fell from the roof of East Hall. We were told that he tripped near the elevator shaft."

"Nicest guy you'd ever meet," Anne said.

Shamus regarded her. He was amused by her unwillingness to be discouraged from conversation.

"We were all devastated," Anne continued. "Just a week before his death, when he arrived for a meeting with Professor Winhurst, he stopped by this office with donuts for all of us. He was that kind of person."

"Well, like I said, just tell Anne if you need me. I've got to go."

Winhurst shook Shamus' hand, turned away, but then turned back. "Please give Meg a hug for all of us."

Shamus lingered in the hallway for a moment.

"How's Meg doing?" came Anne's voice.

Shamus went into the department office.

"She's coming along," Shamus said. "Hell of a guy, that Winhurst. Who wouldn't want a hug from him?"

"Not too many like him," she replied.

"Broke the mold I guess."

Anne chuckled. "If they did, it was no accident."

Shamus grinned. He'd found another compatriot in an unlikely place. "You'd better watch yourself with him. He didn't look pleased when you spoke up."

"He'd better watch himself with me. I've worked here a lot longer."

Shamus smiled at Anne with bemused veneration.

"By all means, call me if I can help," she said. "I used to work in East Hall. I got to know Meg. She is real – nothing put-on about her. If I can be of any help, it would be my pleasure."

"Thanks Anne," Shamus said. "I'll be sure to call."

* * *

Shamus walked from the Atleswood Building to Meg's office, wondering what might have been on her mind as she had taken that same walk. Had she been upset, angry, depressed? If there was one thing he knew his sister hated when they were young, it was people who threw their weight around. She wouldn't have lost that ingrained mindset so evident in her childhood. The Meg he remembered would find a way to flatten a guy like Winhurst. Letting him win would be intolerable to her. But then she wasn't the little girl boys hesitated to anger. She was a young woman in a very strange place and Winhurst was no cringing boy.

Outside of East Hall a group of graduate students were gathered.

"Anybody know Meg Doherty?" Shamus asked.

"That would be most of us," one of them said.

"I wonder if any of you saw her leave East Hall last Thursday."

A gawky young man who looked about fifteen stepped forward, grinning: "You mean the night she tried to off herself?" He glanced back at the others to see how well his humor had been received. No one was laughing.

Shamus restrained himself from taking a swing at him. One of the other students in the group shoved the jokester and shouted: "Shut up, you idiot." He looked at Shamus. "You'll have to forgive my brother. He doesn't know Professor Doherty. And he's a freshman."

Shamus glared at the offender whose embarrassment was palpable. Satisfied, he turned back to the group. "I'm her brother. Did any of you see her at all that night?"

"I'm Jim Shaw," said a tall, dark-haired youth somewhat older than the rest. "Your sister is one of my professors. I saw her leave the building around 6."

"Did she look upset?"

"No." He thought for a moment. "She smiled and waved as she always does."

Shamus nodded in gratitude. "Is a Bill Savage around?"

"Bill hasn't been around for a few days," a woman seated on a stone bench called to Shamus. "Must be sick. He never misses classes."

"I see." Shamus took two slips of paper from his pocket and wrote Meg's office telephone number on both. He handed one to Jim. "Well, if you see him, please have him call me at this number."

"Will do," Jim said. "She's a great teacher."

Shamus walked over to the young woman seated on the bench. He handed her the second paper. "You'll call if you see Bill?"

"Yes," she said. "But I don't talk with him much. To be honest, he's kind of creepy."

"In what way?"

"His eyes I guess. They're weird, like he's looking through you, reading your mind. Maybe it's just his eye color. But he's quiet too and stares a lot. Creepy."

The freshman joker had eased his way out of the group and was sitting on the East Hall steps. Shamus started to ascend them. He stopped. "Looks like creeps come in all shapes, sizes and eye color," he said before kicking the now lone, less courageous "idiot's" backpack down the steps.

When he arrived at Meg's office, Shamus noticed a middle-aged Hispanic janitor who was emptying a waste paper basket into a barrel in the hallway.

"Are you Juan?"

"I am Juan." The janitor looked at Shamus for a moment. "And you must be Shamus. I recognized you from the photo in Meg's office. There's some resemblance as well."

"I want to thank you for saving my sister's life," Shamus said, reaching to shake Juan's hand. "She'd be dead if you hadn't checked on her last Thursday night."

"I usually clean her office earlier. But that night I walked Susan out to her car. I don't like how they work here so late at night. It isn't safe walking to the parking lot."

"It's extremely considerate of you to care about them like that."

"I have daughters. I'd like to think that someone would do the same for them. What goes around comes around. Also, your sister is a kind person."

"That's not what I've been hearing. She's seen as aggressive and irascible by some people here."

"Some people here are very rude and careless with their words," Juan said. He had a gentle voice and bright, caring eyes. He was a breath of fresh air, a stark contrast to Wilkins and Winhurst.

"Meg is still trying to remember that night. And I'm trying to help her piece the puzzle together. If you can think of anything unusual..."

"I only know on that night she was very anxious when I saw her. I was cleaning the alcove by the stairway. She came up the stairs there around 8:30. Her face was pale and she looked almost frightened. She rushed by me, only a slight wave, and went into the mailroom, closing the door behind her. That was unusual. I heard her rustling around in there. She was making copies and running the fax machine. Then she rushed back to her office. I was going to go speak with her to see if she was okay, but Susan was preparing to leave and I didn't want her to walk alone."

"How did you find her?" Shamus asked. "I mean, you know, later?"

"When I got back here to East Hall, I went directly to her office. I knocked. She didn't answer even though her light was on. I thought about leaving so as not to bother her but I felt like something was wrong."

"Thank God for that," Shamus said.

"I opened the door with my key," Juan said, taking a key from his chain and opened Meg's door to demonstrate. He pointed upwards. "There she was, hanging by a scarf from the sprinkler pipe – one of those university crimson and black scarves they sell in the co-op."

Juan's eyes averted from Shamus' in a moment of pained recollection. "I got her down as quickly as I could. *Dios mio. Pobrecita niña.*" There were tears in his eyes now.

"I stood on her chair. I held her up and tried to untie the scarf, but it would not loosen. I remembered my utility knife in my pocket. I opened it with my teeth and cut her down. She was still breathing when I placed her on the floor." Juan pointed to a spot in front of the desk. "Then I called 911 and the paramedics arrived."

Shamus was piecing the bits of information together, mentally replaying the moments Juan had described.

"I've thought about it over and over," Juan said. "It doesn't make sense. She was so happy about her baby coming."

Shamus waited for more, letting the silence grow.

Thinking hard, Juan raised his right hand and pointed his index finger in the air as something popped into his mind. "I do know that one night when I walked her to her car she told me one of her papers had been rejected by a journal. She was quite upset about it."

They stood quietly together for a further moment, Juan looking at the floor and rubbing the back of his neck. Shamus was examining the sprinkler pipes visible only in such vintage buildings.

"Thank you for everything you've done," Shamus said, again taking Juan's hand and shaking it warmly.

"I'm around if you need me. I'm here day and night." Juan left the office and returned to unlocking offices and emptying wastebaskets.

Shamus sat in Meg's chair, rested his elbows on her desk and placed his face in his hands.

* * *

A short while later, Rashid poked his head in the office door.

"How's Meg?"

"She's doing better," Shamus replied.

"I have thought about her so much."

"Thank you, Rashid. I know she will appreciate knowing."

"Have you found out what happened that night?" Rashid asked.

"I've talked to Susan, Ellen, Kent, Wilkins, Jake Winhurst and Juan. All I have is a bunch of loose ends."

"Have you spoken to the dean yet?"

Shamus looked bewildered. "Why would I do that?"

"He runs the school. It might flush the birds from the brush. There would be considerable damage control then. Power makes them stop and think."

"What power do I have?"

"The power to make a big fuss in the Dean's Office over your sister's near demise. The power to make them look negligent, even culpable."

Shamus looked at Rashid with the same kind of respect Denise had in her eyes when he'd mentioned the peer review. This was a route Shamus wouldn't have thought to take. Only an organizational insider, one who knew how things got done, would think of it. He invited Rashid to sit down.

"Rashid," Shamus said with the abandonment of guardedness common only in talking heart to heart with a dear friend, "Did my sister tell you anything about the baby's father?"

Rashid considered his reply as he always did, then spoke: "She did."

"Can you tell me what she said?"

"I cannot."

"Why?"

"I do not share confidences. It is not my way." Rashid gave no indication that he might be persuaded

"Did she also tell you that I'm a lousy brother?" Shamus smiled.

Rashid threw his head back and laughed. "No, she did not. She loves you very much. In fact, she worries about you. That much I can say. She worries that you will never marry, never have children, never know the kind of love I know with my family."

"She's probably right. I'm focused on my work. That's what gives me the greatest pleasure."

"I don't think that is possible."

"You don't?"

"No. I do not."

"You mean because it's only half a life?"

"No." Rashid said before pausing to reflect for a moment. "I mean because you are not the kind of person who can go through life unloved."

"If I don't start working on it soon," Shamus said, chuckling, "There'll be no other choice."

"These things come of their own accord if you allow it."

Shamus laughed lightly. He looked at Rashid with appreciation for one so perceptive. "Do you ever go out for a beer?

"I do."

"I'd like that."

Rashid nodded in agreement, smiled broadly and rose from the chair. "I must go. Please tell Meg I am thinking of her. My family is praying for her too."

"She couldn't have a better friend."

"She is like my wife says. We are south-of-Pico people."

Shamus looked puzzled.

"My wife calls us the 'authentic' residents of Los Angeles. We're the colorful people – not striving for more and more tangible things like so many people in Pacific Palisades, Beverly Hills and Brentwood. That is how we see it anyway. Perhaps it is merely a justification for not being wealthy. But we know our neighbors and we look out for each other. Our children attend public schools. Some of us can afford to live elsewhere. But we choose to be – and to be among – people who are salt of the earth."

Shamus smiled. The description did fit Meg, her apartment, Madeline, Susan, and Rashid. It fit the small shops, tiny ethnic restaurants, and diners lining Pico Boulevard near Pacific Coast University. Meg could probably afford to live in a "better" neighborhood. But she chose to live among little shops instead of designer boutiques and upscale malls, with people who would recognize her – people like Rashid who cared. Shamus knew people with wealth, but Rashid was right. Authentic meant not getting caught up in the climb, like the man with whom he was speaking – as if they'd known each other for years.

"That does fit Meg," Shamus said. "Your wife is very observant."

"That woman doesn't miss a thing," Rashid said with an affectionate smile just before turning to leave.

The acoustics of the narrow hallway exaggerated the sound of Rashid's footsteps as he returned to his office. How quiet it must have been the night Meg came to near demise, Shamus thought. Had Rashid or anyone been nearby, she would have heard their familiar footfalls in this hallway. If she didn't recognize the person, surely, he thought, she would have called security.

* * *

Meg was trying to walk with the help of a nurse when Shamus arrived at her room after visiting his nephew. The nurse helped her into bed, assured her pillows were comfortable and left the room.

"Johnny looks like you," Meg said, smiling.

"You saw him?"

Meg shook her head. "More photos. This time from Denise."

"Motherhood appears to have smitten you," Shamus said.

"It has," Meg agreed as she looked adoringly at the photos. She placed them next to her heart.

Shamus didn't want to upset her but he was thinking children should also have fathers. Not that he had anything against single mothers; he admired them as much as anyone. To choose that life, however, was wrong in his estimation. There was something selfish about it. Besides, what if this mess were to take a long time? What if DCFS did take

Johnny? What then?

"What are you dwelling on?" Meg asked as she returned the photos to the book.

"I don't want to judge your life, Meg. But a kid needs a father. And Johnny needs one even more right now because they're keeping you from him."

Meg inhaled, suppressing her annoyance. She breathed out slowly.

"I should know, Meg – you know that. You had a father. I didn't."

Meg's eyes widened as if a door forever closed had suddenly opened – to a lie. "I know what happened that night, Shamus. Even a child my age could figure out some things and later the rest. But you never forgave him."

"He was the adult!" Shamus said. His face turned red, starting with his cheeks and moving outward across his nose like an angry, resentful rash.

Meg closed her eyes and breathed deeply.

"And why didn't you tell me you knew? All these years I protected you."

"All these years you protected *you* by never talking about it even when you were old enough, even when you weren't a child deeply hurt. And you missed a chance to know our father. And, yes, he missed his chance too. But that's no reason for keeping me at arm's length all these years. But that's what you've done."

Shamus stood speechless studying his sister's intense, angry expression. He wanted to tell her she was wrong, to shout at her, to set her right. He looked down.

"I don't want to fight, Shamus. And I don't pretend to know what it was like to not have a Dad the way I did. But you have to accept that Johnny doesn't have a father."

Shamus paced, brow furrowed, trying to cool off. He turned to face his sister. He had calmed down. "Everyone has a father, Meg."

Meg shook her head, closed her eyes, and then looked up at Shamus. "I went to a sperm bank affiliated with the hospital."

Shamus' eyes widened.

"People do it, Shamus. Every day. I thought a lot about it, did some research, and chose a donor with characteristics I'd like Johnny to have."

"Like what?" Shamus asked harshly. "What characteristics substitute for a real father?"

"Shamus!" Meg protested.

"No. I mean it. Why would you do that – deprive him up front of half of his parents? It's selfish, Meg." He was losing his sense of time and place. They were kids again, him yelling at her to play with her friends, to get away from his clubhouse, to just get lost.

"You're the one who's selfish, Shamus." She sat upright, her face reddening and her eyes dark with indignation.

"For Christ's sake, Meg. You could have waited to have a baby the normal way."

"How long?"

"I don't know," Shamus stuttered. "Longer."

"Oh Shamus, grow up!" Meg said, exasperated.

Shamus resumed pacing, shaking his head. "Johnny may have ten siblings, maybe one hundred!"

"Don't be stupid," Meg said glaring at him.

"I've seen it on television. They find each other now. Did you think that through, Meg? Did you?"

Meg's indignation had usurped her body. "He won't have siblings. I know this. And it's none of your business anyway."

"None of my business?" Shamus shot back. Right now I am his uncle and his father. I'm all he has for Christ's sake. And you think it's none of my business? You can't even see him because you…"

He stopped. "Meg, I'm… God. What an idiot." He was hitting his forehead with the base of both hands. He turned to her. "I'm sorry."

The color had drained from Meg's face. She was holding her head, obviously in pain.

Meg struggled to remove the sheets, pulled the hospital gown around her, and tried to stand. She looked like the twelve-year-old who wouldn't take crap from anyone. Shamus rushed forward holding out his arms to stop her.

"What is going on here?" Denise demanded angrily as she entered the room. She looked accusingly at Shamus, then to Meg for an explanation. "Don't you get out of that bed!"

"I'm going to see my baby. You can't stop me. He's my child." Meg was shouting.

"Meg," Denise said softly, nudging Shamus away and holding Meg by her shoulders. "You can't do that. I know how you feel, but it's against the law. They could remove him from the hospital."

Meg stopped struggling. She looked into Denise's empathic eyes. "How could you know how I feel? He's my child. I carried him. He's my baby and I can't even hold him." Her lips were trembling, her eyes moistening before she took in the full meaning of Denise's words and with her help moved her legs back under the sheets and her head back onto the pillows.

Denise looked over at Shamus, now sitting in a chair, his legs bracing his elbows, head in hands, looking at the floor. He rose slowly and walked out the door.

"I just told Shamus that Johnny's father is unknown, that I went to the sperm bank," Meg said.

"I'll talk to him," Denise assured, patting Meg's hand. "Leave it to me."

"He's such a jackass sometimes."

"Yes. Evidently that is the case." Denise comforted.

"It's just that he hasn't cared about my life up to now," Meg protested as she looked toward the door, eyes still angry but wishing Shamus would come back.

"Well, he cares now, Meg. He does. His timing is off, I'll grant you that. And he is pretty darn sure of things he knows little about, but he loves you and Johnny too."

Meg nodded. She looked at Denise for a moment as if an answer to her impossible situation might reside in her intelligent eyes. She removed the photos from the book and looked at her child. "Shamus wants Johnny to have someone other than me – other than him, too. I understand that. I do. But I can't change the past."

Denise smiled down at the photos and patted Meg's hand. "And when this is all over, and it will be, that little boy will be blessed with his mom. She will be more than enough."

* * *

Outside the room, Denise delivered a stern warning to Shamus. If he wanted to make a political or moral stand, he could do it elsewhere. Meg needed to recover.

When he reentered Meg's room, the two of them sat in relative silence. He offered her water and later to straighten her pillow. They were two siblings from the same family. Yet they were miles apart in so many ways. He watched as Meg began to fall asleep. He reached through the bars so reflective of the resilient distance he'd inserted between them over the years. He'd never stopped to think about her side. Slowly, gingerly, he took her hand in his. "I'm sorry, Meg. I'm really sorry."

* * *

Shamus had a bland dinner in the hospital cafeteria. When he returned to the unit, Meg was awake and he told her his discovery of Jake's appointment in her electronic calendar.

"I don't remember having a meeting with Jake," said Meg. "Why would he ask to talk with me the night before the tenure vote?"

"Actually, I went to his office and asked him that very question," Shamus said. "He says it was to offer you the prestigious associate director position."

"Now there's a laugh! I would have been his last choice. I'm too opinionated for him. He's pointed that out to me right in front of other people on more than one occasion."

"I'm just repeating what he told me."

"You're serious! That creep was using the vote to get me to take the job? Well, I suppose I shouldn't put something like that past him. He *was* getting rejections from every associate professor, and even from some of the assistant professors. He could have been getting desperate."

"Would you have told him where to stick it?"

"I probably told him I'd think about it."

"Well, that's just what he said you did."

"I would have had to consider the associate director position."

"You would have played the game?"

"I would have pretended to play. You know – told him I'll take the position if I get tenure. But not long after taking the job I would surely have found a way to encourage him to replace me. I probably would have engaged in some strategic incompetence causing him to miss an important meeting or two. You have to fight fire with fire in this place."

"Why stay here? Allen says too many assistant professors chase after tenure in universities and colleges where they don't belong."

"Easy for him to say. It can be a real blotch on your record to be denied tenure, and I'd already begun the process. Besides, I have an impressive record. I wasn't going to curl up and die."

"But Jake pulling a fast one like that the night before the tenure decision must have made you angry?"

"I'm sure it would have. If I didn't give him an affirmative answer by the next morning, my chances of getting tenure would certainly have been diminished, likely to zero."

"When I was leaving Jake's office, his assistant mentioned a guy named Harry Dustin," Shamus said.

"Poor Harry. He was a gem of a person. He fell down the elevator shaft in East Hall when he was up on the roof checking it out."

"How could that have happened?"

"I don't really know," Meg replied. "I heard that he tripped."

"Just a freak thing?"

"I guess so. I met him a few times during the meetings our department had with him about the earthquake safety – or lack of it I should say – in East Hall. He was a very rational person. He also struck me as someone who really cared about the safety of people on campus. He was a hundred percent behind our desire for the retrofit they finished last summer."

"Apparently Harry Dustin's death is the only strange one people remember happening at Pacific Coast."

"Most professors and staff die of natural causes," Meg said. "I've been trying to make that point."

"Any chance you stepped on a *really* big toe along the tenure route, Meg?"

"I told you I err on the side of diplomacy whenever possible. Sometimes that's not possible."

"You also told me that Kent Allen isn't talking to you. Maybe he isn't the only one with his back up?"

"People get their backs up all the time here. It's what some researchers do. They protect their turf by demeaning someone else's work. But we don't *kill* each other. It's done career-wise on occasion, but not physically."

"That's what I mean. You've made some enemies and I just wonder if one of them felt threatened somehow – maybe even without you being aware of it. There's Jake wanting to keep you quiet about his attempt to blackmail you into being his associate director; Kent Allen, who was deeply offended by being upstaged and insulted I might add; the creepy student, and God knows who else. The egos here are easily bruised."

"And these enemies would hate me so much that they'd try to kill me and my unborn child?" She looked at Shamus as if he'd read too many thrillers. "This is a strange place, Shamus, but you're spinning a web here that's off the mark. It has to be someone other than my colleagues, no matter how self-important and shady some of them are."

Shamus' forehead creased. Perhaps he was off track. But where was the track?

"You see. It had to be someone who wanted me dead – someone who didn't mind killing a child, and that narrows the field considerably. Don't you think? It has to be someone for whom violence is second nature or who is insane."

Shamus said nothing. Perhaps he was weaving a web all the time, missing what could be right before his eyes – a dangerous stranger on campus.

"Listen to me," Meg said. "Try again to find out where I went after my meeting with Jake. That could tell us something."

"Juan saw you looking very upset at about 8:30. That was the earliest you were seen after meeting with Jake.

"OK. Then I must have gone somewhere after seeing Jake. The meeting with him was at 6 p.m. I wouldn't have stayed with him more than an hour."

"Maybe he took his time trying to persuade you to take the position."

"I doubt it. He had the upper hand. He wouldn't have squandered that by looking desperate. He probably told me what he wanted, answered some questions, dealt with resistance and left it at that. That's how he'd do it."

"Where could you have gone after meeting with Jake? There was some time in there" Shamus said. "You can't tell me you would have taken that lightly and gone to the library to do some research. And then there was the journal rejection Juan told me about. That had to be weighing heavily on your mind, too. You must have been worried that the tenure committee would hold that against you."

"I don't know where I would have gone after talking with Jake. And, yes, I was deeply disappointed about the journal article, but I'd gotten over that."

"I'll try again to find Bill Savage. Some of the others told me he hasn't been in class the last few days. I'll try to get his home number."

"I keep a file of my students' e-mail addresses and telephone numbers on my computer desktop. You should find Bill there. But he's a straight 'A' student so I doubt he'd miss classes unless he was ill or had a family emergency. That's another long shot, Shamus. He's really just a bit odd."

"Meg," Shamus insisted. "Odd is enough for me."

She looked down as if not wanting to challenge him, not wanting to seem unappreciative or to start another battle.

"I'm going to talk to Denise about hospital security. If someone could do this to you once, what's to stop him from doing it again? I should have thought of it earlier."

"Shamus, let's not get dramatic. This is a hospital with lots of people around and I'm not exactly a Mafia informant."

"For God's sake, Meg. Somebody tried to kill you."

She looked at his face, appreciative that he believed her now, realizing for the first time how much the recent events had taken a toll, realizing, too, as a chill surged through her, what his being right meant.

CHAPTER TEN

Meg's eyes were closed but she was not asleep. She was going over the pieces of the puzzle again. If she could only remember some part of that day, then she might be able to remember the rest. She tried to recall what she'd been planning to wear. Being pregnant had made it difficult to wake up, grab some clothes out of the closet and run, given her desire to downplay her condition on teaching days. It took more planning, which was something she usually did the night before. She recalled watching her favorite police drama on television that evening and then reading a book in bed. She tried to remember waking up the next morning but to no avail. She slammed her fists on the bed. "For crying out loud!"

In the hallway, one of the nurses suddenly called out: "Hey! Who are you? What are you doing?"

Meg heard someone running.

"Stop!" the nurse called.

"Are you all right?" Nurse Constance cried, rushing into the room. She looked terrified.

"What happened? Who was that?"

"I don't know," the nurse said. "His face was covered."

"What?"

"He had some strange sort of hat on. I couldn't see his face. He looked dark from head to toe. My God, are you sure you're all right?"

"What's going on?" Dr. Michaels demanded as he strode into the room. "What's the problem here?" Two security guards rushed in behind him.

"He went that way," Nurse Constance told them, going back into the hallway and pointing toward the stairwell. The guards ran down the hall and a shaken Nurse Constance returned to the room.

"He was dressed entirely in black. He was just about to come into Meg's room. A moment later and I wouldn't have even seen him. I called to him and he ran off. It was frightening."

Dr. Michaels turned to Meg. "Did you see him?"

"No." Her heart was pounding, her hands crossed over her chest.

"I don't know what's going on here, but we can't take any chances," he said to Nurse Constance. "Have security post someone at this door. Until we figure out who he was and where he was going, no one gets in here except myself and Dr. Cohen and the patient's brother."

"Yes, Dr. Michaels. I'll call them right now."

"God," Meg said, as Denise walked quickly into the room. "I thought Shamus was off his rocker when he said he was going to call you about getting security for me."

"Shamus called me about an hour ago," Denise said. "I thought he was being overprotective."

"Let's not overreact," Dr. Michaels instructed. "We don't know for sure that he was coming into this room. He may have been sneaking around looking for Mr. Santo."

"Who is Mr. Santo?" Meg asked.

"He shot some people," Denise explained. "He's in police custody, but he was just moved to this wing. It could be a revenge thing this guy was up to. But in any case, we can't be too careful."

"This is absurd," Dr. Michaels said angrily.

"What's absurd?" Meg challenged him. "That someone is after me – or that I didn't try to kill myself?"

"Both."

"Well, you're wrong on the suicide and you could be wrong about my life being in jeopardy too."

Denise shook her head. She tugged on the Dr. Michael's sleeve, trying to convince him to end the confrontation. He angrily pulled away.

"You actually want me to believe that someone tried to hang you in your office?"

"Believe what you like, but I didn't try to kill myself."

"You don't even remember what happened that night," Dr. Michaels insisted.

"I may have lost one night in my memory – but I haven't lost my sense of who I am and what I would and would not do. And I would not kill my child!" She was shouting, her eyes daggers of indignation. "You know that Robert."

"OK," Denise insisted. "That's enough! Both of you be quiet."

Dr. Michaels's eyes were intent on Meg. He pointed as if beginning a lecture. He dropped his hand to his side, huffed, and backed away from the bed.

"Right," Denise said. "We can discuss this tomorrow. In the meantime there will be someone at this door."

Meg was watching Dr. Michaels as if he owed her more, knew her better than to insist that she'd kill her unborn child. "Fine."

Dr. Michaels turned to leave. "Find her brother," he told Denise. "Maybe he'll be able to talk some sense into her."

"Ignore him," Denise said softly after Dr. Michaels had gone. "It's his way of handling worry. Once when I was a kid I stepped on a nail. He actually yelled at me. Do you believe it?"

Meg's anger lingered.

"Fortunately, I knew he was worried or I would have held it against him for a long time. He couldn't do enough for me later that day and for two weeks afterwards."

"He's so damn sure he's right," Meg persisted.

"He is used to being right."

"And because of it, I can't be with my own baby." Meg turned away from Denise to stifle her emotions.

"That's not fair, Meg. The law protects Johnny. Whether it applies here is not Dr. Michael's call. He has some say, but it's really out of his hands. Psychiatrists decide." She paused. "Are you listening to me, Meg? He cares about you very much. He has a strange way of showing it, but I know him. And he cares."

Meg looked into Denise's pleading eyes. She closed her own to calm herself.

"To be honest, it seems to me he's a lot like Shamus, really."

Meg opened her eyes. "They're both stubborn for sure," she said more calmly.

"But they're caring too," Denise added, as women so often do, finding the redeeming feature that erases male outbursts of anger, the way their mothers did, the way they swore they never would.

Denise patted Meg's shoulder. "Listen, I am going to have someone up here to watch your room. Until he arrives, I'll be right outside. And we'll find Shamus. He'll be here soon."

* * *

When Shamus arrived at Meg's room the sun was coming up.

"My God, Meg," he said. "I told you we need security!"

"Take it easy," Meg said, struggling up from the semi-consciousness of fractured sleep. "Dr. Michaels thinks it was probably a guy looking for some murderer who's a patient here.

"Oh sure. Hired killers always poke around hospital rooms before they get to the patient they're looking for."

"Sarcasm doesn't help."

Shamus fell into the chair next to Meg's bed. "I'll just stick around here. Denise is sending security. You shouldn't be alone in here."

"Then you need to go talk with people. Look at it this way, the sooner we find out what happened the safer I'll be and the sooner I'll be with Johnny."

"Johnny should be protected too," Shamus muttered to himself, not thinking of the effect his fears would have on Meg.

She sat upright. Her eyes widened. They looked at each other, silent, each waiting for the other to speak.

"You actually think someone would hurt Johnny?" Meg gasped.

"Of course not," Shamus said emphatically.

Meg stared at the wall, frightened.

"Listen, Meg. I was talking through my hat again. Johnny is fine. They're great in the nursery – always hovering. It's Fort Knox up there."

"If someone really wanted to hurt me, Shamus…I mean if they wanted me to suffer then they could go after…"

"Stop right there. This is getting blown out of proportion. I was upset. What I said about Johnny was stupid." He rose from the chair, clearly annoyed at running off at the mouth. "I'll talk to Nurse Shaughnessy and have them be especially vigilant if that will make you feel better." He watched her face. She had leaned back onto the pillows but had not relaxed.

"And you'll find a way for them to let me see him? Right?" Meg was insistent.

"Yes."

"Regularly."

"Yes."

"You promise."

"Stop Meg."

She took in a deep breath as she placed her two hands on her forehead.

Shamus sat down again waiting for the whirlwind of maternal terror he'd created to subside, searching for a subject that could distract her. He stood and paced about the room.

"Rashid thinks I should talk to the Dean," he said to change the subject.

Meg said nothing at first – still dwelling on her child's safety. Then softly, categorically uttered, "That's a waste of time."

"Why?"

"He's a pompous idiot."

"Seems to be an epidemic."

"His only concern is his career. Anything he tells you should be taken with a large grain of salt."

"I'm not going to see him for information. I'm going to let him know that his business school and the university are in danger if the truth of this matter is not unearthed soon. It's a power move."

Meg's eyes widened. "I didn't think you..."

"Managed people?"

"Yes," she said with a slight smile.

"I'm learning."

"There is a first for everything."

But they could not hold the mood. Their effort at levity dissipated as quickly as it had emerged. Fear had replaced air in the room. There was no escaping it.

"Shamus, if these incidents are more than mere coincidence you could be in danger yourself. Someone out there won't want you getting close. You'll be careful, right?"

"Meg, in a few days, maybe sooner, we'll be talking about how a string of freakish, unrelated, admittedly scary events allowed our imaginations to go wild. But, yes, I will be careful. I promise."

* * *

"Office of Dean Burns." A young, female voice answered the phone.

"This is Shamus Doherty, Professor Doherty's brother. May I speak with Dean Burns?"

Shamus was sitting at Meg's office desk.

"Just a moment, please." Then, after a very brief pause: "I'm sorry, Dean Burns is not available at the moment."

"I'd like to make an appointment."

"Just a moment, please."

This time several minutes passed. Shamus entertained himself by examining the cracks in Meg's walls. A different, more authoritative female came on the line:

"This is Kate Winston, Dean Burns' personal assistant. May I help you?"

"I'd like to make an appointment with Dean Burns. I'm very flexible. He can choose the time as long as it is today."

"May I ask the subject?"

"The subject," Shamus said struggling to sound pleasant, trying not to ask what the hell she thought the subject was with his sister lying in the hospital. "The subject is my sister, Professor Meg Doherty."

"Yes, of course," Winston said more flatly than the subject warranted.

"Dean Burns has been fully briefed on the matter and is looking into the circumstances."

"Fully briefed on the matter?" Shamus mimicked.

"Yes," Winston replied evenly. "He is very concerned."

"I bet he is."

"I beg your pardon?"

"Once again," Shamus said firmly. "I'd like to meet with him today."

"His schedule is quite full this week. Let me look at next week."

"It can't wait." Shamus' tone was adamant now.

"Let's see. He has lunch meetings all week with MBA students, a series of important meetings with contractors for the new building and – I'm sorry but next week is the earliest possible time."

Shamus reflected briefly on Rashid's comments on power being the only language people like the dean understand. "I can speak to him either before or after I speak to the university president," Shamus said. "It's his call."

"Just a moment please." More waiting. "It looks as though Dean Burns had a cancellation and can fit in a meeting later this afternoon," Winston offered.

"How kind of him."

She was briefly silent. "Yes. Well, he can meet you at 3 o'clock. Will that suit you?"

"I'll be there."

Rashid had been right. As Susan had told him, you either play hardball in this place or hand in your bat.

* * *

Shamus had a few hours before meeting with the dean. When he tried to arrange a meeting with the man who'd visited Johnny, he was pleasantly surprised to find himself invited right over. He arrived at the law office in an area of Culver City teaming with auto repair shops and parts suppliers. Attorney Jonathan Nathans was waiting in his own reception area. Nathans was certainly not a dapper man. His tie was askew, his suit wrinkled.

"My receptionist had a doctor's appointment," he said, noticing Shamus' curious glance at the empty reception desk. "Follow me."

They passed three other offices where what appeared to be other, more officious and polished looking young lawyers were meeting with clients or combing through thick legal files.

"We're a small firm, comparatively speaking," Nathans said, stopping in the doorway of an office. "We're exclusively discrimination, wrongful termination and harassment lawyers. It's not a pretty life, and not terribly lucrative, but it puts food on the table. As you may have noticed on your way here, this area isn't Century City or mid-Wilshire."

Nathans' office needed a dusting, but the furniture befitted a lawyer of stature, not someone struggling to get by. He motioned for Shamus to take a seat in a large, mahogany chair.

"I'll get right to the point," Nathans said. "Your sister did not want to sue the university or the business school. She just wanted to understand her rights. At least that's why she came to see me initially. The second time we met things had gotten more serious. According to Professor Doherty, they were pressuring her to leave. Her chairman and some professors were accusing her of 'not being a good fit,' as they called it. Apparently, one professor had suggested that she should either abort the baby or leave."

"She wouldn't have even considered abortion," Shamus said.

"Precisely. And apparently they knew that."

"So she'd have to leave."

"Seems that was their plan."

"And Johnny?" Shamus asked again. "Why did you go to see him?" "I was just worried about the child. Professor Doherty was still in a coma. She's my client and so, in a way, he is too."

"I see."

"I should warn you that there are some things going on at Pacific Coast that are murkier than a layman may be used to, Mr. Doherty. The endowment there has shrunk considerably. A lot of jobs are on the line; some of them held by rather big shots. According to your sister, someone at the University knew that Meg had contacted me, and they were listening in on her phone calls or at the very least checking her phone records. Quite a few organizations do that nowadays with people whom they consider loose cannons."

"Do you have a lot of cases like this?" Shamus asked, skeptical of the notion of phone tapping.

"More than you'd expect. And I don't talk about them to family members but your sister specified, in writing, that you were the only person to whom I could speak about any of this."

"You seem to believe that how 'murky' things can get in these situations is a better theory than suicide."

"Yes," Nathans replied immediately.

"It seems so odd. Academia isn't supposed to be like this."

"I have another case where the woman has won every major award in her field. She's a prolific author and had the support of her entire department when she went up for tenure. She was turned down at the university level."

"Why?"

"Someone poisoned her well. Didn't like her or just jealous. She spoke up at a meeting and got labeled. Differs each time."

"Hard to believe."

"That's why it works. These people operate in the range of

deniability."

"Do these things happen mostly around tenure?"

"Tenure is just one of many opportunities to derail or get rid of people who don't fit – often quite competent ones – male or female. They might tell a targeted professor that he or she needs to write a book to get a raise or promotion. The professor writes a book, and then they say that books aren't enough – that the professor must teach a certain range of courses, or that an article in some particular journal is lacking. The criteria keep shifting, you see. It's a never-ending race with no finish line."

"Meg isn't the type to just walk away from that kind of treatment," Shamus said.

"No. They picked the wrong victim this time."

"Do you think someone directly threatened to deny her tenure?"

"My guess is it's bigger than that. I was only beginning to scratch the surface of Meg's case, but she must have been seen as a threat to someone or something big."

"Big enough to kill her and her child?"

Nathans shook his head in frustration. "I've been over and over this myself, but the answer isn't evident yet."

"I don't mean to offend you, Mr. Nathans, but blocking tenure is one thing and murder is another.

Nathans nodded in agreement. "As I said, I've been over and over it."

"Thank you. You've been a big help," Shamus said, rising to shake Nathan's hand. "I have to meet with a dean," he added while looking at his watch. "If you can get Meg in to see her baby that would be major."

Nathans nodded. "I'm on it."

* * *

Dean Burns was a round-faced, rotund man of 6 feet with sparse, graying hair – a former football player. He wore gold-rimmed glasses, a very expensive suit and a university tie. His office was opulent compared to those Shamus had seen. The shelves were lined with sports trophies, plaques and volumes of books in matched sets, their titles etched in gold leaf.

Dean Burns rose to greet Shamus. "Let me say how very saddened I was to hear about your sister. We have had high hopes for her ever since the day she first interviewed here."

Burns directed Shamus to sit in one of two plush, black leather chairs studded with crimson and gold buttons at the opposite side of his oversized, ebony desk. The rug was crimson punctuated by university emblems in black. The curtains were lush gold. It was what Shamus imagined a college president's office might look like – a bit too ostentatious for a dean.

"My people are my most valued resource," Burns said as he took his seat. "When something happens to one of them, it happens to me. So my time is yours." The smile that followed these words had clearly been practiced. It was broad and held too long.

"I'll come right to the point," Shamus said. "My sister came very close to dying."

"Yes," Burns said, looking at his hands, his fingertips pressed together. Before he spoke, the fingers pushed against each other several times then returned to their stationary steeple position.

"I have a theory," Burns said, looking less at Shamus than above his head and up at the ceiling. "Your sister was very worried about tenure. She became so upset that she lost her perspective. This sort of thing does happen. We try to keep an eye on our young professors and graduate students to be sure the pressure that inevitably results from our high expectations is not getting to them. Frankly, though, Meg fooled us. She seemed to be quite happy here. That's the scary thing about these incidents, you know. Some people give no warning whatsoever."

"Incidents?" Shamus asked, suppressing his instinct for sarcasm.
"What I mean is that on the rare occasions when someone obviously cannot take the extraordinary pressure of top-tier academe, we try to recognize that and help them gain perspective."

"How, exactly, were people helping Meg? Gain perceptive, I mean."

The dean glowered at him in a manner that surely silenced professors who dared to defy his authority.

"As I said, we had no real sense that she needed help."

"Why do you suppose under such ideal circumstances that the promotion committee was planning to go out for more letters? And why do you suppose that she was invited to the committee head's office the night before the vote? Also, why in your experienced opinion do you think a woman with such an outstanding record would be told that she'd better abort her baby or be thrown out of this despicable excuse for a college?"

Burns' face reddened with indignation. He rose from his chair, placed his fingertips on either side of the crimson blotter, and leaned forward. "You are misinformed, Mr. Doherty. I am aware of none of this. Absolutely none of it," he added coldly. "Are we quite clear?" His eyes were fixed on Shamus' eyes as if their poison glare could force submission.

Shamus rose from his chair and planted his hands on the polished desktop. "Listen Dean Burns, I'm not one of your shivering little assistant professors. I'm the brother of a brilliant scholar who also happens to have a real backbone and who is lying in a hospital bed recovering from something very sinister that happened on *your* watch."

The dean's face swelled with fury. The birds had definitely been flushed from the brush. Rashid would be proud, Shamus thought.

"You had better lower your voice," Burns commanded.

"*You* had *better* start working with me here," Shamus shot back, pointing at Burns' nose for emphasis.

When the dean spoke, his voice and demeanor were like ice. "We pride ourselves on providing quality lives for our faculty. We have an elite committee devoted to that issue. We could not attract eminent scholars like the ones we have here if we treated them anywhere near as crassly as you suggest. Your sister's department chairman had expressed serious reservations about her commitment to the field. We're very serious about commitment here."

"Commitment?" Shamus scoffed.

"Yes," Burns replied with the confidence that comes from thinking one has found a viable argument. "I believe it had to do with her spotty attendance at important meetings or job candidate interviews. I don't know the exact details, nor is it necessary that I do. Frankly, such things are handled by the people who report to me."

"You're edging her out."

"Mr. Doherty, I will not be made a scapegoat for your sister's limitations as a scholar and her questionable mental health."

That was it. Shamus could restrain himself no longer. He rounded the desk and stood before the dean. No more than ten inches between them, Shamus stepped closer.

"Kate!" Burns called to the outer office.

A short, middle-aged woman rushed in.

"Yes, Dean Burns?"

"Mr. Doherty is leaving now."

"Come with me, Mr. Doherty," Kate urged.

"I don't think I'm ready to leave yet, Kate." Shamus said, keeping his eyes on Burns. "I thank you for the escort offer, though."

She looked with panic from the dean, to Shamus, and back to Burns again.

"Get out of here before I have you physically thrown out!" Burns shouted.

Kate flashed a look of discouragement at the dean then pleaded with

Shamus, arms out, palms upward in supplication. "Mr. Doherty, *please* leave with me now. It would be best."

Burns hands were clenched by his sides, his eyes locked on his adversary.

"I'm giving you notice, Burns," Shamus warned. "You'd better get to the bottom of what happened to my sister. Whoever did this to her had better pay. Your future happiness and the reputation of this school depend on it. Don't doubt my intent. Unlike my sister who is now lying in a hospital, I can play your dirty game."

Burns' face was nearly as crimson as the rug. A bespectacled, balding, sour-faced, distraught man of about forty-five scurried into the office.

"What's going on?" he gasped, trying to catch his breath. "I got here as soon as I could,"

"Who are you?" Shamus demanded.

"I'm Frank Simmons, Associate Dean of Faculty."

"Get this man out of my office," the dean ordered through clenched teeth.

"Come with me, Mr. Doherty," Simmons said. He clamped his hand on Shamus' shoulder and pushed him toward the office door.

Shamus pulled away. "Does he do all your dirty work?"

Burns took a step forward. "Get out!"

"Don't bother escorting me," Shamus said. "I'm leaving. But this isn't the last you'll see of me. I'm onto you, Burns. You and your crew here had better watch your step."

"It's you who'd better watch his step," Burns threatened. "Snooping around where you don't belong, badgering university officials, making wild threats to everyone – and you're advising me to watch my step. This isn't your sleepy little New England town, Mr. Doherty, and you are in way over your head."

"We'll see who's in over his head," Shamus countered. "We'll see whose limitations and mental stability turn out to be in question." Casting one last threatening glance at Simmons, he turned and left.

As Shamus descended the stairs, his heart pounding, the dean's last comment burned in his mind. He was in way over his head, but it was too late to turn back even if he could.

CHAPTER ELEVEN

Shamus was still mulling over the confrontation with Burns as he opened the door to Meg's office. A familiar voice came from beyond the closed door across the hall. The volume and vehemence steadily increased. Each angry, accusatory comment was followed by a barely audible, measured reply from Rashid. Shamus stood just beyond the doorway of Meg's office to listen.

"Your tail is in a sling!" shouted the visitor.

Rashid replied but Shamus still could not make out his words.

"Don't push me, Rashid!"

Shamus started. He recognized the voice.

"I am not your puppet." Rashid spoke sternly, his volume raised.

"You are what I say you are. Don't fool yourself, my friend. This job is yours only as long as I say it is."

"I am not your friend."

"Have it your way. If you ever embarrass me at a meeting again, you're as good as gone. Is that quite clear?"

It was peacock avenging Kent Allen. There was no denying it. He'd used the same tone with the birds. Shamus went into Meg's office and closed the door gently. He sat down in Meg's chair and could hardly believe what he'd just heard. A scholar like Kent Allen should be above such bullying of an adjunct professor. To be otherwise would be unseemly and unprofessional. What could mild-mannered Rashid have done to incur such wrath? Shamus went back to the door, opened it slightly and began to listen again.

"You may frighten some people and delude others, but I bow to no one and I am no fool." Rashid's voice was steady.

"You are a fool if you mess with me."

The knob on Rashid's office turned. Shamus retreated further into Meg's office, closing the door gently behind him.

"Consider yourself warned, Rashid."

"Anyone who disagrees with you is treated to a diatribe," Rashid fired back. "You did the same thing to Meg Doherty. But I am not a young woman looking for tenure. You cannot bully me."

"Watch your step. You'll find yourself back in New Delhi so quick you won't know what hit you."

"I have tip-toed around you for too long."

"Whatever happened to Professor Doherty she brought on herself. She could have had my support, but she chose to do otherwise. It had nothing to do with me."

"You hung her out to dry simply because she disagreed with your precious opinion. You knew her tenure was in jeopardy. What did you do? Nothing. You are a very small man. You have no power over me. I am not under your thumb."

"We'll see about that," Allen threatened as he walked away. "We'll see."

When Shamus was sure that Allen had gone, he knocked lightly on Rashid's still open door.

"Come in," Rashid said testily.

"Sorry," Shamus said, peering in.

"Oh! My apologies!" Rashid said as he rose to greet Shamus.

"I couldn't help but overhear that conversation, Rashid."

"I'd be surprised if someone around here *hadn't* heard it. The man is a raving lunatic."

"What did you do to make him so irate?"

"I disagreed with him at a meeting. He wanted to hire someone from outside to finish teaching Meg's classes for the semester. I argued that we should wait. The faculty could cover for her. Meg would want some say in the decision in any case. Imagine that, an adjunct professor taking on the imperious Kent Allen. It turned him into a raging imbecile."

"Sure sounded that way. What did you mean when you said he did the same to Meg?"

Rashid did not answer right away. He looked down at his desk and then looked at Shamus. His expression was apologetic.

"I'm sorry that you had to hear that. You have enough on your mind. I hold him partially responsible for what happened to Meg. He knows I do. He could have protected her, and would have had he not been so thin-skinned – so incapable of stomaching anything but awe from a young scholar. She would have easily gotten tenure if Kent Allen hadn't let it be known that he was no longer backing her."

"Did he say that?"

"He didn't have to say it. He withdraws his support as a message. Nothing needs to be said."

"Do you mind if I sit down?" Shamus asked, his tone indicating that he had something important to say to Rashid. "Please do. My manners escaped me."

"I know it sounds strange but is it possible that Meg was in the middle of something bigger than a tenure dispute – bigger than a silent feud with

Kent Allen? Could she have been a serious threat to someone?"

Rashid sat down. "I'm not sure what you mean."

"I know you're more in tune with people and that you know Meg better than I do but something very disturbing appears to have been going on the night Meg was found."

"I will help in whatever way you find useful," Rashid said, looking into Shamus' eyes with intense sincerity.

"I'm sure you will. It's only speculation at this point. The dean was nearly apoplectic when I challenged him. Jake Winhurst met with Meg the night before her tenure decision. He's manipulative at best. Kent Allen let her down over a spat. Some guys tore her place apart either trying to steal things or looking for God knows what. And somebody tried to run me over in the parking lot the other night.

Rashid looked shocked. "Run you over?"

"I know it sounds nuts. But, yes."

"You're sure of this?"

"It didn't look or feel like an accident."

"I will help in any way I can. You know this, of course?"

Shamus nodded.

"But you must be very careful now. Perhaps all of this will seem merely coincidence in time. But for now, you must watch your step."

Shamus stood to leave. "I will."

"You are welcome to stay with my family."

"You're a rare find, Rashid."

"My wife says the same, but I do not think she means it as a compliment," Rashid smiled warmly.

* * *

Meg struggled for some remnant of recollection. When none came, she tried to let sleep envelope her gently, softly luring her mind from its task, escorting it into somnolent stillness. She lingered there resisting the intruding thoughts hovering just outside the borders of calm. The most persistent among them broke ranks, sneaking nearly through to consciousness. Others, as if encouraged, followed suit. Dimly, distantly, then more closely and clearly she saw herself sitting across from a man. His facial features were hazy. His smile seemed patronizing. She could feel the heat of her own indignation. A woman appeared in the doorway. He rose, motioned for Meg to stay seated, and left the office. She looked at the photos on his walls, then at his desk. Protruding from beneath the blotter was a sheet of paper. She tugged it from its hiding place and read it. He was coming back. It was too late to replace the paper; he was at the door. She slid it into her skirt pocket. He came in and sat before her again, lecturing, demanding, and then, as if worried that someone might overhear, talking softly. It was Jake. He spoke encouragingly about the associate director position. Her heart was pounding. She rose to leave. He stood in front of her, blocking her path. His eyes were latched onto hers, holding her gaze with malevolence, saying nothing. When he finally stepped away, she exited his office slowly. Once outside his suite, she ran down the stairs. Her heart was pounding. Surely he'd notice the piece of paper was missing. There was no turning back. Perhaps he'd think he'd misplaced it. She reached her office and locked the door behind her. She removed the paper from her pocket and looked at it again. Slowly it came into focus.

"Meg," Dr. Michaels said. "Meg, wake up."

She opened her eyes.

"You were having a dream, a bad one I'd guess from the way you were moving and sweating. Are you all right?"

Meg edged her way up onto her elbows. Dr. Michaels shifted the pillows so she could sit against them comfortably. He pulled a chair to the bedside and sat down.

"I was dreaming, but it seemed so real."

"The medication can do that."

"But now I can't recall. It was awful. I know that." She shivered. "I'm so cold."

Dr. Michaels pulled the blanket up to her shoulders. "I'll get you one of those blankets we keep warm for special patients." He smiled affectionately.

"Thank you, Robert."

"The best thing you can do now is rest. I'll increase the medication a bit to help you sleep more peacefully."

"I'd rather be able to think."

"Just a bit, I promise."

She wanted to tell him what she could recall of the dream, but knew she'd remembered too little for him to take her seriously – to believe it was anything other than a dream. She wanted to take his hand, hold it, be closer to him, a feeling she'd kept to herself for over a year.

"Meg." His expression had turned serious.

"What is it?"

"You remember our discussion about the sperm bank, Meg? You asked about it and I advised you not to go that route. Remember?"

Meg looked away. She shook her head with annoyance and then turned back to face him. Dr. Michaels' expression had not changed. Perhaps he was fishing. Surely Shamus would not have mentioned it. Could it have been Denise?

"You went there. Didn't you?"

"Robert, what difference does it make?"

"I'd advised you against it."

"I appreciated your opinion."

"It doesn't look that way."

"I chose carefully – a doctor, you'll be pleased to know – someone whose description reminded me of you."

"But that's precisely what I told you. Some doctors think it's a joke or do it on a bet. Some get drunk and later regret they went there. I told you that," Dr. Michaels repeated insistently. "He is likely walking these halls." He took in a deep breath as if attempting to calm himself. "For some people it's fine, but you could have waited. You're young."

"I'm not that young."

Dr. Michaels looked at her. Used to people backing down, he held his gaze.

She didn't flinch.

"I don't know why it bothers you so much, Robert."

"Why at tenure time? You knew they'd hold it against you. It's just one more thing they can use against you."

"I tried a few times to get pregnant. It was beginning to look unlikely. I wasn't going to stop on the long shot that it would happen during the tenure process." She paused. "Besides, Robert, it's done. You and Shamus can sputter all you like, but it's well and truly done. If you want to be helpful, bring my baby to me from the nursery."

Silence descended like a heavy fog between them. Dr. Michaels closed his eyes and took in a deep breath. He opened his eyes, now softer. "You know I can't get involved in that, Meg. I'd have Johnny here in a heartbeat if there were a way. But I'd risk my medical license."

"What happened to innocent until proven guilty? What about that? What law keeps an infant from his mother on an assumption? It isn't as if I'd be with him alone. It's wrong, Robert, and you know it."

"I don't make the laws, Meg. I just follow them. I wish I could do more. I know you don't believe that, but it's true."

She looked straight ahead – away from him. Tears formed in her eyes.

Dr. Michaels patted her shoulder, looked up at the ceiling in frustration and back at her as if wishing to speak, to comfort her, before he turned and walked from the room.

* * *

Denise had suggested that they take a break together – an evening at the beach in Redondo. Shamus had been surprised. He'd considered Denise a workhorse in the hospital. But she brought along a picnic basket and blanket, and they spread them out on the sand as the sun began to set. "How did your meeting with the dean go?" Denise asked as she sliced some cheese and Shamus poured the wine.

"The guy is a snake in the grass."

"You got in his face, didn't you?"

"Am I that predictable?" Shamus smiled like a guilty child. "Of course I did – he was asking for it. He gave me some BS about Meg not fitting in and lacking commitment. He claimed that they do all they can to be sure assistant professors aren't too emotional about tenure. I tell you, the guy is a low-life liar."

"Shamus, you can't go around alienating everyone you meet and then expect to get the whole story about what happened to Meg. They'll just shut you out. You need to play along to get along. Haven't you ever heard of that?"

"You had to be there," Shamus defended. "This guy sits there in his palatial office and patronizes me. He tells me my sister doesn't have what it takes. Do you expect me to just take that?"

"You haven't been dealing with people like this. They viciously defend their turf, and they're not about to let you and your sister get in their way."

"What are you suggesting?"

"Let things cool down. Once you're out of sight for a bit, they'll think you've backed off. Then you can come back and snoop around."

"These guys only understand power. If you're in their face, they fold."

"Suit yourself, Shamus. But if you don't believe your sister tried to hang herself, then there has to be more to it. Right? So I'm afraid of what might happen if you get too close to the wrong person and act like you did with the dean."

"I'm being careful, Denise," Shamus said as he smiled with reassurance. Let's talk about something else."

Denise retained her expression of concern for a few moments. She studied his eyes attempting to comfort her. "Okay. But be smart."

Shamus nodded and smiled. "You got it."

She poured some wine and removed sandwiches from the basket.

"Do you remember Martha from the waiting room in the hospital?" Denise asked.

"Sure I do."

"Well, she remembers you too. She works at Pacific Coast in the public administration school. I ran across her at the faculty club yesterday and she asked me how your sister is doing. Apparently she hadn't made the connection that Meg is the assistant professor who had tried to take her life until I mentioned the stir it had caused around campus. Anyway, she asked me to tell you to call her. She looked concerned."

After the picnic dinner at Redondo Beach, they took a drive to Palos Verdes and walked along the cliffs. Toward San Pedro they could see the colorful chutes of hand gliders hovering in the breeze, catching the last bit of sunlight.

As they hiked along the dirt path, strangers nodded. There was a feeling of friendliness and security in Palos Verdes that Shamus liked. It was civilized and welcoming. They walked along another path dividing the main drive through Palos Verdes. The path weaved through rows of large trees, some of which were labeled. Flowers reached out from low-lying bushes as if a day's worth of being adored by walkers like themselves had simply not been enough. The cars passing nearby on either side of the greenway seemed somehow distant. There was solitude and serenity here. Were he living on the west coast, Palos Verdes might just work for him. He couldn't help but feel that people with poetry in their souls had planned this walkway.

"So what made you become a doctor?" Shamus asked.

"I know what you're thinking: If he really was as distant as I've said, why would I follow in my father's footsteps? A psychologist might say I did it to please him, and maybe that's accurate. I prefer to think I did it to please myself. Truth be told, I come from a long line of doctors, mostly men. My mother was an OB-GYN. She reduced her schedule when I was born, but they didn't have any children after me because of my mother's career – or that's the reason my father gives, but I know better. They grew apart. Why wouldn't they with him always at the hospital?"

"Anyway, when my mother passed away, I guess my father felt some obligation to nurture my career. I went to Stanford like he had. He visited me every few months. We went out to dinner, talked mostly about medicine and bonded a bit – and that was that."

Shamus put his arm comfortingly around Denise's shoulders.

They headed back to Redondo Beach where, on a street lined with t-shirt and surfboard shops, they found an elegant Italian restaurant. With its linen-covered, candlelit tables and well-starched waiters, the restaurant had an ambiance quite contradictory to the casual attire of the inhabitants. They ordered dessert and wine, bantered about the comparative advantages of East Coast versus West Coast until Denise moved the discussion to a more personal level.

"Tell me about Meg."

Shamus' brow fretted. He'd been able to put aside his concern for a few hours and now it came rushing back.

"She was a tomboy. I mean, she played with dolls but she was also one hell of a baseball player, to the point where it used to be annoying. She followed me around, trying to butt in on games I was playing with my friends. Worse still, they wanted her to play. She was a better player. I guess you could say that I suffered from a bad case of sibling rivalry made worse by the affection my parents, especially my father, showered on only her."

"She's easy to like."

"Meg is a very astute observer of human behavior. And she knows how to communicate."

"And her brother?"

"Oblivious."

"I don't think so," she reassured fondly.

Shamus nodded in appreciation. "Why don't we talk more about you?

"You're not getting off that easy. We already talked about me."

"Not enough," he said grinning.

Denise shoved him lightly. "The way I see it, you've kept complications to a minimum in your life."

"I've always prided myself on being able to pack everything I own in my car. You know, no baggage, few responsibilities, free as a bird. But now there's Johnny to think about. Even if Meg does pull through, she won't be a hundred percent right away. There's her cat, too. That little animal is actually getting to me. I find myself looking forward to seeing Sunny in the evening and I enjoy having her sleep at the foot of the bed."

"You're a softy."

"I don't think I ever would have considered myself to be, but I appear to be letting things slip a bit. Maybe when Meg gets on her feet again, I can go back to criticizing everything and basically grumping around."

"You give yourself too little credit."

"You're the first person who's ever accused me of that."

After dinner they passed a club that advertised "Dancing Every Night."

"What do you say?"

"I'm game if you are," Denise responded. "We could work off some calories from dinner."

They danced until after midnight. When they finally walked out into the cool sea breeze along the sidewalk, Denise checked her watch.

"Will you come back with me tonight?" Shamus asked softly.

Denise smiled. She leaned her head on his shoulder. "I thought you'd never ask."

* * *

At Meg's apartment, he turned the key and gestured gallantly for her to enter. He turned on the entry light then held his arm out as if in a posh restaurant, offering to take her jacket. She played along. Shamus gently removed her coat and with the gesticulation of the Four Season's Hotel waiter placed it carefully on a hanger. She reached into her pocket and pretended to tip him.

"Madame is most generous," Shamus said, looking closely at his hand as if searching for something quite small.

She nudged him again, playfully. "You're quite the actor – another side of you I hadn't expected."

"There's more, much more," Shamus teased as he led her into the living room.

"I can hardly wait."

When she was comfortably seated on the sofa, he went to the kitchen and returned with two sodas. He sat next to her. When he looked into her eyes, they were soft and inviting.

Shamus moved his body closer to hers. She smiled. His heart seemed to be skipping beats. His lips touched hers.

"Denise," he whispered, "You're beautiful."

* * *

Meg was surprised to see the sun when she awoke. She pushed herself up and grabbed for the phone beside her bed. It was nearly 9 a.m. She dialed her apartment. The phone rang over and over, but no one answered. She needed to tell Shamus about her dream – about how real it was. Someone needed to tell him.

"Shamus, for crying out loud. Pick up the phone."

She pressed the buzzer. A nurse arrived two minutes later.

"What is it, Meg? Is something wrong?"

"I need to talk to Dr. Cohen," she said anxiously.

"Are you all right?"

"I'm fine. I just need to talk to her. It's very important."

"We can call her on her cell phone."

The memories were pressing down on her now. They weren't yet clear, but she could vaguely remember hurrying, nearly running, across the campus. She had then sat in her office wondering what to do with the note. She remembered leaving the office and faxing the note to herself at the apartment and to Shamus in Ridgefield. What was it? Why had she done that? She'd called Shamus, but he hadn't answered. She remembered searching for something in her desk drawer when she heard voices in the hallway. The doorknob was turning. Why hadn't she called security? She couldn't remember beyond seeing the doorknob turning.

"Jake," she whispered.

Ten minutes had passed since she'd spoken to the nurse. There'd been no response. Twenty more minutes passed with no word. She pressed the buzzer.

Dr. Michaels walked briskly into the room.

"Thank God," Meg gasped in relief.

"I heard you were asking for Denise. She took the day off. Didn't say where she was going. But you're in luck – I'm here instead."

"Do you know where Shamus is?" She was distracted, anxious, her forehead moist.

"No. I'm afraid I don't. Just tell me what's bothering you, Meg. Are you remembering more?" As he lifted his hand, Meg saw it held a syringe. "I'm going to give you this."

"No," Meg insisted. "I need to be alert. It's important that I speak to Shamus."

"When memories of events like the ones you experienced begin to come back, the shock can cause a relapse. We can't take the chance."

He gently took hold of her arm. Meg yanked it away.

"I said No! Shamus needs to hear what I have to say."

"Meg, I'm doing what's best for your health," Dr. Michaels said firmly. "You're upset." He waited. "Give me your arm, Meg."

"Get away from me, Robert!"

Nurse Constance rushed into the room.

"You'll need to hold Miss Doherty's arm, I'm afraid," Dr. Michaels said emphatically. "She's becoming agitated."

"Robert, I am not upset. Just leave me be," Meg insisted.

As she turned to the nurse to plead her case, a sharp pain shot up her arm.

"Robert!"

"I'm sorry, Meghan."

She pushed him. "How could you?" Her eyes began to blur. Her head grew heavy. Dr. Michaels took her by the shoulders and gently placed her head on the pillows. Meg tried to talk through the increasing delirium. Nurse Constance, now taking Meg's pulse, looked with certain incredulity at Dr. Michaels.

"It was for the best," Dr. Michaels said to her.

Nurse Constance was not convinced. She busied herself straightening Meg's sheets. When she finished, she cast the doctor one more skeptical glance and left the room.

* * *

Denise entered the room followed by Shamus. They were arguing.

"He was going to call you, wasn't he?" Shamus demanded. "You said if there was a change he'd call."

"Yes I did," Denise responded angrily. "I don't know why he didn't call."

"I'm not blaming you."

"Yes you are."

"I just don't see why he'd tranquilize her without calling you, that's all."

"He must have had his reasons."

Meg opened her eyes. She could make out Denise and Shamus, but could not see them clearly.

"Meg," Denise said. "How are you feeling?"

"Meg, it's Shamus." He took her hand and held it tenderly in his. "Are you feeling okay? I'm sorry I wasn't here."

"I started to remember," Meg mumbled.

"What, Meg? Tell me," Shamus said urgently.

Denise shook her head at him.

"...Desperate." Meg said, straining to stay awake.

"Who's desperate?" Denise asked.

Dr. Michaels appeared behind them. "She isn't ready for company."

"Why didn't you call us?" Shamus demanded.

"I had things under control. She was beginning to remember that night and I didn't want those thoughts to come rushing back all at once. The damage to her emotionally could be extensive, to say nothing of the danger to her physically. I made a professional judgment. I do not want you pumping her for information.

He turned to Denise. "I'm surprised that *you* do not understand or appreciate the gravity of this situation to the patient."

Denise patted Meg's hand before turning to face Dr. Michaels. She was not pleased. "Let's talk outside," she said.

Shamus followed them out of the room.

"I do not understand," Denise said to Dr. Michaels. "You were supposed to call me. That was very clear."

"You were taking a much needed day off. I had everything under control. There was no danger to Meg. There was no need to call."

Denise took a long, deep breath.

"Meg *is* in danger. The presence of a security guard outside her room is a clear indication of that. Anything she can tell us enhances her safety. By putting her in a fog in order to reduce potential trauma, you increase the likelihood of her being unable to remember what happened to her. In that way you open her up to greater harm. It's a treacherous trade-off."

"The only harm that can come to her is the harm she might inflict upon herself if she suddenly remembers that night – trying to hang herself with an infant inside her."

"Are you still clinging to that theory?" Shamus angrily interjected. "Someone skulks outside her room, she's obviously being targeted, and you still insist that Meg tried to kill herself?"

Dr. Michaels looked at Shamus as a disgruntled parent would look at a truculent child.

"Your sister was in the grip of clinical depression. She didn't know what she was doing, and she attempted suicide. If you believe otherwise, you are deluding yourself and putting her at risk. The man in the hallway was looking for a criminal who had taken his brother's life – he was not after your sister. You've managed to create a fantasy in order to protect yourself from the truth, which is that your sister tried to hang herself. You need to face that or you won't be able to help her get the help she needs. If you insist on collaborating in her delusion, you are killing her yourself, because she will surely try again."

Dr. Michaels's conviction was total. Shamus started to speak, but the doctor continued.

"She was emotionally vulnerable from the pressure of the tenure process when I last saw her. If I thought for a moment it would lead to this, I would have done something. You see. She did not intend to harm her child. She simply was deeply depressed."

"Michaels, you're way off track here."

"*Doctor* Michaels," he corrected. "I'm not going to go around and around with you again, Mr. Doherty. I do not enjoy the exercise as much as you do."

"This isn't getting us anywhere," Denise interrupted forcefully. She glared at her father. "I don't see how one emotional afternoon indicates suicidal tendencies. Some days I wonder if I'll get through my shift. Why don't I stick a needle in my arm?"

"People who are clinically depressed do not think straight. In many cases, they live in impenetrable darkness often invisible to those around them, even the people who love them." Dr. Michaels paused. "You know that from your training, Denise."

Denise looked down, shaking her head, torn.

"Let me ask you this, Mr. Doherty. Did you really know your sister so well that you are one hundred percent convinced that she did not try to commit suicide? You know as well as I do that you did not know her. You do not know her now. That woman lying in there might as well be a distant cousin. You shut her out of your life a long time ago from what I've heard. You abdicated your right to say that you know what she is thinking."

"I may not be the best brother in the world, but I know her better than you do."

"One hundred percent, Mr. Doherty? That's my question."

"Nothing is one hundred percent."

"That's what I thought." Dr. Michaels turned and left the room. Denise threw her arms in the air, exasperated. "I'll talk to him." She turned and followed her father down the hall.

Shamus was grateful to Denise but concerned about her loyalties. He watched her begin to talk animatedly to her father. If it weren't for his feelings for her, he'd replace Dr. Michaels with another physician. He returned to Meg's room. Her eyes were open. She was looking up at the ceiling as if in a daze.

"How are you feeling, Meg?"

She turned to face him. Her expression was one of resignation.

"Meg, what's going on?"

"It keeps slipping away," she said with intense frustration. "I can't remember."

"Tomorrow you'll remember, Meg. For now, just get some rest."

* * *

Two nurses entered Meg's room. "We need a few minutes, Mr. Doherty," one said. As he came out of the room, Shamus saw Martha waiting across the hall. He slapped his head with his palm.

"Martha, I'm sorry. I was going to call. Things have been crazy."

"I know what it's like. That's why I'm here. How's Meg?"

"Better. How's your family handling your sister's death?"

"It's not easy, especially for the children."

"I'm sorry, Martha."

She nodded in gratitude. "Do you have time for a coffee?

They walked together to the hospital cafeteria discussing Meg's condition, purchased two coffees and found a corner table.

"I'll get right to the point of why I'm here," Martha began when they were seated in an empty waiting room. "You need to keep your eyes wide open when you're at the business school."

"I already figured that one out."

"I'm serious about this. Until a few months ago, I worked there as an assistant to Dean Burns. Do you know him?"

"Unfortunately, Martha, I do."

"He'd sell his mother at bargain basement prices to get what he's after. He also likes to keep files on people. He uses them when he wants to hobble or gag someone who gets in his way. When I stopped working for him, I felt that I needed something on him just in case he decided to make my departure a difficult one. So when no one was around, I copied a few choice files. There's one among them that should interest you."

She handed him a manila folder. Shamus read the tab: Meghan Doherty.

"It didn't occur to me when we first met that this file was in any way connected to *your* Meg. But now it's a gift from me to you. And what's in it will tell you what you're up against."

"The guy actually keeps special files on people like J. Edgar Hoover did?" Shamus asked, incredulously.

"Exactly. One professor might make a mildly derogatory remark about another, for example – they do that all the time just like kids in a schoolyard. If the remark is about someone in the dean's inner circle, it just passes. If it's about someone they want to hurt, Burns has one of his stooges suggest to the critic that he ought to put his observations in a confidential memo. From there it goes into the file. Then, when the opportunity presents itself, they pull the file, make sure certain people see its contents, and the poor sucker is done before he even realizes he's a target."

"Pathological."

"We have a copier. The copies are in Burns' files. You're holding the originals."

"Do you think you can get away with this?"

"They probably won't even notice. It's a very good copy machine. And very few people see these files. Besides, what would they do if they did suspect I'd taken them? If they confront me about the files, they'll be admitting to their existence."

Shamus went through the folder as Martha sipped her coffee. It was rife with recent memos about Meg failing to show up for graduation ceremonies; about her "uncooperative attitude" when her department chairman happened to schedule all of her classes at night; about the concern one professor had because she hadn't taught a certain management course. Other memos were from one or two faculty who'd criticized Meg's research for being "out of the mainstream."

"Most of the accusations and criticisms may seem minor," Martha said. "But when Burns accumulates enough of them, he turns them into patterns of incompetence. Before they know what hit them, the targets are packing their bags and leaving quietly. A memo usually goes out explaining that they wanted to spend more time with their families or that they chose to move to a university closer to an ailing parent. My own policy is to never keep a job long enough to piss off the wrong person, to keep moving from department to department. We administrative types tend to stay below the radar, but in that place I figured it was only a matter of time before they'd turn their cannons on me. So as soon as I found another position at the university, I was out of there in a flash. An old saying fits the situation at the business school: 'The fish stinks from the head.'"

* * *

"We're making progress in my getting to see Johnny," Meg said as Shamus entered her room.

"All right then! Who do we thank?"

"My lawyer. And I believe Nurse Shaughnessy has been making a nuisance of herself telling everyone in hospital administration that it's wrong to keep me from Johnny. She's wonderful. She even walked by the room with him in her arms earlier today. They'd probably fire her if they knew about it upstairs."

"She would not go softly into that dark night," Shamus laughed.

Meg smiled. "No she would not."

"And that attorney of yours, Nathans, is committed to helping you."

"He's an understated genius when it comes to issues of discrimination, civil rights and wrongful termination. A little lawyerly pressure on the hospital and the DCFS can't hurt."

"I'll go see the little guy after I leave here."

"Meg smiled warmly. Her eyes moistened but she blinked the tears away.

"You know, Shamus, you are a very good big brother."

He smiled. "I ..."

"Don't say some smart ass thing back to me. I'm being serious."

Admonished, he nodded and smiled appreciatively. "Thank you, Meg."

"We don't agree on some things, that's for sure."

He nodded.

"But on the big things we do. And no matter what happens, I want you to know that Johnny and I appreciate what you're doing. You should be in Connecticut with your clients. I know this has to be hurting business for you. And so I want you to know that I love you very much. I thank God for you every night." She smiled.

"God must be rather shocked."

"You just can't help being a smart ass, can you? Not when someone is telling you something good about yourself."

"The jury is still out on that. I'll have to get back to you. There isn't enough data – not enough events of this nature have occurred." He was clearly enjoying himself and deftly intercepting the emotions that had begun to envelope him.

"Well, at least you know. I don't blame you for keeping me at a distance for so many years. Dad really hurt you and he was inept at putting things right."

"No use going over that spilt milk again. I'm learning what I should have learned years ago. Not forgiving can eat away at life and fracture a family."

"If only Dad had thought of that," Meg said sympathetically.

Shamus smiled and squeezed her hand.

CHAPTER TWELVE

At the apartment Shamus fed Sunny and the two settled on the sofa. He opened the file Martha had given him. A letter from Kent Allen described Meg's standing at the university during her third-year performance review. "Her teaching is the best I've ever seen in a young scholar. Her research breaks new ground," Allen had written nearly three years ago. Clearly things were good between Meg and him then.

Shamus noticed that a small, tinted plastic sticker had been attached to the upper right corner of the memo. He had found them handy when specking out lists of building materials, since they came in a dispenser, were semi-transparent and could be easily removed without damaging the original document.

Deeper in the file, a recent letter described Meg as "uncooperative" and "not promising." That same professor rated her research "below expectations at this stage," opining that "granting her tenure would lower our standards and harm our chances of remaining a top-tier business school." The letter also sported a similar sticker to the one Allen had written, though instead of purple it was tinted blue.

Wilkins had contributed a letter as well. It read:

"As chair of the Management Department, I must express some hesitation in recommending Meg Doherty for tenure. Her research record appears on the surface to be quite extensive. She has, for example, published in some leading journals. Similarly, on the surface, her teacher ratings suggest exemplary accomplishment. Were these our only criteria for promotion, she might be a viable candidate. We must also consider, however, whether her research and teaching fit with the goals we have established for ourselves.

"Her teacher ratings are comparatively high. Here again, however, the numbers are deceiving. She teaches four courses each year. Of those four, three are courses we will likely cease to offer within the next two years. The narrowness of her research and its peripheral nature does not bode well for her ability to develop or teach new relevant courses. Moreover, we have had a policy in our department that professors teach the basic course sometime in their careers. She has not done so to date. Being nearly six years out from her Ph.D. now, her ability to teach crest-of-the-wave materials has been compromised. I would be remiss were I to assign her to the basic course under these circumstances.

"Recently I mentioned this policy to her. She became argumentative and claimed both that no one had told her about such a requirement and that she had never been asked to teach the basic course. This is the kind of attitude she takes whenever the advice given her doesn't match with her own view of the situation. In fact, it is her responsibility to know our rules.

"I would not be surprised if letters from outside reviewers regarding Meg's work are positive. She is well liked within the academy. She is active in the Academy of Management and served as

secretary of the Organizational Behavior division and she is chair of the Western Academy OB division. This effort at self-promotion has achieved a modicum of success. Yet, some well-placed members of the academy have told me in private that they do not expect her to reach beyond the secretary level in the national association because of her obvious self-serving intentions.

"I recommend that Meg be passed over for tenure. She is not a good fit with our efforts in the department. Her scholarship is peripheral; her teaching not central to our mission, and her potential for future external, high visibility service is limited.

Bill Wilkins,
Chair, Management Department"

A second memo from Wilkins followed:

To: Dean Burns
From: Bill Wilkins
Subject: FYI
Following on my earlier memo, I am writing to let you know that Meg Doherty has requested maternity leave for the upcoming fall semester. I have informed her of the challenges this will pose for her.

Bill

Both memos bore blue stickers somewhere in the margins, as did a memo from Jake Winhurst that described Meg as a *"borderline tenure case."* He'd written,

"Despite the positive recommendation of her Management Department peers in the Peer Review Report, I have misgivings

regarding Professor Doherty's scholarship. Her research reveals an increasing preference for qualitative rather than quantitative research methods and the discussion sections of her latest work reveal unacceptable limitations of her findings."

He further explained that this *"unfortunate turn of events"* would curtail the number of high quality journals in which Meg might publish. The final line read: *"A rising star, I regret to say, has become a falling one."*

Shamus returned to the living room to peruse the remaining contents of the file. He separated them into two piles. In one pile were glowing recommendations all with purple stickers. In the other pile were all the memos and letters that could be construed as positive but with reservations, on the fence or downright negative. Each had been tagged with a blue sticker.

Shamus went into the bedroom and dialed the phone.

"Hello?"

"Martha, this is Shamus. I have a question about the stickers that were placed on many of the letters."

"Yes?"

"Is there any reason why they are different colors?"

"I should think you would have figured that out yourself."

"I'd like to hear it from you."

"Blue stickers are for letters to be included in the dossier – the tenure package. That's all I can say. I will deny forever that I had anything to do with you obtaining them."

"I hear you, Martha. So some of these letters are dropped from the dossier and the candidate is none the wiser?"

"After being reviewed and voted on in a department at Pacific Coast, a candidate's tenure package is sent on to the university level, where the final tenure decision is made by a committee of cross-discipline full professors and the provost."

"And none of them would have previously seen Meg's dossier."

"That's a fair statement."

"And therefore none of them would know whether any of the materials had gone missing."

"All I can say is, I think you are beginning to understand why I moved on."

"Thanks, Martha."

The kitten entered the room, pleading for food.

"You're a bottomless pit," he said scooping her up and petting her. Shamus took her into the kitchen to feed her. As he filled the dish, he wondered how snakes like Burns, Winhurst and Wilkins rose to such high levels in academia. Was everyone oblivious to files like the one they were maintaining on Meg? They weren't just collecting dirt; they were manufacturing it. All for what seemed to Shamus minuscule stakes.

* * *

Sometime after midnight, Shamus awakened to a rustling noise emanating from Meg's room. He'd fallen asleep on the couch, and the file on his chest had slid to the floor, its contents spread on the carpet. His body yearned to stay put but, struggling against inertia, he managed to stand up.

"Mow," he heard as he went into the room.

"Oh," Shamus said. "It's you."

Sunny was under the table with the fax machine. She was batting something between her paws.

"What do you have there, you little rascal?"

Shamus reached down and removed a tattered piece of fax paper from her paws. As he straightened up, he noticed that the fax machine was missing paper. Then something white under the adjacent bureau caught his eye. He got down on his knees near the confused feline who – believing Shamus wanted to play – scampered over to his head and batted at his hair with her paws.

"Get away," Shamus laughed, gently nudging her with the back of his hand.

Under the bureau, Shamus found another curled up piece of paper. It was only about four inches in length, with a dark line down the middle. The machine must have run out of paper before the full page had come through. Shamus sat on Meg's bed and turned on a lamp to read it:

February 12
TO: Jake Winhurst
FROM: Harry Dustin
Our meeting yesterday was totally unacceptable. I now have no choice but to place my concerns about this matter in writing. We must act now. There is not a moment to lose. Lives are at risk. Where the money has gone is not my business. I am only concerned about what could happen in the case of a major earthquake. We must retrofit East Hall now.

Shamus leaned his head back and closed his eyes.

* * *

"I hear you guys work all kinds of hours," Shamus said as he entered Rawlins' small office. Rawlins looked up from a morass of paperwork and rubbed his eyes.

"Those rumors are absolutely true as you can see for yourself."

He gestured for Shamus to sit. Rawlins reached for the 'cleanest' coffee mug among an array of undesirables behind his desk.

"How about some coffee?"

It wasn't really a question. Rawlins was out of his chair and on his way to a coffee maker just outside his office before he'd finished asking. He returned with a concoction more akin to mud than coffee.

"It ain't much, but it's home brewed," Rawlins said, returning somewhat reluctantly to his desk chair.

"I've got some more information about my sister's case," Shamus said with a degree of conviction he hoped would get the officer's attention.

Rawlins inhaled deeply. "Listen, Mr. Doherty..."

"Call me Shamus."

"Have it your way. Listen, Shamus..."

"I just want you to take a look at the death of a man named Harry Dustin," Shamus interrupted. "He fell from the roof into an open elevator shaft in the building where my sister works." He took the crumpled fax paper from his shirt pocket and handed it to Rawlins. "I found this near Meg's fax machine at her apartment."

Rawlins looked it over, then pulled his chair in to his desk, put down his coffee mug and read it once again, more closely.

"Harry Dustin was the university engineer," Shamus said. "He died shortly before my sister's supposed suicide attempt. He uncovered a big lie, a dangerous one."

"And your sister knew this guy, this Dustin?"

"Somewhat."

"Mr. Doherty," Rawlins said, his voice betraying his growing annoyance, as he slowly and deliberately placed the memo aside on his desk. "I've already told you we can't chase around after weak assumptions. We don't have the time."

"I think my sister, Meg, pissed off the same people Harry Dustin did."

"That's some story."

"Look into Harry Dustin's visits to a professor by the name of Jake

Winhurst. You'll love Winhurst – you'll want to arrest him on sight. Then consider that Dustin was a conscientious professional in good physical shape. Yet right after he writes this memo, he falls to his death from a roof he's been on a hundred times. So he picks that time and place to screw up and take a header? Not long before my sister, who is about to have a baby, decides to hang herself from a water pipe in the same building?"

Rawlins was studying his watch, but there was no question that he was listening.

"Look at the sequence," Shamus persisted. "For no apparent reason, someone sends her a copy of a memo – and let's even say it's from a complete stranger – a memo from Harry Dustin to Jake Winhurst. Maybe she even sends it to herself. Then she goes back to her office to hang herself. Why would she do such a thing?"

"It happens."

"No." Shamus looked squarely at Rawlins. "*Shit* happens. But *this* kind of thing doesn't happen. Not in my universe – and I don't believe in yours – unless somebody wants it to."

Rawlins returned Shamus' intent gaze, waiting, it seemed, for Shamus to flinch. He sat forward, pointed his forefinger as if about to give a lecture, then thought better of it. He reached for his mug and took a long sip of coffee – all the while his eyes on Shamus who had not lessened his challenging gaze. He placed the mug back on his desk, following it with his eyes before looking at Shamus.

"I'm not saying this isn't of interest," Rawlins says calmly. "But I'm gonna tell you something straight. A lot of people come in here with reasons you wouldn't believe for why their relatives' suicides weren't really suicides. They blame the neighbor they've always hated or the ex-boyfriend who never really got over the break-up. I could go on at length. After listening to theories like these for years, I've come to understand why people construct them. Deep down they're afraid that if a relative of theirs, especially a close one, commits suicide then maybe, just maybe, they might do it too. They worry that it runs in the family, like it's in their blood or DNA or something."

Shamus was silent. He sensed the positive change in Rawlins' demeanor and focused on that instead of his words. "That must be a tough part of your job, distinguishing who is in denial and who may actually be onto something."

Rawlins leaned back in his chair.

"All right, listen, I'll do some checking into this guy Dustin," Rawlins said. "But I'm telling you, it's a long stretch from a workplace accident to a hanging. Don't get your hopes up."

Shamus nodded.

"Thank you."

Shamus took an obligatory sip of coffee, cringed and placed the mug gently on Rawlins' desk.

"That'll put hair in places you don't want it." Shamus pushed the mug toward Rawlins. "No doubt it's an acquired taste."

Rawlins smiled. "Leave me your phone number and don't call me. I'll call you."

"This has to be high priority," Shamus pushed.

"So are all of these." Rawlins lifted a pile of folders from his desk. "Every damn one of these is a high priority murder."

"But my sister is still alive. And since she didn't try to kill herself, someone else did, and may try again. I'd call that a higher priority."

Rawlins looked at Shamus with restrained appreciation. "Maybe."

Shamus rose and reached to shake Rawlins' hand.

"I won't be sitting at home waiting."

"Don't go playing amateur cop," Rawlins said rising from his chair, pointing his right forefinger at Shamus.

"Then call me," Shamus said. "The sooner the better," he added as he exited Rawlins' office and headed toward the reception area.

"For Christ's sake Doherty," Rawlins shouted after him. "Don't do anything stupid!"

* * *

Shamus arrived at the university at 10 p.m. and parked in the garage. He opened the glove box and took out a mini flashlight then removed a jack handle from the trunk and put both in a briefcase he'd found in Meg's apartment. He planned to examine the elevator shaft in part to check on the earthquake retrofit done there. But if Harry Dustin was a threat, there was the chance that he hadn't fallen. It wouldn't hurt to look, to see if it was possible to easily trip.

A walk across campus past the huge white stucco library from which students were exiting in large numbers, a guard at the door about to close the massive bronze doors inherited from the building's predecessor, across the Business School green bathed in light from antique lanterns he hadn't noticed in the daytime, brought Shamus to the steps of East Hall. Three landings up the stairway, Shamus had to make a choice. He could exit and go to Meg's office – what Rawlins would call the more sensible choice – or he could ascend to the roof. There would be no better time to take a look at the elevator shaft and the entry to it, since it was not in use. Soon it might be up and running again. If he were going to check to see what might have happened to Dustin, where he might have tripped, or been pushed, he'd have to do it now.

He reached the roof and worked his way to the small shack over the elevator. An old electric motor had received a recent coat of industrial gray paint but there was little doubt that it was in use beyond its years. Exposed gearing and a thick, rusty steel shaft led to a large sheave pulley. Steel cables emerged from a hole in the floor, wrapped over the cable and disappeared back into the shaft below. A trap door, perhaps a yard square, was located a few feet from where he was standing. Beside it was a pile of hazmat suits used for asbestos abatement. All but two were still in plastic.

Shamus looked for something on which Dustin might have tripped, but found nothing. He squatted over the trap door cover and tried to pull it open. It was locked. He opened the briefcase and took out the jack handle then wedged it between the floor and trap door and put all of his weight on it. What seemed an eternity of grinding resistance from years of having its way, the trap door finally relented. He retrieved the flashlight from the case, turned it on and pointed it downward.

The elevator was on the first floor. There were cracks in the grimy, rust-streaked masonry lining of the shaft walls. Numerous steel bars crossed the compact space like a lattice. A ladder reached downward to approximately the fourth floor. If he got on the ladder and slipped, it would be all over. He attached the still-lit flashlight to his belt and gingerly stepped onto the top rung. He worked his way down. With each step, he found more cracks, some extending for several feet. He barely touched a hole about 2 inches deep and the mortar crumbled in his hand. East Hall was a disaster waiting to happen.

Suddenly, an intense grinding sound sent a painful pulse through Shamus' ears. The hatchway slammed shut.

"Who's there?" Shamus called. He started to climb up. His foot slipped. He dropped but caught a rung of the ladder and hoisted himself up. For the moment at least, he was alive. The grinding sound again and the hatchway swung open. A dark, shadowy figure of a man holding a large flashlight was peering menacingly down at him.

"For God's sake, give me a hand!" Shamus called, squinting. The hatchway slammed shut again. Shamus reached in vain for his flashlight hanging now just out of reach. Suddenly, without warning, the bolts holding the ladder to the wall began to give, one then another. The ladder lurched outward throwing its unwelcome guest free. Shamus caught the cable with one hand, just as the ladder plummeted down the shaft to the elevator below.

He was clamped onto the cable, both arms and legs around it, all aching. His whole body was screaming. "For God's sake help me," he called. But all was silent.

A high-pitched whine slashed through his already traumatized eardrums. The cable began to move. Thirty or so feet below him, he could see the elevator edging upwards, the ladder being pushed about like a toy. He tried desperately to shimmy up the moving cable; he might have a chance at the top. A loud crunching sound dashed those hopes. The ladder had been snapped in two between the ascending elevator and a wall. He watched as one part was crushed then heard it drop to the basement floor. To his horror, Shamus saw that the other piece was now vertical with the sharp jagged metal moving ominously toward him. He tried again to climb the cable, this time reaching the top, but the hatchway would not give. He pushed on it again and again, the insistent ladder edging closer. Pounding furiously, his fate nearly sealed, he closed his eyes to await its inevitability. The sharpest point of the ladder was a foot away now. He could fall on it rather than die slowly. One finger then another loosened their hold as if making the decision for him. His right foot slipped from the cable, coaxing his reluctant left just as a large hand clasped his wrist and yanked him from the shaft.

* * *

"You are a crazy man," Rashid said when Shamus opened his eyes. "What if I hadn't heard you from the hallway?"

"Rashid?" Shamus said, blinking back the bright light tearing at his eyes.

"One man losing his life in this place was one too many. You were trying for two?"

"Was that you looking down at me?"

"Looking down at you?" Rashid said puzzled. "Who had time to be looking down? I heard terrible noises coming from the elevator shaft and then you calling out. When the door wouldn't open I ran like a madman to the roof, opened the hatch and here we are."

"Did you see anyone?" Shamus said, painfully sitting upright.

"There was no one. Only you."

"Rashid," Shamus said. "Someone was here."

"You were probably wishing someone was here."

"No. He was here all right."

Shamus held his head with both hands as he sat up.

"All the more reason to stop snooping around," Rashid said. "I'm not going to report this, but you have to promise to stay off the roof."

"This building is dangerous," Shamus insisted.

"So that's what you were doing, playing building inspector in the elevator shaft."

"Harry Dustin knew how dangerous this place is. He tried to pressure the wrong people – Winhurst."

"Your imagination is running wild," Rashid said. "East Hall passed inspection just four months ago. I told you about that. Winhurst heads the retrofit committee and the capital campaign. He has been pushing for the retrofit for years. You must have hit your head. There were scaffolds and men working everywhere during the summer."

"You were all duped," Shamus said. "They were not retrofitting the building. They may have been filling some cracks and painting, but that's about it."

Rashid thought for a moment. "Are you actually suggesting that the administration told us the building had been retrofitted when it hadn't been?"

"I'm telling you that this building hasn't undergone a retrofit. Harry Dustin would have known that just by looking, as I did, beyond the surface."

Rashid's expression of skepticism gave way to reluctant belief. "I'll need to report this."

"Not yet."

"Why not?"

"Trust me on this, Rashid. Keep a lid on it until I tie up a few loose ends."

Trying to stand, Shamus faltered and Rashid helped him to his feet.

"I'll keep quiet – briefly, but not if I see you skulking about on roofs again and not if it looks like anyone else might be in danger. Do I have a deal?"

"You have a deal."

* * *

It was late by the time Shamus arrived at Meg's apartment. He showered, changed, took a beer from the refrigerator and, exhausted, flopped onto the sofa. When the phone rang he toyed with the idea of heaving it against the wall, but answered it instead.

"Rawlins here. The autopsy report indicates no heart attack or stroke," the officer reported dispassionately. "Nothing medical caused Dustin's death. He tripped on a ladder. May have left it there himself."

"You don't think a professional engineer would remember doing that?"

"Can't say. There are times when I don't remember where I put my pencil."

"And you still don't think his fall is suspicious?"

"I think it's odd."

"What's the difference?"

"Odd means unusual. Suspicious means a little too unusual."

"I was in that elevator shaft tonight. I saw what Dustin saw – there hasn't been a retrofit. Somebody tried to kill me – trapped me in the elevator shaft. I'm sure of it."

"If I put aside for the moment the fact that you were trespassing and risking your life, what the hell were you thinking?"

"Put tonight together with the memo faxed to my sister's apartment and Dustin's untimely demise. That's more than odd."

Rawlins was silent for several moments. "I'll do some checking around campus tomorrow. I'll visit a few big shots."

"You do that for me and I'll buy you a new coffee maker," Shamus offered.

"And screw up my digestive system?" Rawlins quipped. "Not on your life."

* * *

Shamus fell back on the sofa, his aching body beginning to relax, sleep tantalizingly close, when the doorbell rang. Wearily, he trudged to the door and peered out the security eye. It was Ellen holding a bottle of wine. He opened the door.

"I thought I'd drop by, but you look a little harried. I can come back later," Ellen said smiling. She was relaxed, as if she'd had a few drinks before the one she proposed to have with him. She tilted her head and pouted slightly.

"Come on in," Shamus said, endeavoring to be hospitable. "Have a seat in the living room. I'll get us some glasses."

He returned with two wine glasses, unscrewed the wine bottle cap and poured.

"How did the detective work go today?" Ellen asked as she raised the wine glass, crossed her legs and pretended to be embarrassed by the shortness of her skirt.

"Slow."

"Why are men like that?"

"Like what?"

"Give them a chance to talk about what's troubling them, and most of them are monosyllabic."

"I'm sure an intellectual social scientist like yourself has a better explanation than I do."

"Women process talk, you know," Ellen said, sipping the wine. "Men are more outcome-oriented. They talk to accomplish things more than they do to just relate to other people or deal openly with their feelings."

Shamus was not in the mood to talk about this stuff with Ellen or anyone. His head was pounding.

"I'd like to get to the outcome of this visit," he said, only half smiling. "I don't mean to be rude but I've had a rough day."

Ellen placed her hand on Shamus' knee. She studied his eyes, his face, and smiled invitingly.

He cupped Ellen's chin with his hand and looked into her eyes. "You're lovely, Ellen," he said, smiling in an attempt to convey sincerity. His fatigue revealed the gesture as kindness bordering on pity. "You really are, but..."

She pushed him away with one hand and straightened her skirt with the other. Her eyes flashed with antipathy.

"Don't do me any favors," she sputtered.

"Ellen," he said, placing his wine glass on the coffee table. "I'm sorry." Her lips were tight with anger, her eyes unwilling to meet his.

"I came here to tell you something."

"What?" Shamus asked, still trying to be kind.

"I was in Wilkins' office today. When he stepped out for a moment, I checked his calendar. He played golf with Dr. Michaels and Jake Winhurst two days ago."

Shamus sat upright. "You're saying Michaels is wrapped up with those guys?"

Ellen removed a band from her hair and replaced it. She moved to the edge of the sofa signaling her intension to leave. "You'll see soon enough."

"What do you mean?" Shamus asked, placing a hand on her arm.

She pulled away. "You'll see – I'll make sure of that. Those guys are going to wish they hadn't messed with me. Wasn't it you who told me to not let Wilkins chase me away?"

"I don't understand."

"I'm taking your advice." She stood up abruptly.

"Ellen, sit down," Shamus insisted. "You can't just drop a bomb like that and leave."

"You're all the same," she said, grabbing her purse from the sofa. "All of you."

Shamus stood watching, eyes glazed over in pain, wondering as she opened the door and slammed it shut what had just happened.

CHAPTER THIRTEEN

It was nearly 11 p.m. when Shamus arrived at the hospital. The security guard outside of Meg's room recognized him and signaled for him to enter.

"What's up?" Meg whispered. The only light in the room was from a reading lamp.

"East Hall was never retrofitted for earthquakes," Shamus said.

"How could that be?"

"Think back, Meg. You faxed a letter to yourself that night. It was from Harry Dustin. He sent it to Jake Winhurst. Do you remember?

"I remember taking something from his desk."

Shamus' forehead furrowed and his eyes tightened. "When were you going to tell me?"

"Today," she said. "I was so angry, so tired after last night. By then I wasn't even sure of what I'd remembered – whether it was a dream."

"It was no dream. Dustin sent a letter to Winhurst telling him that East Hall hadn't been properly retrofitted. He knew that it was all a fraud and that people were in danger."

"You mean to tell me that Harry Dustin was killed because someone didn't want it known that East Hall was never retrofitted – that a mistake was made or that the company that did the work messed up?" Meg tilted her head and raised her eyes as if Shamus had lost his grip on reality.

"I'm pretty sure no one messed up."

A nurse could be heard walking toward the room. Shamus ducked. Meg held up her book and then smiled as the nurse slowed to check on her, nodded and moved on. He stood up.

"Did you think she was going to hit you?" Meg laughed softly.

"You never know with Nurse Constance."

"She's okay. Believe me." Meg smiled.

"Just trying to keep a low profile so they won't send me packing."

Meg laughed. You're like a boy sometimes, I swear."

"One of my many charms."

She nodded. "Tell me. What could Harry Dustin have to do with me being here?

"I'll keep looking into it," he said. "You've had enough for today."

"I have not had enough for today!"

"Fine, have it your way. Okay. Change of subject. Why do you suppose Dr. Michaels played golf with Winhurst and Wilkins the day before yesterday?"

"You mean do I think he's in on some nefarious scheme concocted by Winhurst and Wilkins?"

"I didn't say that."

"You didn't need to."

"Never mind," Shamus said.

"No! I want to finish this conversation. Robert is not like them. He probably went to find out what he could about the link between the tenure process and that night. Denise probably told him that I saw Jake that night. Besides, he sometimes sees other big shots on committees and it wouldn't be the first time a few of them ended up playing golf or tennis."

Shamus did not look convinced.

"They socialize together too sometimes," Meg continued. "Tomorrow Robert is having a gathering at his home. You should go. Everyone who is anyone will be there. No one would miss it. They might need a doctor like him some day. The president of the university will no doubt be there too. It's to celebrate a big donation. Jake Winhurst will be there. You can see for yourself if they're cozy."

"I'll go. But that kind of thing and golf are two different things in my book. One's a job requirement and the other is what your said – cozy."

"Shamus, you're starting to imagine things are dangerous that are simply normal."

"Nevertheless, I'm going to stay here tonight with you."

"But you look exhausted. You need to go back and get some rest."

"I'm staying here – that's all there is to it." He moved the cushioned chair to a darker part of the room, settled back in it and closed his eyes. "But if you remember anything at all, wake me."

Meg could see that further efforts to persuade him to leave would be futile. Shamus quickly dozed off. Meg took out the photos of Johnny. She held them to her heart. She had no regrets. Biological connection was not fatherhood; she'd assured herself of that many times before deciding. That's why she did it. He was her responsibility – no one else's. Only Johnny was owed the truth and not for many years to come. But how she'd get him back, become his mother as she so longed to do was the thought that tortured her daily even more than what had happened to her that night. Progress was being made, but it was too slow. A part of her was missing. She looked over at Shamus. He snored intermittently. She smiled and watched him breathe in and out. At least another part, long gone, had returned.

* * *

Dr. Michaels' home was less elegant than Kent Allen's estate. It was in Santa Monica – the prestigious north of Montana section. Each house had been given careful thought in construction and décor, and all the lawns were manicured. There was a peaceful ambiance about the area, a sense of safety and comfort. It even smelled safe. Shamus guessed eucalyptus and roses. Young and elderly couples strolled the streets holding hands. Beaming new parents were pushing designer strollers. Montana Avenue bustled with activity. Each corner seemed to have a sidewalk café. This was, indeed, a different Los Angeles than the suburb surrounding Pacific Coast University.

Dr. Michaels was at his door greeting people when Shamus arrived.

"Good to see you, Mr. Doherty." Michaels was wearing a Pacific Coast tie. He was not surprised to see Shamus. He glanced furtively to his left and right like a child about to abscond with candy. "Be sure to meet Richard Small. He's the one with the pipe. Can't miss him. He's the university architect. I told him you were coming." The doctor smiled. "He won't be looking forward to meeting you. He's a friend of Dean Burns."

"Thanks," Shamus said.

"See what you think of him," Dr. Michaels said before turning to greet other arriving guests.

He wondered for a moment if it was the festivities that had altered the good doctor's demeanor. Why would he want him to meet Small other than their mutual interest in architecture? He shook his head in puzzlement and entered the foyer.

Shamus slowly moved to the living room. As in Meg's apartment, the furniture was mostly white, with the exception of a large, cushioned blue, white and gold striped chair that had provided years of service. Shamus could imagine Dr. Michaels sitting there nights reading journals – a scotch by his side. The rug was a rich burgundy, the walls off-white edged in pure white. The scent of homegrown roses, plush and perfect, wafted throughout the house. There was a marriage of utility and style, not so perfect as to be uninviting but not so informal as to welcome long visits. The kitchen was art deco, a green and black combination that had no doubt once been a selling point.

Shamus caught sight of a man with a pipe. He was tall, gray-bearded and likely in his late fifties, wearing a professorial tweed jacket of light brown color. If Broadway were casting a play about academia, Shamus thought, Small would land a leading role. Offstage, though, he looked out-of-place, too perfect a stereotype, trying too hard. He was holding court with a group of young men who were likely graduate students. His voice carried over the hum of the crowd that nearly filled the spacious living room.

"It is best, of course, to publish a book after one has been promoted to associate professor. Even then might be a bit early. The safer time is after promotion to full professor. That is my view. And it is one widely shared, I might add."

The students nodded in unison.

Shamus worked his way over to the group. Small glanced at him. His eyes revealed a hint of recognition.

"Who have we here?" Small asked.

"I'm Shamus Doherty." He reached to shake Small's hand and once again was confronted by the Pacific Coast tie. The room was a sea of crimson and black.

"Of course. Dr. Michaels told me you'd be here. I am sorry about your sister. I hear, however, that she is doing better."

"Thank you. Yes, she is." Shamus nodded to the young following. They each shook his hand and said their names.

"I was giving these young ladies and gentleman some career advice.

There is so much pressure during the university promotion process." Small cast a glance over the group as if expecting them to agree. They did not disappoint.

"You think my sister was under that much pressure?" Shamus asked directly and before Small had completed his full reception of accord. Small looked at Shamus as though he'd stepped over some invisible line. He removed the pipe from his mouth, slowly, which allowed him time to scrutinize his interrogator.

"I can think of no other explanation."

His eyes held fast to Shamus' with intrepid superiority.

"It is the easiest explanation," Shamus replied as if he had not even noticed Small's expression. "It is not, however, the most plausible one."

Small was glaring at Shamus. Then, as though suddenly aware of the inappropriateness of his fixation, he segued to feigned empathy. "It must be a very trying time for you, Mr. Doherty. If there is anything I can do, anything my office can do, we are at your service."

"There may be something you can do, Dick." Shamus watched as his informality took effect. Small stood more erect, as if he'd been affronted.

"Oh, pardon me. May I call you Dick?"

"I do not use that nickname, Mr. Doherty."

"Please, call me Shamus."

"Shamus, I prefer to be addressed as..." Small stopped, seeming to rethink his inclination to demand formality. "Call me Richard."

Shamus smiled over a subliminal sense of victory.

"Perhaps we'd better talk privately," Small said, signaling his devotees to vanish. They merged into the crowd.

"How may I be of service, Mr. Doherty? I mean, Shamus."

"Richard, I need to know something. As the university architect, you would know when East Hall was retrofitted. Can you give me the approximate date?"

"I do not, of course, carry such details around in my head." Small chuckled and looked about the room as if to see if his efforts to appear amiable were being noticed. He placed the pipe in his mouth and puffed.

"Of course not." Shamus coughed and waved Small's smoke away from his face.

Small took his pipe from his mouth and held it by his side. He looked perturbed.

"The faculty was told that the retrofit took place last summer."

"There's your answer then," Small pronounced, replacing his pipe in his mouth and shifting it to the left side, away from Shamus, with a self-satisfied smile.

"But I have to tell you that they were misinformed."

Small removed the pipe, held it beside his right cheek. He squinted then latched his pin-point eyes onto Shamus' eyes and held fast. When Shamus did not flinch, he continued.

"Are you an earthquake retrofitting expert, Mr. Doherty?"

"No."

"I see."

"But I know enough to be sure of this."

"The faculty would not have been informed of a retrofit if it had not occurred."

"That's what I figured. That's why I'm asking when it did occur. Perhaps it wasn't last summer. Perhaps it was many years ago and they misunderstood or were mistakenly misinformed."

"Mr. Doherty, I came here this evening to enjoy the celebration. Large donations like the one Dr. Michaels obtained for us are rare indeed. I would be delighted to speak with you in my office. You may call my secretary, Grace. She'll give you an appointment. Tell her I said we should meet. We can look into this and get our facts straight."

"That sounds very good. I'll do that, Richard. You enjoy the rest of the party. I'll call Grace and you and I can walk over to East Hall together. It would be my pleasure to learn more about retrofitting. I'm always anxious to learn. And a university is a place of learning. Isn't that right?"

Small frowned at Shamus as if he were a petulant student. Then he smiled insincerely. "Of course, Mr. Doherty." He looked over Shamus' head. "Ah," he said waving. "I see one of my colleagues is here. I must excuse myself. So good to have met." Small nodded to Shamus, forced a broad smile, commandeered immediately by his true feelings, and turned away. He joined a group of people who seemed less than pleased to see him.

Shamus saw Denise coming his way through the crowd. She was wearing a long, black velvet dress that clung to her perfect figure. Her hair was tied up; her ears sparkled with small diamond studs.

"You are stunning," Shamus said as she joined him.

"Thank you." She smiled flirtatiously.

"I would not have missed this for the world. Surprised you didn't invite me."

"I didn't think you needed this kind of company."

"But I'm making so many new enemies."

"Are you? I'm delighted to learn that my father isn't the only target of your disdain."

"Actually, he's growing on me again."

"I'm glad to hear it."

Shamus caught a glimpse of Winhurst standing in a corner talking to a group of people. He seemed to be telling a joke. His listeners were captivated.

"He arrived about twenty minutes ago," Denise volunteered.

"Hello there, Shamus."

The voice was familiar. Shamus turned to find Kent Allen holding a drink, looking as though it was far from his first. His face was flushed, his eyes liquid.

"Good to see you, Kent. You may have met Denise Cohen."

"Ah, yes, the lovely 'daughter doctor.'" Allen reached for Denise's hand. When she offered it, he lifted it to his lips. "A pleasure, my dear," he said, stumbling slightly as he spoke. Denise smiled patiently.

"Nice to meet you Professor Allen."

"Anyone as lovely as you, my dear, should call me Kent. Don't you think so, Mr. Doherty?"

Shamus attempted a smile.

"Denise, perhaps Professor Allen will excuse us for a moment."

"I would not wish to intrude," Kent huffed. As he turned to leave, his glass tipped and the remainder of his drink spilled onto the carpet. "My goodness. I didn't mean to do that. These glasses are shallow indeed."

"It's not a problem," Denise assured. "I'll get something to wipe it up. Don't worry about it for a moment."

Kent nodded, then wobbled his way across the room to verbally accost other guests.

Denise caught the eye of one of the waiters and asked him to clean the spill off the carpet. "He's certainly had a snoot full," she said to Shamus.

"He's not the Kent Allen I met at his home."

A female guest tapped Denise on the shoulder. Shamus excused himself. He decided to check on Meg to put his mind at rest. He took out her cell phone. When he called the hospital, a nurse told him Meg had been asleep for over an hour. The nurse offered to awaken her to take the call, but Shamus declined. It was better for her to rest.

"Just tell her I called. She knows where to reach me."

Shamus milled about the reception.

He was drawn to a conversation to his left. Several people were gathered around a small, rotund, balding man in his late forties or early fifties. He was telling jokes. "Have you heard the one about the princess,

Marilyn Monroe and Greta Garbo?" He waited for the crowd to indicate their unfamiliarity and to urge him on. The joke that followed disgusted Shamus. It was vile. The laughter was mixed – raucous and forced, the latter principally from the females who, one by one, moved on to other groups. What an ignorant lout, Shamus thought. Where do they get these people? Do they actually teach? He wanted to take the offender by the lapels and throw him out the door, but he restrained himself. There were bigger fish to fry.

Hearing Winhurst's voice, Shamus walked in that direction. His attention was briefly drawn to the door where Dr. Michaels was welcoming Ellen. She tripped slightly upon entering as if she'd already been drinking. She disappeared into the crowd.

"I don't care what you think," Winhurst was snapping at a fortyish man.

"You aren't running my life," the man returned abruptly.

"I'll run your career into the ground if you mess with me."

"Gentlemen, gentlemen," a familiar voice interrupted. "I see we have an academic dispute arising. I'm no stranger to them myself." It was Kent Allen. He continued to address his words to both men as well as onlookers, but his eyes were principally on Winhurst. They were admonishing him, warning him to consider his next move very carefully, exerting a power that few others had over the imperious Winhurst. Shamus wondered if perhaps Kent Allen was overestimating the weight of seniority.

Winhurst took in a deep breath and then smiled as if grateful to Allen. "You're absolutely right," he said. "This debate is best saved for another time. Professor Sherman and I are forever battling about one theory or another." Anticipating agreement, Winhurst glanced over at the seething Sherman.

Kent Allen shifted his gaze to Professor Sherman. "Bill, you are too long in the tooth to let Jake get to you. You are worthy adversaries indeed." Allen patted the still angry professor on the back. "But this is a celebration. We should do our best to set a good example for our students. I know you agree, Bill."

Bill Sherman remained rigid.

"Professor Winhurst was well-matched, my friend. You may have been the victor." Allen patted the professor again. "Will you join me for a drink, Bill?"

Sherman relented. Shamus watched Kent steer him cross the room. Any hint of inebriation in Kent's gait had faded away like a shell taken suddenly by a determined tide. He'd risen to the occasion. Certainly a man of many sides, Shamus thought.

Winhurst was standing by himself, recovering from the altercation. Shamus approached him.

"That was a close call."

Winhurst's expression shifted ably to cocktail party pretense. "Oh, hello Mr. Doherty. It's a pleasure to see you. How is Meg?"

"She sends her regards," Shamus said sardonically, watching Winhurst's face.

"And mine to her," Winhurst said raising his wine glass.

"She remembers being at your office that night."

Shamus dropped the comment as a magician drops a handkerchief into a hat, knowing the outcome will marvel.

Winhurst raised his drink to his mouth – buying time. He swallowed. "That's a good sign. Although it may be quite unsettling when she remembers the entire night."

"Unsettling for whom?"

"For her, of course," Winhurst replied. "Who else?"

"I have my suspicions."

Winhurst placed his glass down on a table. "I need to visit with a few people. I wish you luck, Mr. Doherty."

Shamus watched Winhurst stride angrily across the room and climb the stairs. Shamus milled about for nearly fifteen minutes, then climbed the stairs himself and proceeded stealthily down the second floor hallway. He passed one open bedroom. The door to the second was closed. As he reached to open it, he heard voices coming from a further room at the end of the hall. It was a man and a woman. The door to that room was slightly open. Shamus was nearly at the doorway when he identified the voices. He peered in.

Winhurst had Ellen against the wall. Her head was back, her blouse open. Shamus recoiled in disgust and disbelief.

"You're a smart girl, Ellen," Winhurst said. "You know how things are done."

"You said you would help me get tenure," she said pitifully.

Winhurst laughed loudly. "And you believed me. Which is why, my dear, you don't deserve tenure. You are not only a slut, you are an ignorant one."

"You son of a bitch," Ellen sputtered.

Shamus peeked in again. Ellen pulled awkwardly at her dress, attempting with her other hand to shove the smirking Winhurst as he zipped his pants. One retaliatory body blow from Winhurst and she slumped to the floor in tears. Indifferent to her misery, he turned, shook his head in disgust, and walked toward the door.

Shamus wanted to help Ellen, but thought better of the potential embarrassing effect on her. He hurriedly slipped into an adjacent open bedroom. After Winhurst was gone, with Ellen following shortly thereafter, he went back downstairs to the party.

"May I have your attention?"

It was Dr. Michaels speaking from a makeshift podium. Half of the assembled masses heard their host and responded with silence, while the other half continued to talk. Dr. Michaels pulled the microphone toward him and tapped it. Most people stopped talking.

"I'd hoped not to use this, but you are an unruly crowd," he joked. "I'm forced to rely on technology. Something you all know I detest."

A few people snickered and nodded knowingly.

"I want to thank all of you for being here tonight. Had I known so many of you would break with Los Angeles tradition and actually show up, I would have rented a tent for the backyard."

Laughter again. One man raised his glass.

"No one here wanted to miss the first party ever given by you, Robert."

Amid the laughing and explaining, the gracious Dr. Michaels continued.

"My cover is blown," he said jovially. "I am not a party animal. That is well known. But tonight marks such an important occasion that I was delighted to be the host."

He glanced about the room.

"Adele, would you please join me up here?" He waited as a dressed-to-kill woman of about forty worked her way through the crowd. As she and Dr. Michaels embraced, he whispered something to her, and she smiled at everyone.

"I want to thank the Westlake family, especially Adele, for our wonderful new hospital wing."

Cheers erupted from the audience. Adele Westlake stepped to the microphone.

"I want to say that this day would not have been possible without the work of Dr. Robert Michaels. His medical skill and the accolades his research has brought to Pacific Coast are in large part the reason why we chose to build this wing in my father's honor at Pacific Coast Hospital. Also, President Fuller gave us his complete support on this, as he has on so many other important projects. Please join me in applauding his leadership."

After the applause had subsided, Dr. Michaels returned to the podium: "I wonder if our president would say a few words?"

A tall, slender man in his early fifties pretended to look surprised, then stepped forward.

Shamus saw Dr. Michaels in a new light. This was a politically savvy man.

"Very impressive," Shamus whispered to himself. "Didn't think you had it in you, old boy."

"I have a question," came a loud voice from the crowd. All eyes turned to Ellen, her hand raised, stumbling toward the president.

Shamus stood erect. He knew this couldn't be good.

"I want to know, President Fuller, what it takes to get tenure around here."

Ellen's words were slurred, her make-up smudged and her posture unsteady.

Dr Michaels stepped to the microphone.

"Go ahead, Dr. Michaels," Ellen interrupted. "You've been on the committees. You answer for the president. He doesn't know what goes on at this university. So, tell me Dr. Michaels, what does it take?"

"This isn't the time or place for a discussion of tenure, Miss …"

"Nelson," she spurted, nearly falling over. "Professor Ellen Nelson, assistant professor of business, and about to be assistant professor of nothing. I'm the brains and work behind the lucrative online seminars at the business school, President Fuller. I'm the first author of articles your big shot, big wigs have stolen from me."

Shamus began to work his way through the crowd, slowly so as not to startle Ellen.

"Dr. Nelson, I'd be delighted to answer your question a little later on."

"No! Damn it! I've waited long enough! You're in with them. I know it. I know… about your little golf outing."

The silence of the room gave way to mutterings, and then silence again.

"You put Meg Doherty in the hospital; you and your friends. And I know why." Ellen laughed deviously. "I know what all of you are up to. I'm not playing along anymore. I'm done. Do you hear me?" She was nearly shouting now. She reached upward feebly, as if to strike Dr. Michaels.

Shamus grabbed her by the wrist and pulled her hand back. Then he took her by the shoulders and turned her to face him.

"Ellen, it's okay. Come with me."

"Get your filthy hands off of me. I'm not going until all of them wish they'd never been born."

She struggled to free herself but his grip was too tight. Dr. Michaels took one of Ellen's arms and he and Shamus managed to escort her from the living room.

Ellen wrenched herself away from them. "Don't touch me!" She brought her face nearly to that of Dr. Michaels and lowered her voice. "Meg thinks you're different from the rest, but you're not. You're a user too. And that baby will grow up to be one, too."

"Stop it, Ellen," Shamus insisted.

Ellen's eyes, pooled in misery, turned to his with disdain. Her body folded. As Shamus caught Ellen, her head fell on his shoulder. Shamus picked her up. He and Dr. Michaels hurried her away to a small guestroom where he checked her pulse, her eyes and her breathing.

"What was that about?" Shamus asked.

"I don't know. I don't even know who she is, but she's as drunk as a skunk."

"It appears that she knows you."

"A lot of people do."

"She's convinced that you're not who you appear to be."

"That wouldn't come as a surprise to you," Dr. Michaels said flippantly. "You've suspected me of one thing or another from the day we met."

"If you're so trustworthy, why *were* you golfing with Winhurst and Wilkins the other day?"

"So that's what she was referring to," Dr. Michaels said. His expression was earnest, his stance solid. "I've had suspicions for some time about Jake Winhurst. He throws his weight around the university. People fear him, and rightly so. He ruins careers at the drop of a hat. I learned Meg had met with him the night before her tenure decision was to be made. There was no doubt in my mind that he'd been up to no good. He invited me to join him and Wilson for golf, as he'd done several times before. This time I accepted to see if I could learn more. I got very little from them. But they're up to something. Perhaps this young lady even knows what it is."

"You're actually beginning to believe Meg?"

"I'm telling you that I'm suspicious about who and what either drove Meg to almost take her life – or who it was that nearly killed her."

Shamus could have enjoyed his victory, but instead merely said: "That puts us on the same team."

Dr. Michaels nodded. "What was that about a baby?" He placed his hand on Ellen's head, and then took her pulse again.

"That *was* odd," Shamus said, looking at Ellen. "Mean, too."

"Yes, it was," Dr. Michaels said slowly, as if he was now beginning to recognize as real something that he'd only speculated existed before. "She did," he muttered.

"She did what?" Shamus asked.

"Nothing," Dr. Michaels said brushing the thought aside. "It will keep."

He left the room. Shamus sat in a chair near Ellen. "You've certainly gotten in over your head," he said as he removed one of her hairs from her mouth.

"She's not the only one," Denise said, entering the room. "I just talked with Meg. Winhurst's former secretary called her at the hospital."

"Former secretary?" Shamus asked.

"Seems her unwillingness to be obsequious caused her to be canned shortly after your visit. When she left that scum's employ, she took along a few sensitive files and a copy of his calendar so she'd have something on him if she needed it."

"Secretaries at this place seem to do a lot of that," Shamus said.

"Maybe it's a smart move in some quarters. Anyway, according to Anne, Winhurst has been sluicing funds from one university account to another. The two accounts had nearly identical names. That's why she hadn't noticed it in the past.

Anne also said Meg called her today to ask why Harry Dustin had been to see Winhurst. Anne wasn't sure of the exact reason, but she said she did hear them arguing and that Harry was accusing Winhurst of something. She said he told the professor, "You're putting lives in jeopardy and I know why.""

"Anything else?"

"Anne didn't remember much more, but Meg did – that's why she called me. She now remembers a memo from Dustin she'd taken from Winhurst's office that night. She said to tell you she remembers faxing it."

"East Hall wasn't really retrofitted in the summer," Shamus said. "None of the buildings were. That memo confirms it. Cosmetic stuff was done, but that's all. Harry Dustin discovered that. Since Winhurst was the head of the committee that oversaw the retrofitting, he held the purse strings and made all the big decisions. Meg stumbled onto his way of filtering millions of dollars into his pockets – and likely those of people in on it with him."

Denise shook her head as if trying to make it all go away. She then looked over at Shamus, concern in her eyes. "I'm worried about Meg. She was upset when she called me. She's starting to remember that whole night."

Shamus took in her words, glanced at Ellen and then back at Denise. "Watch Ellen, will you? I'm going to the hospital."

As Shamus reached the front door, Kent Allen blocked his way.

"Well, well, well," Kent said, his words slurred.

"Congratulations on your mastery in breaking up that argument," Shamus said. "It was very impressive, I'd love to discuss your technique, but I have to go."

"So, one of the Doherty siblings finds me impressive. My oh my."

Shamus tried to move past him.

"Do you know what true genius is, my friend?" Kent's eyes were afloat. His body was wavering. "Do you?"

He moved his face in so close that the stench of alcohol made Shamus feel ill.

"Of course you don't. How silly of me to think you might. You're young. You don't know the value of experience. You've never read the Greeks. Why would I ask you? No doubt you're cut from the same cloth as your brilliant sister."

Shamus wasn't about to engage Allen. This was a man of many sides. He'd seen that at his home, listening outside Rashid's door, and this evening. There was no time to discover which Kent Allen he was with at this moment. He needed to talk to Meg.

"I have to be somewhere, but later perhaps we can resolve all our differences."

"It's beyond that my boy. Far beyond that."

Allen staggered and nearly fell before regaining his footing.

"Listen," Shamus said. "Maybe you should go home. I'll drive you on my way."

"You'll do no such thing. I'm perfectly capable. You should go back in there and mind that girl – Ellen. A university is no place for someone like her."

"Please excuse me," Shamus said – pushing Kent aside.

"Well pardon me," Kent said indignantly. "I shall not burden you further." He tripped, regained his balance, straightened his tie, and headed to the living room where he would surely accost some other poor soul.

CHAPTER FOURTEEN

Meg lay in her hospital bed warmed by the tender embrace of somnolence – familiar hospital sounds meandering through subdued consciousness. Footsteps. She was in her office, frantically rummaging through her desk drawer. Her heart was pounding so hard that she could barely breathe. Surely Juan was around somewhere. If only she could hold the intruder off. But the doorknob was turning. He had a key. She felt the sharp point of a letter opener that she had never used – a faculty research creativity award, useless until now. She gripped it, watching the door, praying that it would not open. She knew who it was but his identity would not come to her in this half sleep accepting of horror but resentful of detail.

"Juan is that you?" she called.

"No, Meg. It's me."

She tightened her grip on the letter opener, brought it out from the drawer and leaned back against the wall. The voice was familiar.

"Meg, I wasn't thinking. Let's talk. Open the door."

"Go away. Just go away!"

Meg struggled to awaken. She saw herself crouched behind her office desk reaching to remove the phone receiver from its cradle. Her hand flopped about like a terrified fish on the end of a line. Nothing. She reached again. This time successful, she punched in his number. The ringing was interminable.

"Shamus here. Leave a message."

She dropped the receiver, panicked now.

"*Juan*," she cried out. "*Juan*, please come!"

The door opened and he stood, ugly with hatred, two feet away, smirking through what seemed like clear plastic surrounded by white. She lifted the letter opener, tight in her fist – shaking. Behind him, someone laughed. Her attacker turned quickly, whispered an order, and then shifted his full attention to her. Infuriated. His eyes were threatening dark pools of disdain. He lunged. She stabbed out with the letter opener. He jumped, pulled back, checked out a slit in his left sleeve. His smirk was venomous as he sized her up with new respect. She sliced at him again. He grabbed her arm, yanked her toward him, glared into her eyes and violently smashed her against the wall. The room spun. The other man moved, anxious to do his part, but was signaled to stop. Eyes still seized on hers through the blur, her attacker reached and clutched her neck. He squeezed. Pain surged through her body. He lifted her slowly like a curio collector examining a potential addition. She tasted her own blood warmly trickling into her mouth. Was she breathing? She couldn't tell. He spun her around, slamming the back of her head into the metal file cabinet. Her body collapsed to the floor. The pain was excruciating, hot. But in that brief moment, she was able to catch a breath. Kicking up and out, she slammed her right foot into his groin. His body folded at the waist in agony. She pulled herself across the floor desperately seeking a chance to escape. The second man blocked her. He laughed. Her attacker revived. His large, bloodied glove grabbed her by the hair like the jaws of a loader, lifted her torso slowly from the floor, pulled her to his right and with a powerful thrust slammed her head into the wall.

* * *

Shamus was on San Vicente Boulevard when the cell phone rang. He braked and moved to the side of the road, other drivers honking and cursing as they went around him.

"Shamus," Meg was breathless. "I remember now." She breathed deeply and quickly out. "My God, they tried to kill me. They must have killed Harry Dustin – Jake and Bill Wilkins. Some of it is vague – hazy around the edges, but I remember most of it. They were dressed in white – like space suits. That part doesn't make any sense."

Shamus recalled the hazmat suits from the opening to the elevator shaft. That's why Rawlins hadn't found a shred of evidence. "No, it makes sense."

"What?"

"They wore hazmat suits, Meg. With those on there wouldn't be evidence of a struggle, no hair, no skin, nothing under your nails, so no indication that you didn't try to kill yourself. Just as there was no evidence that they killed Harry Dustin."

"They probably went down the fire escape stairwell outside of Rashid's office," Meg speculated. "Jake must have had a master key. No one would have seen them. They wouldn't have run into Juan. It's out of the way and pitch black at night. I've never liked being in that far off section of the building with that fire escape being there. Rashid's window doesn't lock."

He wanted to tell her she shouldn't have stayed there, that she should have demanded to be elsewhere, especially since she worked there at night. But he stifled his sibling criticism. It would keep.

"Meg. You need to stop thinking about it for now. I know this is upsetting and you want to remember it all, but it's not a good idea. Some of it may still be, like you said, a bit hazy." The last thing he wanted right now was for Meg to remember hanging, helpless, death inevitable for her and her unborn child and not being able to do a thing. "Your job now is to settle down. You can't risk a relapse. Think of Johnny."

"He could do the same to you, Shamus. He's so powerful. He has connections everywhere. Everyone owes him. You've got to..."

"Listen Meg, is the security guard there?"

"Yes."

"Are you okay?"

"Don't worry about me," Meg insisted.

"Then I'm going to find Jake Winhurst."

"You've got to call the police first."

"I will," Shamus lied. "Promise me you'll relax."

"How can I do that?"

"You can, Meg. I'm fine. I'll call Detective Rawlins. He'll believe me now. He'll put two and two together and realize that it happened just as you said. It'll be fine." The call ended with a promise to call her back within the hour. His heart was pounding. The antipathy was coming to a boil in his head. He gritted his teeth and pressed his foot down hard on the accelerator.

* * *

The trip to Winhurst's house in Pacific Palisades proved fruitless. Shamus had located the house through a friendly telephone operator and had waited outside for two hours.

It was nearly 1 a.m. when he arrived at Meg's apartment. He'd called her as promised. She'd been sedated. This time he was glad. As he pulled into the garage, he saw two dark, female figures struggling at the entrance to the complex. One of them saw him, broke loose from the other and ran frantically toward the car. It was Ellen. He slammed on the breaks. She pounded on the passenger seat window before collapsing.

Shamus exited the car, ran to the opposite side. "What the hell are you and Ellen doing here?"

She insisted on seeing you – a condition of cooperating," Denise said, clearly exhausted from dealing with Ellen.

Shamus shook his head as if this was all he needed. He managed to get Ellen into the passenger seat of the car and then parked in the garage. They managed to carry Ellen to Meg's apartment and put her on Meg's bed. Shamus went to get a wet cloth for her forehead. Denise covered her with a blanket and sat on the edge of the bed – defeated.

"I don't know what to do about her," Denise said, as Shamus returned with the cloth. He placed it on Ellen's forehead.

"She's a train wreck in progress," he said, squeezing Denise's shoulder to assure her none of it was her fault.

"We should bring her to the hospital. She may be a suicide risk."

"She may be a drunk"

"That's heartless," Denise countered.

"Sorry. But I have a lot on my mind and this isn't helping."

Denise closed her eyes and shook her head. "I know, but she's in bad shape. Winhurst and Wilkins used her. They promised her tenure if she…"

"I know," Shamus interrupted. He squatted next to the bed, chastened. "I'm sorry. I *was* being heartless."

Denise touched his hair and ran her hand gently down his cheek.

He smiled, appreciative of her forgiveness.

"On top of everything, my father is all upset. He was pacing after you left. I haven't seen him that anxious in a long time. I finally pried it out of him. He told me that he donated sperm at the request of his youngest brother. He and his wife weren't able to get pregnant and so reluctantly my father helped them out. He agreed to be an anonymous donor. He chose somewhere in town where he wouldn't be recognized – not the best of options. They weren't going to tell the baby about the sperm donation so anonymity was the best route – legally as well. My aunt and uncle would know it was his sperm by some information he'd provided on the form. Anyway, it's very complicated, but before using the sperm my aunt and uncle got pregnant – with twins. He should have done something then. He didn't. A young woman became the recipient of that sperm.

Shamus looked at her concerned eyes as the realization of what she was saying sunk in.

"So you think the young woman was Meg?"

"It's possible."

"Your father thinks so?"

"He didn't say."

"He didn't have to," Shamus surmised."He probably found out for himself."

"How would she have known?"

"He didn't tell me. I'm his daughter. It was enough to reveal what he did. But he may have shared the story about my aunt and uncle with Meg." Shamus ran his right hand through his hair and scratched the back of his head. "So it's possible that my nephew's father is your father?"

Denise remained silent.

"Why would she…?"

"Because your sister loves him." Denise said as if he were dense.

"But it looks like she betrayed his confidence."

"She loves him and admires him. That's probably why she did it. And he never would have known if circumstances had been different. No harm, no foul."

"But she could have …"

"She could have what?" Denise looked annoyed. "Married him?"

"Maybe," Shamus challenged.

"Life isn't that simple, Shamus. My father doesn't date let alone get married. His life is the hospital."

Shamus sighed.

"Besides, who are we to judge?" Denise said.

"And that's why Ellen was raving about a baby?"

Denise nodded. "To hurt my father, I suppose. Maybe she did it to embarrass him. And it would have if she'd said much more at the party. I think she just wanted to make someone at his level suffer. Jake would have been the more rational target."

Shamus nodded. He sat on the floor, took Denise's hand and pressed it to his cheek. "You mean I'm now related to your father?"

Denise moved her hand to his chin and raised his face to look into his eyes shining at her with affection rather than the anger she'd expected. She reciprocated. "The family picnics should be fun."

He chuckled. "I bet."

"Besides, we have much worse to worry about," Denise said. "Meg called me after she remembered what happened."

"Then you know what Winhurst and Wilkins did.

"I can believe using people like Ellen. It happens. I get the money," Denise said. "But killing one person and trying to kill two others – one an unborn child – is not something you expect in academe – in real life, for that matter. Jake Winhurst is an evil monster."

"Evil people can be brilliant scholars too. Depravity comes in all shapes and sizes. A Ph.D. doesn't make you a good person."

Denise sighed in disappointed agreement.

"I can find out where he teaches tomorrow. I'll wait outside his classroom. If he isn't there, I'll find him. I'm going to beat the shit out of him."

"No you're not. We're going to call the police – tonight. This guy's reputation and his entire career are on the line. He may sense that you've figured it out or that Ellen spilled her guts to us about what she likely knows about that night."

A crashing sound came from the living room.

Shamus motioned for Denise to stay put. He lowered to his knees and crept out of Meg's room into the hallway. Denise followed. As they approached the door, Shamus suddenly pulled Denise back against the wall.

"Go call 911," he mouthed silently. Denise retrieved a cell phone from her pocket and edged her way back into the bedroom. Shamus worked his way closer to the living room door. He peered in. A searing pain shot through his head. He tried to turn and ward off the next blow; too late. He fell to the floor, twitching. A foot slammed into his gut. He thrashed in agony. His vision went from blinding white to a gray blur.

"If you make a sound, you're dead."

"Winhurst," Shamus grunted, trying to catch his breath and regain his sight. "So the – dimwit – with the gun – must be Wilkins."

Winhurst jammed a revolver muzzle into Shamus' right ear.

"He isn't the only one with a gun. Where's the memo?" Winhurst growled, forcing Shamus' head against the floor with the heavy barrel of cold steel.

"I forgot to ask you, Winhurst," Shamus said sarcastically. "Are you going to cut Wilkins here a full share of the millions you skimmed off the retrofitting budget and those lucrative faculty grants, Shamus embellished, or are you just going to throw him a few dimes?"

Wilkins looked with surprise at Winhurst. "What faculty grants?"

"Shut up!"

Winhurst twisted the barrel of the pistol in Shamus' ear. "The only thing I want to hear from you is where you've put that memo your sister stole."

"You think I'd only keep one copy?" Shamus winced.

"Do you know what happens to the bodily functions during slow strangulation? Believe me, you will give me that memo and copies," Winhurst snarled.

"I wouldn't count on it."

"With you gone, and then your sister, there won't be anyone to give it to the police anyway," Winhurst said smirking.

A loud crash came from the bathroom near Meg's bedroom. Winhurst started.

"What the hell is that?" gasped Wilkins, visibly trembling now. Screwing the revolver further into Shamus' ear, Winhurst hoisted his prisoner to his feet. "You first, smart-ass."

Another noise came, this one from the bedroom. Winhurst signaled Wilkins to check it out.

"Get moving!" Winhurst ordered, shifting the gun to the back of Shamus' head. He kept the barrel pressed there as they moved into the hallway. Blood seeped from the top of his head into Shamus' ear. He moved slowly toward the bathroom door, pushed it open gingerly and peered into the dark. Something moved on the top of the medicine cabinet.

"Well, what do you know?" Shamus pulled back and smiled at the floor as if reviewing a private joke.

"I have Michaels' daughter." Wilkins called from the kitchen. "And I've found Ellen – unconscious."

"If either moves, shoot them."

"C 'mere," Shamus called gently into the bathroom. At his feet appeared the purring, preening kitten. "She's probably hungry. Why don't you shoot her, Winhurst? Isn't that what you do? I mean you hang pregnant women, why not kill helpless animals?"

"Shut the door," Winhurst snarled.

"Okay, back in you go." Shamus said gently as he picked up the terrified kitten.

"What's going on?" Wilkins called.

"Will you shut the fuck up in there?" Winhurst shouted.

Shamus felt the gun barrel wander slightly away from his head. He grabbed the cat tightly and turned on Winhurst. The struggling feline – its back arched and its fur standing on end – shredded the professor's fleshy cheeks with its outstretched paws. With a vicious kick, Shamus sent Winhurst's legs out from under him, hurling him to the hallway floor. The cat scrambled out of the way just as Winhurst raised his gun. Shamus grabbed the barrel, and wrenched it back. It fired, shattering the popcorn plaster ceiling. Shamus twisted the barrel further, a snap and Winhurst screamed; his right index finger fractured. The gun fell to the floor.

"What the hell is going on?" came Wilkins' panicked voice. He appeared with Denise in tow.

Shamus held the pistol on Winhurst, who was writhing in pain on the floor.

"Don't – don't shoot me! Please, I beg you!"

Shamus squatted down and aimed the gun at the center of Winhurst's face. The high-powered academic skittered backward against the wall

"Tell Wilkins to let Denise go."

"No!"

Shamus inserted the gun barrel into Winhurst's left nostril. The professor's eyes widened with terror. "Let her go," Winhurst called weakly to Wilkins.

Wilkins had Denise pinned to the wall, acrid sweat drenching his clothing.

"I can't," Wilkins whined back. "She knows too much."

"DO IT!" Winhurst commanded.

"But the memo…"

"Screw the memo," Winhurst bellowed.

"Let her go." Shamus ordered. "Now!"

Wilkins was looking at Winhurst for a sign.

"Forget it," he said. "It's over."

"Remember what you told me?" Wilkins said. "'No witnesses,' you said. 'No witnesses ever. No evidence to find.'" Wilkins was shaking violently, tremors wracking his body.

"You fucking idiot," Winhurst shouted. "Let her go, I said. Do it or I'll kill you myself."

"I'm sick of doing things your way." Wilkins was staring wide-eyed at Winhurst, then frantically back at Denise and back again. "You would kill me for the money, wouldn't you?"

"I'd kill you now you jackass if I had a gun."

Wilkins held Denise more tightly, slowly turned the pistol and aimed it at Winhurst.

"He's not worth it," Shamus said.

Wilkins stood frozen, the gun shaking, a man possessed by fear and hatred.

Winhurst jabbed Shamus in the gut, sending the gun flying across the floor. Wilkins fired. Blood gushed from Winhurst's chest. He stood for a moment, his face contorted in shock. His mouth open, he looked down at the wound and then at the trembling Wilkins. He closed his eyes, grimaced in agony and crumpled to the floor. Denise slowly moved along the wall to a bookshelf. Shamus stood frozen as Wilkins raised the gun.

Denise grabbed a bronze bookend, raised it high and slammed it into Wilkins' head. Shamus tried to grab the gun as Wilkins fell to his knees. It fired, missing Shamus' face by a fraction of an inch.

"Go!" Shamus called to Denise, struggling with the frantic professor regaining his strength.

She didn't move.

"Go! Get the police!"

Denise scrambled to the door and vanished.

Shamus grabbed Wilkins' hand with the gun. He delivered a knee to Wilkins' midsection. But he could not wrench the gun free. Wilkins was getting stronger, raising the gun slowly. Shamus kneed him again, and took off across the living room, through the hallway, into the bedroom and out onto the back balcony. Wilkins, in pursuit, fired as Shamus vaulted over the balcony railing. A sharp pain seared Shamus' left thigh as he fell to the bushes below.

On his back, caught in a tangle of branches, Shamus saw Wilkins lean over the balcony and take careful aim. He moved just as a bullet seared past him. Wilkins steadied himself to take aim once again. Shamus slipped further into the branches. Another shot and Wilkins twitched, folded over the balcony railing, fell forward knocking Shamus from the grip of the branches and slammed to the ground. Shamus rolled to his side and looked up. Ellen was peering over the balcony, dazed, holding a gun in both hands pointing it downward.

"Ellen," Shamus said. "Don't shoot him. It's over."

Ellen stared at Wilkins, distracted – deranged.

"Ellen, I need you to help me up. Can you... ?"

He watched in horror as her arm moved slowly, robotically, until the gun pointed directly at him.

"Ellen! It's me, Shamus!"

She leaned on the railing, steadying the gun.

Shamus tried to get up. Pain ripped through his arm. His legs were lead. The rest of his body shivered with the penetratingly cold awareness that he was going to die.

The gun was now pointed at the center of Shamus' face. Ellen tightened her grip and curled her index finger around the trigger.

"Ellen, you're not yourself. ELLEN, LISTEN TO ME! IT'S ME, SHAMUS! They're all gone now. They can't hurt you anymore.

ELLEN!"

It was too late. Shamus tightly closed his eyes. It was over. He looked up with one eye closed. The balcony was swaying, Ellen holding on, the gun still aimed downward. The ground beneath him was churning, the apartment building shuddering, threatening to engulf him. But he couldn't move. "Earthquake" he heard a man yell. He reached out his arm, took hold of the grass and watched Ellen, now two hands on the gun, body wrapped around the balcony railing for support, face and gun fixed on him. Shamus closed both eyes again.

A shot rang out, then a thud from the balcony above him. The gun fell to the ground beside his head just as Shamus opened his eyes. The shaking had stopped, but the ground was not solid. He felt adrift in a foreign place somewhere between a dream and death. Officer Philips was looking down at him from the balcony.

"Mr. Doherty?"

Shamus took a deep breath.

"Two seconds later and you wouldn't have been here anymore. You're one lucky SOB. Hold on buddy. There's an ambulance on the way." Another officer was wrapping Shamus' arm.

"You've done it this time, Doherty," Rawlins said as he leaned over him. "I told you not to go playing cop." He pointed the forefinger of his right hand as if about to lecture, looked at Shamus long and hard, and then simply smiled and shook his head. He patted Shamus' shoulder. "Hang in there, kid." He motioned for a young police officer to put pressure on Shamus' wound. "The ambulance is almost here. So, just keep breathing."

Shamus' heart was pounding. He managed a slight smile. He lifted his head – the only part of him that could move. "Ellen – what about her?" he uttered through excruciating pain.

"She's alive, for now," Rawlins said. "Officer Philips is working to keep it that way."

Shamus rested his head on the ground, put his hand on Rawlins' forearm in gratitude, breathed deeply and let the world go black.

CHAPTER FIFTEEN

It was good to be in Ridgefield again. Shamus drove past the old
Ridgefield Inn. Turning at Main Street and West Lane, he saw the
beautiful Cass Gilbert fountain, donated to the town by the architect who
designed the U.S. Supreme Court building. Nearby stood the historic
Keeler Tavern, once a favorite stopping place for travelers from the late
1700s to the early 1900s. As Shamus passed by, he recalled from his
childhood learning about the cannonball lodged in a corner post. It had
arrived there during a battle in which Benedict Arnold's horse had been
shot out from under him. Shamus smiled. He derived a certain pride from
Ridgefield's rich history – something Los Angeles with all its Hollywood
glamour could never match.

He drove up Main Street, lined with pre-revolutionary houses and
mansions from the late nineteenth century. Churches, museums, parks, and
a village burgeoning with charming shops and restaurants that had been
built over 300 hundred years prior came next. The street was in full fall
regalia. Red, orange, and caramel colored leaves danced across his
windshield. There was a biting New England chill in the air, a pleasing

freshness. Soon the holiday season would arrive. How many holidays had he spent alone? Many. This year would be different.

One sharp turn and he'd be home. It was starting to rain. Several months had passed since his return to Ridgefield from California. He pulled into the driveway, put the car in park, and sat taking in the fall evening and thinking about California.

Allen, still hateful of peacocks, had softened somewhat. He'd apologized to Denise for his behavior at her father's party and to Rashid. He was bringing Meg books again, but no longer insisting that she read them or agree with him. She was, after all, tenured. Shamus had stayed in L.A. for that decision, to get Meg back on her feet and Johnny brought home with her.

He and Meg called each other regularly now. She was back to teaching and had an office with a window far from remote corridors and rickety fire escapes. She and Susan had visited Ellen a few times, but there'd been little sign of improvement. She was alive, but psychologically diminished. Still, there was hope.

Small had been dismissed from the university and was due to appear in criminal court for having helped Winhurst with his scheme. Wilkins was headed for years behind bars. Shamus would return to L.A. to testify. He was looking forward to seeing Rashid again who, with his wife, checked on Meg regularly. Shamus would never think of the vicissitudes of life in the way he had before meeting Rashid. He would no longer simply run.

Shamus cheered on a single auburn leaf as it fought for freedom from an unmerciful wiper blade. He turned off the ignition and watched the tenacious leaf break free. It scampered jubilantly across the hood of the car and, as if aware of its inevitable destiny should it linger a second longer in the moisture, leaped high into the air onto a benevolent nocturnal autumn breeze.

He still couldn't say confidently that he knew his sister well, but their past had become just that. Coming so near to death – hers and his – had altered several of his perspectives. It would take a while, he thought, as he exited the car, but he had a sneaking suspicion that he might even come to appreciate Robert Michaels. After all, he'd been helping Meg with Johnny – going on walks with them to the park – actually being the kind of person Meg considered him to be – like a father to Johnny and surely a friend to her. More would depend on whether both of them would come to want that. Shamus and Denise had decided to never mention what they believed they knew about Johnny's origins – to let human nature or destiny take its course.

Before emerging from the car, he reflected on the others who'd turned his life around in a massive city for which he'd held such disdain. Martha, Anne, Nurse Shaughnessy, Nathans, Rawlins, and Susan were all salt of the earth. More, he now believed, the rule than the exception. He missed Denise.

Talking by phone worked to keep their relationship developing – along with occasional visits. Once he'd almost convinced her to apply for a position at a Connecticut hospital.

He wondered about going back to college in California – earning a degree in criminology – teaming up with Nathans and Rawlins. He smiled. Perhaps it was far-fetched, but not impossible, he reasoned. Stranger things had happened. He walked toward the front door and stopped to scan the bucolic street lined with willow trees shimmering in the light of antique lamps. He gazed upward, momentarily losing himself in the familiar indigo, starlit sky. "Nah," he said, smiling and shaking his head as he stepped onto the porch. "Some things are better left as they are."

Acknowledgments

First and foremost, I'd like to thank my husband, Chris Noblet, for believing in this story all along and for being there in my writing endeavors as editor, coach, critic and muse. He taught himself book cover graphics in order to create sample art from three of my paintings. Thank you, Chris.

Special appreciation also to renowned author Roddy Doyle who told me several years ago at the Bantry, Ireland Writers Festival that I should never give up on this story. Anyone who tells me differently, he advised, should simply be ignored. That was a gift.

Thank you especially to David Koslow for believing in this story from the start and Aviva Layton for excellent advice and encouragement.

My gratitude to friends and relatives who have read versions of *Shadow Campus* and to those who encouraged and perhaps pushed a little.

Author and fellow professor, Michael Keith, introduced me to Blue Mustang Press. Many thanks. And, of course, my appreciation to publishers Walter Chalkley and Tony Savageau of Blue Mustang Press for inviting *Shadow Campus* to your library. My appreciation also goes to Carole Groepl, copyeditor at Blue Mustang, for her diligence and enthusiasm.

My three children, Devin, Ryan and Shannon, were truly joyful on learning about the publication of *Shadow Campus*. That was a lovely moment – one of so many.

This is a first novel. I hope all who read it are almost as pleased as I am that it found such a good home.

CPSIA information can be obtained at www.ICGtesting.com
Printed in the USA
LVOW13s0753090813

346815LV00002B/5/P